Sprinkle of Love

The Sunshine Breakfast Club
(Book 3)

KARICE BOLTON

Sprinkle of Love

Copyright © 2023 Karice Bolton

ISBN: 979-8-9872814-2-0

Exterior: Adobe Stock © polinaloves

Sprinkle of Love

For My Family,

You're my everything!

Cover Design by Didi Wahyudi

Interior Formatting: BB Formatting Adobe Stock © Natalia Iachimova

Chapter One

Nina

"I seriously cannot believe this." I groaned and stared at the old, rusty truck parked sideways in front of the house. My only shot at getting inside our home before I froze to death was to climb on top of the truck, jump to the roof of the house, and pray my grandmother never fixed the guestroom window from when I was a teenager. If a person wiggled it just right, they could spring it open, and voila. My life would be saved from bitter cold temperatures and a life of humiliation.

This tricky maneuver had to be accomplished without sliding off the snowy roof and falling to an early grave, all because my key wouldn't open the front door any longer and my family refused to answer their phones and texts in the middle of a blizzard where most of the town had shut down.

This wasn't quite what I'd imagined when I thought about living closer to my sisters.

"Cheesus Mice. This sucks." I wiggled my frozen fingers inside my gloves and marched onto the crunchy snow surrounding my truck when I suddenly realized I sounded exactly like my Grandma Millie.

How did Wisconsin seep into someone's soul so easily, and how did I turn into an eighty-year-old woman after only a couple of months?

Kicking some of the sparkly flakes off the top of my purple boots, I jogged in place for a quick second to get the blood flowing and warmth streaming through my appendages before any attempt at finding a way not to freeze to death. I felt like a fighter about to step into a ring, except my opponent was a Wisconsin winter.

Besides, who was I kidding? It was January in northern Wisconsin. There was no such thing as heat. Warmth evaded even the puffiest of coats and squishiest of gloves and, once again, became a shining reminder of what my life used to be like in New Mexico before everything turned upside down on me.

But the one thing I knew was that I wasn't going to go down without a fight. I didn't want my obituary to read, *Nina Bailey, our beloved granddaughter and sister, blazed her trail to Wisconsin, only to be met by a Wisconsin Winter. Unfortunately, she came, she saw, she failed. Please direct all donations to "Snow Jackets for Wisconsin" in her memory.*

I shivered at the thought, and for the first time since

arriving at Buttercup Lake, I wondered if I was cut out for this type of living.

For years, I'd made decisions based on the heart and not the head, and things had turned out better than I could ever have dreamed until this summer when my life became more of a mess than I could ever hope to understand.

I shook off the suffocating feelings swelling through me and opened the tailgate with fierce determination, hopped into the bed of the truck, and slid my way to the cab, where I very gingerly propped one foot on the truck bed and hoisted myself belly first to the top of the cab. If Travis hadn't completely destroyed me, I certainly wasn't going to let a few snowflakes and chilly weather take me out.

My pulse pounded heavily as I felt the slippery crunch of snow underneath my stomach, lying sprawled across the top of the truck, praying for some miracle.

Like, I don't know . . . someone answering a text or something?

I tilted my head up and got a good look at the roof of the covered porch, which would be my best shot if I fell. Not that I was a glass-half-empty kind of gal, but if I tried to jump to the other section of the roof while closer to the window, the landing wouldn't be nearly as forgiving if I slid off.

I sighed before spitting off the fresh snow stuck to my

lips.

"You can do this, Nina. You've got this." I slowly pulled my knees under me and curled my spine upright as I leaned forward on my hands as if I were readying to prop myself on a paddleboard in the warm weather of New Mexico on the New River, taking in the beautiful red rocks and bright green foliage hanging off the cliffs.

Oh, how life had changed.

My mouth puckered into a grimace as I glared at my surroundings covered in thick, white, freezing, puffy stuff while I straightened my spine.

I slowly moved the tip of my boot and didn't feel like I was going to slide off, so I took another step forward to inch my way toward the side of the truck in order to get as close to the roof as possible before jumping.

It all seemed reasonable.

Usually, I enjoyed the snow, but I'd never been in a life-and-death situation stuck outside the one shelter that promised me continued life with no other alternatives.

Holding out my hands, I straightened my arms and drew a slow breath as a huge blast of icy cold wind smacked my cheeks like a cold, dead fish against my flesh. The chill made my bones feel hollow, my legs turn brittle, and the opportunity in front of me more daunting with every passing second.

I clenched my fingers together in a ball and wiggled them straight again, willing them to no longer feel numb.

"You've got this, Nina." I couldn't even hear my words as another blast of cold air blew a cyclone of snow in front of me. "Now or never."

Without thinking, which was the initial problem, I jumped toward the roof. My body splayed like a flying squirrel as my life flashed before my eyes.

The moment my knees hit the snowy shingles, tears sprang to my eyes.

I did it! I landed it!

"Gouda job, Nina." I chuckled, completely horrified and relieved at the same time and grateful for my horrible sense of puns.

But the moment the tears of joy started rolling down my cheeks, they froze.

They froze.

Oh, how I missed New Mexico.

My hands shook as I slowly shifted on the roof, unable to trust myself not to tumble down and hit the ground as I wormed my way toward the window.

With every centimeter closer to the old farmhouse's window, a little less panic thrummed through me.

I stared into the guest room that I'd been calling home for months, and relief spread through me. I only needed to get through this window, and I'd be warm.

I'd live.

The thought brought a smile to my lips as I slid my gloved hands along the ridge of the window and dusted fresh-blown snow away before pulling my truck key out of my pocket. Never again would I let the gas in the truck get so low that it couldn't sit idle and keep me warm.

With my gloved hands, I went to slide the key along the window when the key fell into the snow, leaving a stab to my heart.

"No." I hissed air and quickly worked my gloves along the roof, feeling for anything that felt like the key.

Crap.

What was it the weatherman said for exposure of bare skin in these minus temperatures? My cheeks had already taken the brunt of it. What about my fingers? I needed those. I was an artist.

But I had to take my gloves off to have any shot at finding the keys and keeping hold of them.

I drew a deep breath and felt the sharpness of the air slice into my lungs as my helpless fingers dug around the fresh, powdery snow until the slippery metal of the key stung my index finger.

"Bingo," I muttered to the blizzard wind that swept over my body.

At that moment, as I slid the key along the wooden window and heard the familiar *pop*, I realized that I was too cold to shiver. I was too cold to care.

However, I was still a lucky Bailey girl. I lifted the window up and squealed as I pushed my body through the opening just as the house phone rang and rang, finally getting picked up by voicemail.

I had never loved this room as much as I did now, crawling through the window headfirst, more grateful than anything in the world not to have been found frozen solid with icy tears stuck to my cheeks, purple boots anchored into a bank of snow, and a key stuck to my blue fingers that no longer opened any door on this house.

As I worked my upper body into the room like a snake slithering into its den, I heard several honks outside while attempting to drag my legs through the window.

The moment the warmth coated my exposed cheeks and hands, my skin burned just as much as my fury when I heard another set of honks.

Some warm body decided to show up now?

Not thirty minutes ago?

Not ten minutes ago?

Now?

After my skin threatened to fall off, I'd lost all sense of touch, and my sense of dignity had frozen to death along with my soul, I had a visitor?

I quickly turned around to look out the window to spot a vehicle I didn't recognize honking away as my body prickled from the cold. I waddled close enough to the window where I was certain whoever was making all the noise could see my disapproval.

When the noise finally stopped, I glanced out the window again to see the car pulled right up next to my truck, with my grandma beaming as she hopped out of the passenger side of the vehicle, along with my sisters and soon-to-be brother-in-law in the back. They jumped out of the car while my grandmother stood, gabbing with the driver. As blissfully ignorant as Grandma Millie looked, I'd have to say she still hadn't looked at her text messages. She appeared warm and cozy with her bright red earmuffs and matching red gloves to go with her white parka while she slowly made her way toward the porch without a care in the world, but my sisters scurried in front of her.

The truth was that it was absolutely impossible to be upset with Grandma Millie. Even if I drew my last frozen breath outside with icicles hanging from my nose and saw her pull up in front of me ten seconds too late, I still couldn't hold a grudge. Not just because I'd be dead, but because she was just too important in my life. After all, she and Grandpa were the only adults who were our true guardian angels. So, even though she was out gallivanting in a snowstorm while her granddaughter nearly froze to death because the key no longer worked, I still loved her. That was always how she got away with so much.

My grandma glanced up at me in the window and cocked her head slightly with a grin before ducking out of sight under the covered porch.

I turned my attention back to the vehicle, but instead of backing out of the driveway, the car turned off and the driver-side door opened.

A man stepped outside.

My breath hitched, and I quickly slammed the window shut.

He was the most attractive person I'd ever seen in my entire life, and I'd surrounded myself with lots of good-looking men. Call it a perk of being an artist.

His eyes connected with mine, and I quickly shut the drapes on him.

Chapter Two

Beckett

"Oh, dear," Millie muttered under her breath as I turned down the driveway to her old farmhouse. My fingers gripped the steering wheel with everything I had to stay on the road. This blizzard had knocked power out to most of the town, and the major wind and ice hadn't even rolled in yet. "What in heaven's name is my Nina doing up there?"

"Up where?" I asked, glancing through the snow veil in front of us when I finally saw two purple boots sticking out of a window, flailing and swinging, on the top floor. "Is that Nina, as in your granddaughter?"

If it weren't so cold and in the dead of winter, I would have cracked up.

Nina's two other sisters, Maya and Grace, groaned behind me while Maya's fiancé chuckled at the sight in front of us. Her fiancé happened to be one of my younger brothers, Cash, and he rarely kept in a bout of laughter since he'd met Maya.

I suppose love could do that to a person.

10

I wouldn't know.

Millie's eyes widened. "Oh, yes. I'd recognize those splashy boots from anywhere. I wonder what the heck she's doing now. Curious. Just pull up there."

I followed Millie's slender finger to the vacancy next to the truck when Grace tapped her grandmother's shoulder.

I glanced at my rearview mirror to see Grace holding her phone. "Uh-oh. Nina has been trying to get ahold of us. She's been locked out of the house."

"For how long?" Maya asked, panic etching her voice.

My eyes flicked to the second-floor window to see no sign of the third sister as I put the car in park.

My brother hopped out of the car, followed by Maya and Grace.

Millie craned her neck to get a better look at the second story of her old farmhouse and chuckled again. "Nina has always been a very creative child when it comes to entering and exiting homes, and that has obviously spilled into adulthood. But with as fast as those boots were kicking, I'd say she's just fine."

"I have to confess that my apartment in Paris looks pretty inviting." I laughed, letting the car idle. The last thing I needed was to turn it off and have it go dead because of the

11

subzero temperatures and then be stuck at the Bailey home.

I hadn't been back to Wisconsin in the dead of winter for years, but fond memories weren't exactly pummeling through me from the last time I'd ventured to Buttercup Lake in minus temperatures.

"Most of your family loves it here." Millie's silver brows scrunched together. "You are the oddball who doesn't appreciate the Northwoods. Right here, right now, is downright magical whether you choose to see it or not."

I shrugged, smiling. It was always fun to get under Millie's collar a little, but somehow, she got under mine. There were many reasons that drove me from Wisconsin, and feeling like I never belonged was certainly one of the top two that kept me away.

Millie reached over and blared the horn several times as Cash, Maya, and Grace jumped straight up into the air from the noise.

I chuckled.

"Are you sure you should keep doing that?" I joked as she kept pounding the center of the steering wheel while I attempted to navigate the snow.

"I always like to refer to it as a love tap, then everyone knows it's me and not some burglar."

"Is that really a worry in the middle of nowhere

during a blizzard warning?"

She winked at me. "We are very much somewhere, dear."

Millie opened the door and jumped out of the car without waiting for my assistance. Wind swirled around her small body as she stuck her head back inside as the others huddled on the porch. "Turn the damn car off, Beckett. You're not going anywhere in weather like this."

I shook my head. "I need to get back. The weather is only going to decline. I can't stay here all night."

"At least come in and grab some coffee until the worst is over." Her eyes pierced through me, and I nodded.

"The worst hasn't happened yet." I glanced at my brother, happily holding Maya in his arms as Grace attempted to open the door.

"Beckett, don't make me call your parents. Cheese Whiz." She slammed the door in my face before letting me answer, but it suddenly didn't matter that I was a grown man, nearing forty, with a successful business and a toasty vacation home on the lake beckoning me back on this cold winter night. No one crossed Millie Bailey, even if it meant having cheese slang slung your way.

I watched Millie stare briefly at a figure in the window I couldn't make out from this angle before she stomped her way to the covered porch while I turned off the vehicle. This wasn't exactly how I'd planned to spend my Friday night.

But with every passing second, the storm was worsening, and I didn't know that I truly wanted to drive back on these old, windy country roads anyway. I wasn't even sure how I got roped into driving everyone to Millie's house from my parents' home.

Turning off the car, I unbuckled, zipped up my coat, and pulled a hat over my head before stepping outside to feel the burn of the frigid air sear my lungs while my feet attempted to hold me up.

There was a reason I didn't visit this place often.

Millie turned around and waved me toward the group as she pushed open the front door, and another blast of Arctic air blasted through my coat.

I quickly crunched my way through the foot of snow and stomped the ice crystals off my boots before making my way inside.

The warm air did little to defrost my body as I stood like a frozen turkey in Millie's foyer as she closed the door behind me. Grace shivered and glanced up the stairs before rubbing her very pregnant belly.

"I'm going to check on Nina and maybe steal a few

minutes of sleep before dinner," Grace told us.

Millie nodded. "You do that, honey."

I blew warm air into my hands, and Millie eyed me as Grace made her way to the second floor.

"It's not even twenty below yet," Millie sang with a twinkle in her eyes. "Come on, we'll get you warmed up."

I laughed. "I was plenty warm in the car, Millie."

"And imagine the guilt I'd feel if you went to drive home and got stuck on the side of the road somewhere and turned into an icicle that the police found tomorrow morning. I couldn't live with myself, and I'm still aiming for a hundred, so I'm not going to let guilt take me down. Besides, have you had dinner? No. You haven't. So, it's settled."

I sighed, realizing there was no winning as I smelled the delicious roast. "Fine."

My brother laughed and squeezed my shoulders. "Welcome back to Wisconsin, Brother."

"Nina," Millie called up the stairs. "We have visitors."

"*We* don't have visitors, Grandma. *You* have visitors, and I'm too busy trying to thaw my ass cheeks to worry about—"

Hearing the woman's response drove a smile to my lips. She seemed like a firecracker, kind of like Millie.

15

"What's that, dear?" Millie called up the stairs.

Maya wandered down the hall, leaving my brother standing next to us.

Millie looked at me and smiled. "She's an artist, you know."

I shook my head, smiling. I knew nothing about the oldest Bailey sister.

Nina's voice echoed through the home again. "I nearly froze to death trying to come up with a plan to get inside this house, and now, I can't feel anything. When I sit, I don't even know it. My cheeks just tingle."

Millie bit her top lip with her bottom set of teeth and grimaced. "I'd better go talk to her. She's a bit melodramatic at times."

I chuckled and nodded. "Well, it is pretty cold outside, and if you can't sense your cheeks, that's not a great feeling."

Millie shrugged. "Fresh ground coffee beans are on the counter next to the coffeemaker. Be a doll and make us a fresh pot, you two."

I nodded, unable to hide my smile. "Absolutely."

It was incredible how easy it was to get back in step with the rest of Buttercup Lake. It was unnerving.

Millie charged up the stairs as my brother and I

wandered slowly down the hall toward the kitchen. Family photos hung from every square inch of the walls. It reminded me of my parents' place. At my family home, every surface was covered with grinning mugs of my younger sister, brothers, and me. Here, I saw three little girls growing into beautiful young women, and I could feel the love spilling from the gallery wall.

"The Baileys are good people," Cash said, smoothing his palm over his jaw. "Maya loves having Nina in town. It's like we used to be when you lived here, the Three Musketeers, only a female version."

I laughed, thinking about the crazy things we used to get ourselves into, and oddly, hanging out a window in subzero temperatures wasn't totally out of the realm of possibility.

"Remember that one time we took out the snowmobiles, and you didn't check the gas tank?" Cash asked, glancing at me.

"Do you remember that one time, you forgot to take the ice fishing hut down at the lake before it thawed like Dad had asked you to do?" I chided, thinking back to how mad Dad got when he realized his expensive setup had sunk to the bottom of Buttercup Lake.

Cash patted my back and laughed. "It's good to have

you back."

"Don't get used to it," I growled, walking to the kitchen.

I spotted the empty coffeemaker and reached for the carafe as I heard females murmuring upstairs. It didn't sound like Nina wanted to make an appearance, and if she'd been locked outside for an extended period of time, I didn't doubt she was frozen solid and needed somewhere to thaw.

Maya was peeling potatoes as Cash placed a kiss along her cheek.

My stomach tightened at the sweet gesture as I pushed the twinge of jealousy away. In my entire dating career, I doubted there was one time that I shared any sort of couple moment like that. Usually, my evenings encompassed sliding into a booth at a cafe to meet up with a client or a casual date with a woman who had absolutely no interest in a future once they found out I was American and had a great family back in the States. No matter how many times I screamed I wasn't interested in moving back to Wisconsin, they all predicted I wouldn't be staying in Europe long-term. Never mind that I'd been living in different parts of Europe for well over a decade.

As I filled the coffee filter up with grounds and turned the machine on, I heard Millie humming behind me.

"Nina will be down in a few minutes," she said,

grinning suspiciously at me.

I shook my head. "She doesn't have to come down on account of me."

Millie eyed me. "Yes, she does. The roast is almost done, and she needs to eat."

I nodded, glancing around the homey kitchen.

It felt like so many of the warm and well-loved farmhouse kitchens that peppered the old properties around here, and it was a complete contrast to what I had living abroad. There was an odd sense of nostalgia rearing its ugly head.

"How long are you planning on staying this time, Beckett?" Maya asked, rinsing the peeled potatoes. "Your brother said you're very seldom here for long. Something about you being allergic to small-town life."

"Two weeks."

Since I hadn't been back to Wisconsin in too many years to count and my house at the lake housed more strangers than me over recent years, I knew I needed to stick around a little longer than normal. Ideally, I'd be in and out for my parents' anniversary party, but I knew that wouldn't fly. I needed to at least give the impression that I was happy Beckett, living his best life with no regrets. Never mind the fact that I'd embraced the feeling of being numb and couldn't

19

remember the last time I'd felt something.

Anything.

"Wow." Cash looked surprised. "Is that some sort of record? I'm surprised you're not taking a red eye the night of our parents' party."

I rolled my eyes and placed my car keys on the dining table.

"I'm not that bad. I would have waited until the next morning," I joked.

Millie looked extremely tickled about something, but I had to remind myself that Buttercup Lake seemed to thread that mystical expression through people. It was completely different from where I'd lived for the last several years, where people tended to keep to themselves and didn't provide an overly enthusiastic response to life.

"Do you believe in coincidences, Beckett?" Millie asked, pouring herself a cup of coffee before the machine was done brewing. She slipped the carafe back under the drip and stared at me over her mug.

"They happen all the time. Why?"

She swallowed her coffee and closed her eyes before taking a deep breath in. "Just curious."

Millie blinked her eyes open at the sound of her granddaughter trotting her way down the stairs. I glanced toward the hall and saw the most gorgeous woman I'd ever seen stride into the kitchen. She was breathtaking, even with the vivid scowl attached to her face. Her dark hair had been swept into a braid, and the white flannel nightgown flowing behind her made her look like an angel as she looked my way in absolute horror.

Her hands flew to her mouth as she attempted to cover her breasts with her elbows and a gasp escaped her lips. She had two pink bunny slippers that she slid next to one another and stopped in her tracks.

"You didn't tell me there was someone here who wasn't family. I'm not . . . I'm in . . ." The woman's soft hazel eyes locked on mine as she dropped her hands from her mouth and crossed her arms over her chest, squishing her breasts in the process. Without warning, she flung her hand toward me. "Nice to meet you. I'm Nina Bailey, but I thought you left."

Nina's icy fingers clutched mine, and I pretended I didn't notice she was in a nightgown as I kept my gaze locked on hers. Her high cheekbones and pouty lips were exactly the temptation I'd vowed to avoid since my last breakup. We shook hands before she quickly hugged herself with a shiver.

"Beckett Knox."

"Nice to meet you, Beckett." She looked over at Cash. "So, he's with you? Your brother?"

Cash laughed and nodded. "He's the oldest brother, a little rough around the edges, but we're happy when he shows up."

Nina nodded. "Just an FYI to anyone trying to call me for the rest of the winter. I can't find my phone anywhere, which means it must be buried in the snow somewhere between the porch, truck, and roof."

Maya chuckled. "Sounds about right. Does that make this the third or fourth time this week?"

"Second," Nina corrected. "But this time, I'm afraid I've really done it."

My brother chuckled. "Maya will short-circuit if she can't text you for the next three months. I'll go find it. Maya, you call it, and hopefully, it will light up in the snow before it gets buried."

They went to the door as Millie stared at Nina, still hugging her upper body.

"Oh, Nina. Since when are you such a prude? Nobody can see anything under your flannel grandma gown." Millie shocked me right out of my thoughts.

I snickered as Nina scowled and stomped to the coffee machine. "It's not a grandma gown."

Millie turned the pot of potatoes on high over the stove and spun around.

"It actually is a grandma gown, Nina. Super cute, though," Maya called from the entry hall.

I could feel the love pouring through these women, and it reminded me so much of my own family.

Within minutes, my brother reappeared.

"Got it," Cash hollered. He stood with Maya and the missing phone. "It was right in front of the truck."

Nina beamed and snatched it from my brother. "You're the best, and I never acted like I was a prude, Grandma. I'm just freezing."

"Good. Let's not forget you've been to *Burning Man* in the middle of the desert three times. I've seen what goes on there." Millie chuckled, glancing at her granddaughter. "And I'm sure Beckett here has seen the curvature of breasts before. Right, Beckett? It's not like you came down in a negligee, Nina. We're all adults here."

Burning Man?

Cash grinned and wiggled his brows at me. I knew what he was thinking.

I had a vivid imagination and couldn't shake the thoughts roaming through my male brain of Nina tromping through the hot, dry desert dressed in very little.

Maybe even naked.

Nina poured herself a cup of coffee and turned to look

at me with an impish look in her eyes, and I was inclined to believe her grandmother.

"You ever been, Beckett?" Nina smirked.

"Nope, but I've heard a lot about it."

Her eyes gripped mine. "It's a trip for sure."

"I can only imagine."

"I bet you can," she shot back.

"You seem a little snippety," Millie chided her granddaughter.

"Almost dying of hypothermia can do that to a person."

"How long were you outside?" I asked.

"I don't actually know," Nina said, eyeing her grandma. "I sat in the truck with the heater running as long as I could without running out of gas, and when no one would text me back, I knew I had to get inside one way or another. Maybe ten or fifteen minutes? Maybe five? It felt like hours. But when I started slinging cheese curses around, I knew I was in trouble. Time wasn't on my side."

I laughed, wondering what that could possibly mean, but when Nina's lip curled into a scowl, I stopped. But I swore on my life, her gaze held the laughter her lips did not.

My heart pulled for absolutely no reason, but I stepped closer and glanced toward the family room, where I spotted a fireplace. "Should we get you in front of a warm fire?"

Nina shook her head. "I don't have one going."

"I can start it," I offered, seeing the red rash of frostbite against her cheeks.

Cash looked amused as he draped his arm over Maya, which told me I was laying it on too thickly.

Millie nodded. "Sounds perfect. You four get settled in the family room, and I'll finish up dinner."

Nina suddenly spun around and whipped her hands to her hips. "Grandma, I love you dearly, but I know what you're up to."

Millie plucked up her brows with a bewildered twinkle in her gaze. "I have no idea what you're talking about, honey."

I laughed nervously and shrugged. "And neither do I."

Cash and Maya exchanged a funny look as I waited for us to head to the family room.

Nina stopped next to me, and I could smell the faint aroma of vanilla. The brilliance in her eyes canvassed over me before flicking back to her grandma. "I know what the Sunshine Breakfast Club does to people." She eyed my brother and her sister. "Just look at those two. All happy and clingy."

I laughed, shaking my head. "Are you talking about the book club? My mom's a member."

Nina's gaze narrowed on me like I was a traitor to part of something bigger and far more nefarious than flipping a few pages.

Maya and Cash walked by me and laughed.

"Is there something I need to know about?" I questioned.

"Don't you know how Maya and Cash wound up together?"

I nodded. "Yeah. She rented a vacation home from him."

"That's what you've been told?" Nina's brows rose.

I glanced at my brother. "Is that not true?"

Cash grinned. "No, it's true. But there were a lot more things pulling us apart than pushing us together if we hadn't been repeatedly—"

"And relentlessly," Maya added.

"Put in each other's way more times than not."

Maya glanced at her grandmother. "And I'm not complaining."

Nina rolled her eyes and let out a grunt as she moved to the couch, snagging a yellow crocheted blanket to drape over herself and moving a Frank Lloyd Wright book next to her before setting her cup down on the coffee table.

Unable to follow even a little of that vague narrative about my brother and his fiancée, I knelt down to get the fire going, but it was hard to pull my eyes away from Nina.

"Some members fancy themselves as matchmakers," Nina continued, pulling the blanket closer. She shivered and reached for her coffee cup.

"Is your grandmother one of those members?" I asked.

Nina pressed her full lips into a thin line and nodded. "She is."

"I think she's the ringleader, if you want my honest opinion," Cash explained as I lit the fire and retreated to a recliner in the corner.

I smiled, propping my elbows on my knees as I studied Nina.

"Well, Millie did ask me if I believed in coincidence, and it was completely out of the blue," I said with a lowered voice. "It almost felt like she was on the verge of telling me that everything happens for a reason."

"Ah, the ol' chance meeting trick." Nina laughed and shook her head. "Never mind that she's always the reason two people bump into one another. I'm sorry about this. But I have a feeling you and I both have a target on our backs, and they'll be relentless while you're here."

She brushed back a piece of dark hair and took another sip of coffee. There was an energy about her that rocked me to my core as her words settled around me. The idea of getting thrown into her orbit a time or two didn't seem so bad.

"Wait. You're telling me that this is all part of a plan?" I asked, disbelieving as I glanced at my brother and soon-to-be sister-in-law.

"I don't know that me nearly freezing to death outside was part of the plan, but I think my grandma's suddenly preparing dinner for me in a blizzard while having you drive everyone here certainly is . . . suspicious."

My brows furrowed, and I shook my head. "Why's it suspicious that she had me drive her home in a snowstorm?"

Nina chuckled and shook her head. "Because Grandma Millie doesn't really live here. She's shacking up with Jackson Senior across town and has been for quite some time, and it's not Sunday, which is the only day we spend eating dinner together as a family." Nina grinned wider. "And she's probably Buttercup Lake's most skilled driver in the snow. She's no damsel in distress."

My mind flashed back to Nina's boots sticking out the

window almost like a little witch who crashed her broom into a window. "That could be said for both of you. I'm really impressed by your fortitude."

She tilted her head and shook it. "I'm not following."

"Those were some remarkable moves up there on top of the roof. Most people would have wound up in the ER or worse."

"True story." Cash laughed.

I shot my brother a warning look. I didn't need him rehashing my bright ideas that led to several emergency room trips when I was a kid.

Nina nodded and drew a breath. "Desperate times call for desperate measures. I generally like to enter homes through the front door, but I knew I was on borrowed time, and I'm not *most* people."

"I see that." I smiled and nodded. "It's life and death here in the winter. Definitely not something I have to deal with to this degree where I live."

Nina watched me closely, and I felt the heat of her gaze when her eyes met mine. "And where's that?"

"Currently, Paris."

Shock registered over her delicate features, but she attempted to hide it.

"So, you've been to *Burning Man* three times?"

"Actually, six. My grandma only knows about three of them."

"I heard that," Millie called from the kitchen.

I couldn't hide my chuckle as Nina twirled her hair around her index finger and traded a look with her sister. "And now I'm living in my grandma's house in the middle of nowhere, trying to thaw out so my fingers and toes don't fall off while wondering how my life turned out so completely opposite of what I imagined it would be." She gave a shiver as her eyes met mine.

"It seems to be a trend with us Bailey sisters. It's like Buttercup Lake is our homing beacon." Maya flashed a sympathetic smile to her sister. "But things always turn out okay."

I sat back in the recliner and nodded. "Life has a way of throwing us curveballs when we least expect them," I stated flatly, watching Nina. She looked uncomfortable yet determined all at once.

"It really does," Nina said over the top of her mug. "And now I just have to figure out how to hit a homerun."

Chapter Three

Nina

Beckett Knox was nothing short of sensational to look at with his green eyes, but I knew nothing about him apart from the fact that he had two really sweet brothers and a sister. The one thing that made him especially appealing was that he lived out of the country.

Paris, of all places. The city of love.

Blech.

But I had always wanted to visit the Louvre and the glorious bakeries with striped awnings dotting the city sidewalks. I was already in awe of the architecture, but seeing it in person would be truly remarkable. And even less of a reality since my life imploded back home, and the trickle effect hadn't found a way of coming to an end yet.

There wasn't a week that went by where I didn't get some surprise in the mail. Speaking of, I reached for the phone and listened to the voicemail from when I was attempting to save my own life through the upstairs window.

31

Silence.

Silence and breathing.

And then *click.*

This hadn't been the first time.

With everything that happened back in New Mexico, I'd been lucky enough to have any money to get across the country to Buttercup Lake. And now, did the debt collectors follow me, or was that my awful ex? But he shouldn't be allowed to make calls, right?

I brought my eyes back to Beckett. The sexy guy in front of me didn't need to hear my woes. I didn't even want to hear them any longer. I hung up the phone and let out a sigh.

Grandma Millie called us into the kitchen, and I kept the blanket wrapped around me as I trundled to the table, where only two place servings had been arranged. I spotted a plate of food on the counter and my grandma grinning as if she'd just won the lottery.

I scowled and slid into a seat. "Why is this a candlelight dinner, Grandma?"

"Because we're in the middle of a snowstorm, and the power could go out at any second."

Beckett hid a grin as Grandma Millie picked up her already full plate.

"What about Grace, Maya, and Cash? Where are their place settings?"

"Grace can eat after she naps. Besides, Jackson is coming home tomorrow from that golf promo thing, and she needs to have enough oomph to greet him, and Maya and Cash told me they wanted to eat in the family room. Didn't you?" She eyed my sister like a lioness protecting her cubs, but I wasn't sure whom she was protecting. I was one of the cubs!

"Uh, yeah." Cash nodded, cupping his hand over Maya's.

"Then where are you headed?" I asked her, feeling a knot in my stomach.

I still felt like an icicle, I was exhausted, and the thought of having to entertain this person was intimidating.

No, it was downright scary.

Because I had a bad tendency to get swept up in good looks and great one-liners, and I was overwhelmed with the endless looping of everything I needed to square away before my life could start over.

But ever since I'd arrived at Buttercup Lake in October, I'd found a new sense of *hermitism* that I quite liked. If I could add it to Webster's Dictionary, I would.

Back in New Mexico, I was always attending parties or throwing them. Here, I just got to reflect on life and not worry about the next big trend to chase or piece to sell.

"I am going to eat in my bedroom now that Maya moved out. I need to have some peace and quiet. Jackson is exhausting. We're always running around, and he's always taking a dang blue pill."

My eyes widened, and I snuck a look at Beckett who was trying to hold in his laughter.

"Besides, I need to catch up on all the shows that he doesn't want to watch with me. Now, you two eat as much as you want, and don't knock on my door unless it's life or death."

"What am I supposed to do with Beckett?" I muttered louder than I realized.

"Figure it out, dear. We can't send him out in weather like this."

"This looks delicious," Beckett said, attempting to break the awkward tension spinning through the air. He made a point to look at the spread of sliced roast, veggies, mashed potatoes and gravy, and rolls laid out on the table between the candles.

"Well, this isn't awkward or anything," I mumbled, scooping some mashed potatoes onto my plate.

"It's not every day that I get to share a homecooked meal with someone so beautiful," Beckett told me.

If my cheeks still had blood in them, they would have blushed. Instead, I felt nothing but an intense burn.

Maya squeezed my shoulders from behind as Cash fixed her a plate.

"Dude, could you just wait until we get to the family room with our plates?" Cash teased his brother.

I chuckled, but my eyes flashed to Beckett's, and I felt a charge run through us as I plopped a lump of mashed potatoes onto his plate too.

"Here you go," I said, simultaneously ignoring his compliment and handing him a gravy bowl.

"Tell me more about this matchmaking club," Beckett said, smiling as he stabbed a few carrots and celery. "Because I think we can clearly say that somebody set us up."

"I'm guessing many a someone, which is crazy considering that you don't live here and I'm just here while I try to figure out my life."

Maya and Cash retreated to the family room.

"And I think your brother and my sister are involved," I added. "Things like this don't just happen because of one person."

His eyes stayed on mine, and I felt another thrill run through me. My body shivered a delightful thrum, and I couldn't figure out if it was because of the way he looked at me or if I was still on the verge of losing limbs from the outside elements.

Beckett smiled. "But you're certain that's what is going on here?"

"Wouldn't you say so?" I glanced around the dimmed room. "We've got a candlelit feast where the chef retreated to her room for the duration of the night and our siblings have been banished to another room. Plus, you can't leave."

"Why's that?" He looked intrigued.

"Because Millie took your keys." I eyed the place I'd last seen them. "Which is kind of worrisome because I didn't have the heart to mention to anyone that I also lost mine out there too. So, we're stuck here in a blizzard, keyless."

Beckett's eyes landed on the dining table where he'd last put his set down, and then he eyed the kitchen counters. "I'll be darned."

"Sorry about all this," I muttered, feeling completely ridiculous. I'd left behind a mess of a life and a boyfriend I'd rather forget, only to land in a place that was supposed to be void of distractions.

He smiled and ate some pot roast. "It's my lucky day. Honestly, it's nice to talk to someone besides my family. I don't know that many people here anymore."

I nodded. "I've been extremely surprised at how

friendly everyone is here. I only came to visit my grandma and grandpa during the summers while growing up, but the moment I landed here a few months ago, the town welcomed me with open arms."

Beckett nodded, keeping his eyes on mine. I saw a flicker of something dart through his gaze, but I couldn't tell what was behind it.

"I've never been one for small towns." He kept his gaze locked on mine, and I felt my body warm from the attention. Maybe I was beginning to thaw.

What was it about this guy? His confidence level oozed from his every action and word, and the little dimple in his left cheek turned his otherwise strong jawline and cheekbones a little softer.

"And that's why you left?" I asked, scooping some delicious mashed potatoes onto my spoon.

"One of the reasons." He glanced around the kitchen before swinging his gaze back to mine.

Without thinking, I glanced at his ring finger, and a little rumble of laughter filled the air between us.

"No, I'm not married."

I scowled and brought my eyes to his. "I didn't ask."

"I saw you check out my ring finger."

"Please." I smiled, rolling my eyes. "I totally didn't

do that."

I took a bite of pot roast and happily drifted to thinking of my grandma. She was such a strong soul and so courageous. She didn't have a problem telling people like it was or lending a helping hand to a community member in need. When Grandpa Renny passed away, my sisters and I didn't know how she'd handle things. But to our surprise, she found love again with an old flame. But since then, I'd noticed she'd become almost obsessive when it came to finding a match for each of her granddaughters.

It made me wonder whether Grandma Millie would ever tire of playing Cupid.

At first, I thought it was a fluke that Grace fell in love with her first love again. Yet when Maya found herself head over heels for Cash, also known as Beckett's brother, I became worried.

Worried that I'd be her next target, but months had gone by without an accidental run-in with the single fireman or the son of one of her close friends, and I thought I was off the hook.

Apparently not.

And here in the middle of a nasty blizzard sat the sexiest man to roam the earth like nothing was out of the ordinary.

Hand-delivered.

"You said you live in Paris?" I asked, avoiding the elephant in the room like how he was going to get his keys back. Would this be considered kidnapping or hostage-taking, and could I be considered an accessory? Because I really didn't need that to add to my already horrible six months.

"I do. I also have a place in Portugal." He wiped his mouth with a napkin and cocked his head slightly. "What about you?"

I chuckled. "Ah, nope. Just the upstairs bedroom for me." I nodded, taking another bite of potatoes and buying myself time. Was this the part where I reveal how screwed up my life became? How I'd lost everything? How I didn't even know how to put one foot in front of the other any longer?

"Sorry. I didn't mean for it to come off like that." Beckett smiled tenderly, and my stomach clenched. I knew he didn't, which made me wonder what expression I was wearing this time.

Tired.

Annoyed.

Distracted.

Alarmed.

Confused.

Those had been my go-to expressions recently,

especially confusion. Some people had one certain resting witch face, but I liked to sample a variety.

I shook my head. "Having all my sisters come back to Buttercup Lake made me a little homesick for a simpler time. Granted, as an adult, I shouldn't base expectations on a childhood town filled with only happy memories."

Beckett nodded, but I could see that answer didn't give him enough. "You're just here temporarily?"

I cleared my throat, feeling a lump between my vocal cords tighten as I pushed away the tears that suddenly wanted to throw me back to New Mexico, to my gallery, my home . . .

"Yes. No. Maybe."

"Where did you live before Buttercup Lake?"

"New Mexico," I answered, feeling a bit of my old life sprout into my world again. It was like if I pushed the memories away, I wouldn't feel the hurt of losing everything I'd built back there, but if I even uttered the name, the things I'd successfully managed to bury came nipping at my memories again like a vine curling around me, threatening to pull me underground and bury me forever.

"For how long?"

"Forever, nearly," I said softly. "I landed there in my early twenties, and even when I caravanned across the country, I'd always return. It's just so beautiful."

"You still love the place," he said softly but didn't press.

"I do, but times change, and so do people. It's time for me to be close to my sisters and niece and the new one on the way." I smiled and straightened in my chair, noticing the way he watched me. It was like he thought I was some complex equation that needed an answer. "How about you? Your entire family lives here, yet you live out of the country."

"True." He nodded and took a deep breath. "I have an amazing family, but Wisconsin never gave me a reason to stay. I wasn't thrilled with the cold winters, and it felt like I knew all the people I could possibly know here while an entire world waited for me outside of these borders."

"Were you right?"

"About what?" he asked.

"That there was more beyond the borders of Wisconsin?"

He nodded and laughed softly. "Yeah, I'd say so. But . . ."

Beckett's voice trailed off, and he didn't attempt to pick up his thought.

"Well, I only knew Buttercup Lake from summers with my grandparents and an occasional visit in between," I added. "But it's home for now. Maybe forever."

"That makes complete sense."

"Does it? Because there are moments like the one a few hours ago when I wonder why I decided to home with the polar bears."

He smiled, and I felt a zip of electricity when his gaze dropped to my mouth for a brief second. "What made you go for that window on the second story?"

I chuckled. "Let's just say I'm grateful the window could still be jimmied like back when I was a teen."

Beckett laughed. "You did a lot of sneaking out in the summers here?"

My mind drifted back to the warm and carefree summers at Buttercup Lake and the camp we spent several weeks at toward the end of the season. It was the one place that offered the security I'd always craved.

But growing up with addicts for parents did that.

"You could say that," I said softly with a quick nod and the last bite of food.

"Okay, we're putting on a movie." Maya stuck her head into the kitchen. "You two game?"

I looked over at Beckett, who looked marginally disappointed, so I smiled and nodded at my sister.

"Count us in." I stood from the table and rinsed my plate, knowing I didn't need any more alone time with Beckett

Knox.

Chapter Four

Beckett

I stared at my parents in the living room of my house. They brought lunch over and wanted to go over a few things for their anniversary party next Saturday. My parents were admiring the view of the lake with nearly two feet of snow piled on my deck and even more leading to the water.

"You planning on shoveling that soon?" my dad asked, glancing over at me. "Don't forget, the longer you wait, the icier it gets."

He was standing in front of a series of black and white photographs that hung on the wall by the brick fireplace. The built-in bookcases surrounding the fire had been filled with some of my favorite books for guests to read when I was renting the place, which was ninety-nine percent of the time, but I'd just put a few more onto the shelf from my flight over here.

My place back in France was filled to the brim with books. Reading was one of the only things that let me lift up

44

the lid and peek inside at a new way of existing, to dare to imagine a life that was fulfilling. All secrets I'd keep safely tucked inside my mind.

I smiled. "Once I get to the hardware store for a new snow shovel and a lock today, but I just got home from Mrs. Bailey's. Are you sure Carter doesn't want to come inside? It's freezing out there."

My dad nodded as if it was a relatable problem. "You probably need a couple of bags of salt too. And no, Carter took his sandwich and is sitting on the porch in the rocker."

Carter was one of the old timers around town, and he happened to be the great uncle of Jackson, who was dating Grace, Nina's sister. Relationships like this were extremely hard to follow in small towns.

"Why is he with you again?" I asked.

"Daisy is down in Madison, and Grace and Jackson had Grace's baby checkup all set up, so Millie asked if we could take him to the appointment. He didn't want to head home, so here he is."

"Makes sense." I shook my head. "But I really don't want him freezing to death on my porch."

"It's a balmy thirty-nine right now," my dad assured me. "He's fine."

"Here's hoping." I grinned, noticing my mom

45

wouldn't look me in the eyes.

"Why were you at Millie's?" my mom asked, staring outside.

I laughed. "I was hoping you could tell me that, being a book club member and all."

She smiled as my dad wandered to my kitchen and opened the fridge for a pop to go along with his sandwich. They'd stopped at a local deli, which was news. The Buttercup Lake I knew never had a deli. Shoot! We didn't have more than one food option. It was the diner or nothing.

My mom shrugged. "How would I know?"

The lilt of her voice raised on the last word, and I knew she was definitely hiding something from me.

"It seems her oldest granddaughter is in town, and somebody was worried I wouldn't run into her, so they made sure we met each other at Millie's house. You know, after Cash's car suddenly didn't work last night and I wound up driving everyone?" I thought back to Nina and how incredibly good-natured she was after nearly freezing to death in a Wisconsin snowstorm.

"Nina is so lovely. She's been here since the fall." My mom turned to face me, but I saw a speck of amusement flit through her gaze.

A knock sounded at the door, and I stood. "Must be

Carter."

I walked to the door, and sure enough, there was the old guy, grinning. "Great sandwich. Do you have a carrot and two Oreos for my snowman?"

I looked over his shoulder. "Sure. Maybe not Oreos, but how about some grapes? Wanna come inside?"

Carter shook his head. "Nah. I'll wait. Too much of a hassle to bend over and take off my damn boots."

I chuckled and dashed to the fridge to grab everything Carter needed. "Want some hot coffee or anything?" I asked when I handed him the fruit and vegetables.

"Nah. Good lad." He shut the door on me, and I spun around thinking I really had stepped into the Twilight Zone.

I walked into the family room and saw my mom smile.

"Funny how you ignored everything else I just said but managed to give me a pretty decent bio on Nina Bailey." I chuckled, thinking back to how little I still knew of Nina. Once we started watching movies last night, we all fell asleep in the middle of the night and woke up to brilliant blue skies and the aftermath of a blizzard. Snowplows were busily clearing roads and dumping salt and sand like nothing ever happened. The electricity had been restored to most of the town, and my keys magically reappeared where I'd last placed them.

Cash and I had whipped up our family's secret recipe of scrambled eggs with fried potatoes and peppers before I took off, dropping Cash, Maya, and Grace at my parents' house to collect his car. Had I known my parents were going to stop by with lunch, I would have just brought everyone here.

"She's such a talented artist," my mom added.

I hid my smile. "I wouldn't really know. Millie said the same thing about her being an artist, but Nina and I didn't really talk much."

A frown etched my mom's features as my dad took a seat with his drink. "What do you mean you didn't talk to her much? You were with her all night."

"Who said I was there all night?" My brows rose as I looked at my dad. "Did you hear me say that I was there all night? I don't recall saying I was there all night. All I recall saying was that I was at Millie's. That could have been yesterday, this morning, last night . . ."

My mom elbowed my dad, and he coughed out his answer. "I think you might have mentioned you spent the night or something."

I chuckled and nodded, wondering if that was the key to success for a marriage to last as long as theirs had.

Always have each other's back.

"All I know is she is an amazing girl, and it wouldn't hurt if you took her out once or twice before you hightailed it out of Wisconsin."

I looked in the sandwich bag and then over at my parents. "Why's there an extra sandwich?"

"Your father is really hungry."

"Should I bring it over?" I asked, sliding my own out of the bag.

My dad shook his head. "No. I'm fine."

Taking a seat on the couch, I took a bite of a sandwich that my parents swore was the best ham and brie sandwich in the world. They were right. The moment the buttery goodness swept over my tongue, I realized I had a new favorite in town.

"Wow. Who knew such a great sandwich place could exist in the middle of nowhere?" I smiled, watching my dad take a bite of his.

"We aren't the middle of nowhere, you know." My mom smiled and shook her head. "The resort is thriving. New businesses are popping up all over. In fact, Nina's sister opened an amazing antique store that also features local artists. You should stop by there and check it out. Nina even has some of her work in there."

My ears perked up, and I nodded. "I'll have to do

that."

"So, how's business doing?" my dad asked, kicking his feet in front of him while he stretched his legs and enjoyed his sandwich.

"Business continues to grow. I was worried we might go a little stagnant with all the competitors jumping into the field, but so far, we've remained the clear leader, and Wisconsin is still our number-one state."

"Don't you find it incredibly ironic?" My mom's eyes landed on me just as I took another bite.

I shook my head. "What's that?"

"That you swore up and down you needed to leave Wisconsin, yet the people of Wisconsin like what you have to offer?"

"Shh." I shook my head and laughed. "That's the worst kept secret out there."

My mom's voice turned tender. "How about dating? How's that going?"

"I'm too busy. I just don't have the attention span to focus on my work and fostering a relationship."

"I don't buy it." My mom eyed me. "It all falls into place when you open your heart."

I chuckled. "Then that's the problem. I haven't opened my heart. It's sealed like a vault with no hope of anyone finding the combination."

My mom laughed and nodded. "You're probably right. But do me one little favor. Consider it our anniversary gift."

"Okay. What's that?"

"One date with Nina. That's all I ask."

I shifted uncomfortably in my seat and shook my head. "Mom, there's no doubt that Nina is beautiful, smart, and extremely interesting, but I don't live in Wisconsin. Trying to start something up with someone from here while I live on another continent is a bit too risky for my blood."

My mom rolled her eyes. "Oh, please. You love risky things."

"Jumping out of an airplane is a lot different from trying to fall in love with someone from thousands of miles away."

"Interesting." My mom's smug look couldn't be ignored.

"What now?" I groaned while my dad laughed.

"I just asked you to do one simple thing for our anniversary. A simple date. No strings attached." She grinned like she'd eaten the Cheshire Cat and loved every second of the furry meal. "And the next thing I know, you're talking about love."

I put my head in my hands and growled. "I just know what the end game with you always is, Mom." Raising my head, I let out a deep sigh. "Fine. I'll ask her out, but if she turns me down, I'm not going to beg."

My mom laughed. "She'd be crazy to turn you down."

"No, she'd be smart." I shook my head. "Like I said. She's an intriguing woman, but she doesn't have any interest."

My mom squinted her eyes at me. "How do you know?"

I lifted my shoulders. "I just know."

"Well, if our son thinks the Bailey woman doesn't have any interest, we shouldn't press it." My dad jumped in. "I mean, let Beckett leave with his dignity."

I flashed my dad a grateful smile just as my mom chuckled. "Beckett wouldn't know how to read the signs of a woman falling head-over-heels for him if it were printed as the day's top headline in the local newspaper."

"Mom, I'm not that clueless. I might be into Nina, but she's . . ." I licked my bottom lip and sighed. "Reserved."

"Nina Bailey, reserved?" My dad shook his head. "Are we talking about the right Bailey sister?"

"Just one dinner. That's all I ask." My mom cocked her head slightly.

I shrugged, wondering what my dad knew about

Nina. "Fine. I'll give it a shot."

"Now, let's move on to the speech we want you to give at our anniversary." My mom stood and walked over to the kitchen to pick up a small notebook she handed me. "I've made some notes."

"You don't think I can handle it myself?"

"I think you can, but I'm pretty sure I'd be the butt of most jokes and your dad would get an extreme kick out of things."

"I see your extreme type-A personality still hasn't mellowed as you aged."

My mom grabbed a small bag of potato chips from the sandwich shop's bag and walked over to take a seat.

"And you can thank me for it. If you didn't follow in my footsteps, how would you run a business? A wink and a prayer?" She winked at me, and I chuckled.

"News flash. A wink and a prayer work ninety-nine percent of the time."

"Maybe you ought to try it when you date. You're a cute winker, and then you could start believing in love."

It was like the same conversation I'd had with this woman for years. Around and around we'd go. Circles and loops and talk of love and then *bam*. Still no answers for either of us.

"I do believe in love, and I have you two to thank for that. I just don't see it in the cards for myself." I licked my lips. "And it's not like I haven't tried. I've gone on a lot of dates, but once they find out I'm American, it fizzles pretty quickly."

My dad scowled before a thoughtful expression moved over his face. "Why would living in America be a problem?"

"They don't want to move, and all the women always wind up thinking that I'm going to come back to live in America. It doesn't matter what I tell them about planning to stay over there. None of them have believed it."

"That's odd." My mom shook her head. "Well, it's good to hear you're at least dating. Usually, when I ask you on the phone, you change the subject."

"I wonder why," I teased.

The doorbell rang, and I glanced at my parents, who pretended not to notice. "Are you expecting someone? We've already figured out that Carter knocks."

"Why would we? It's your house." My mom yawned and stretched her arms to the ceiling. "I'm getting sleepy."

"You are?" my dad asked as I wandered out of the family room to the front door.

When I opened it, Nina's big hazel eyes stared back

at me, and all words fled my mind.

She had a pair of pink leggings on with an oversized white cashmere sweater, scarf, and matching hat. Her silver snow jacket hung from her shoulders like a superhero cape.

"Hey there, Beckett," Nina said, smiling. "Grandma Millie wanted me to drop this off. She said you might need it. Hey, Carter." She waved at the older man, who was finishing up his best version of Frosty the Snowman.

"Hello to you too," he replied gruffly.

Nina handed over a key ring with an image of Buttercup Lake embossed on the leather. "She said yours was worn out. Apparently, she noticed when she stole your keys."

"And I see you've found yours." I grinned. "But I prefer the term hijacked. It makes me feel less emasculated." I smiled, taking the key ring from Nina. Our fingers touched, and a thousand little jolts of electricity ran through our fingertips.

Her gaze flashed to mine, and a sexy curl of her lip made my heart skip a beat.

Damn it. She felt it too.

I drew a breath. "Did you want to come inside? My parents are here and brought an extra sandwich for lunch."

The moment the words flew out of my mouth, Nina and I both laughed, realizing how we'd been set up again.

"How convenient." Nina sucked on her lip for a brief second and shrugged. "Sure. Why not? I don't have to be at the store until two."

"Great." I stepped aside as she came into my house and slid off her jacket.

"You look a little less frozen than yesterday."

"And fully clothed," she added.

I smiled as I hung up her coat in the closet. "That too."

We made our way into the family room, where my mom pretended to be surprised at Nina's arrival. My dad shook his head once he figured out what was going on.

"Hi, Nina. It's so lovely to see you today." If my mom's smile were any bigger, it would have wrapped around her head.

"You too, Nancy." She glanced at my dad and did a quick wave as half a sandwich hung out of his mouth.

He mumbled a reply as I handed Nina the extra sandwich wrapped in brown paper.

"So, Beckett told me he didn't get to talk to you much last night," my mom said, beaming.

I flicked a look of concern toward my mom. What else was she going to say?

"Oh, he said that?" Nina glanced at me. "What did you want to know, Beckett?"

My dad flashed my mom a warning sign to cool it. I could see he wanted to be a good wingman, but my mom had absolutely no clue.

I shrugged. "You know. Just the normal stuff. Favorite color, holiday, birthday, occupation."

"Oh, is that all? Turquoise, Groundhog's Day, April 9th, and Artist."

"Good answers." I nodded as my mom and dad exchanged looks when I took a seat next to Nina.

"Well, they're all mine, so . . ." Nina chuckled, unwrapping her sandwich as my mom popped up from her chair.

"It's time for us to head out, Harold. I'm exhausted, and I need a nap."

My dad looked surprised but held his sandwich in the wrapper and stood. "You haven't napped in years."

My mom scowled at my dad, and I grinned.

"We'll catch you later," my mom said, yawning again.

But this time, Nina and I traded a smile as my parents trundled out of my house.

"Well, that's one way of getting us alone." Nina shook her head and took a bite of the sandwich.

I laughed. "So, turquoise, huh?"

The thought of small talk suddenly escaped me, and Nina laughed.

"What mediums do you use in your artwork?" I asked, hoping to bring the conversation around to something she'd enjoy.

"Mostly photography and collage."

"I'd love to see some of your pieces sometime."

She nodded as her cheeks blushed, and she took another bite of her sandwich.

Damn. What was wrong with me? I'd gotten so used to feeling absolutely nothing when talking to females that when a spark finally ignited, I was a mess.

"I have a little space rented out from my sister," she said, smiling. "It was so nice of Grace to carve out an area for me. Her place is booked. She even has a waitlist, but she gave me a booth right away."

"That's what siblings are for," I said, thinking back to my family and how lucky we were.

"For sure." She nodded. "It's been tough figuring out how to downsize and what to put up here versus in New Mexico. There, I understood the art market and what tourists and locals loved seeing. I don't have a clue here, but my stuff is selling, so I have no complaints."

"It sounds like you had a really full life back in New

Mexico."

Her eyes connected with mine, and for the first time ever, I saw a thread of sadness weave through her gaze.

"I did. It wasn't easy to leave, but it would have been harder to stay." Nina's smile disappeared, and I nodded, realizing I wanted to know so much more about Nina Bailey

Chapter Five

Nina

Six feet of full-on Beckett sitting only a cushion away was a lot to handle. Between his blazing green eyes, chiseled jawline, scruffy growth along his chin, and broad shoulders, it was difficult not to imagine a no-strings-attached romp before he went back to France. The act might even give me a confidence boost.

I thought back to Grandma Millie's comment about me not being a prude, and she was right. All sorts of thoughts were flying around my mind about this guy, but I wasn't going to be foolish enough to do anything with the Sunshine Breakfast Club lying in wait.

And while I was sitting on the couch, talking a good story to myself, I knew better. I'd been broken and trampled on, and there was no tidy way to heal my soul.

"Maybe I'll swing by to see your work later today. I have to get a shovel to dig my way out of the sliding glass door out back, and I'd imagine the hardware store isn't too far away from your sister's antique store."

I swallowed down a wave of nausea. It was one thing to have complete strangers look at my art, but to have someone like Beckett view it was an entirely different story.

"Sure. Yeah. It's super close. Just on the other end of the main street in town . . . a little past Buttercup Java."

Beckett looked surprised. "Buttercup Lake has a coffee shop?"

I smiled, nodding. That was how I felt when I first came back to town a few months ago. "Technically, they have two. One in town and one at the resort. Same owners for both. How long have you been back in town that you haven't seen the new and improved Buttercup Lake?"

He sat back on the couch, and I noticed his long, lean body stretched out in front of me. I ripped my gaze away and looked outside to see the beautiful lake view.

"I drove an hour right off the plane, picked up my brother and his fiancée and your sister, and finally pulled into my parents' driveway around noon. Then the blizzard hit, and somehow, it was imperative that Grace, Maya, and Millie get to your house, and Cash's Jeep suddenly didn't start." Beckett flashed a wry grin.

"Okay. I guess you're off the hook, but I think you'll be pleasantly surprised." I stretched my spine and glanced toward the kitchen clock. I needed to get going to the antique store. "If you stop by later today, I'll take you over to our coffee shop. I'm positive it beats anything you can get in your fancy bakery shops in Paris."

His eyes caught mine. "Have you been?"

"To the coffee shop? Of course. How else would I know it's incredible?"

Beckett smiled. "No. Paris."

I waggled my finger in the air. "That is on my bucket list, along with most European destinations. But all that will have to wait until I get my head back on straight."

Beckett nodded. "You seem pretty put together to me."

"That's because I'm the best actress in the world, my friend." I hopped up, knowing I absolutely, positively had to avoid the topic of conversation surrounding what pulled me back to Buttercup Lake.

"You have a wonderful house here. I'm surprised you'd rather spend more time in another country than sprawled out here," I blurted out, and it was true. The family room had a lovely view of the lake, an enormous brick fireplace flanked by built-in shelves, and an oversized couch and two chairs in neutral colors. The entire home was put together really nicely.

Beckett let out a low grumble. "It's a special place,

but it's still hours away from civilization."

I chuckled. "Hey, I take offense to that. We are completely civilized. You just haven't seen our growth yet."

"Even though I detected a hint of you longing for your life back in New Mexico, something tells me Buttercup Lake has worn off on you." His eyes dropped to my lips unexpectedly, and a frisson of excitement ran through me.

I shook my head and then nodded. "Maybe. It happens. I'm pretty fond of the people and the place." I shrugged. "But the one thing I won't be doing is joining any book clubs here. They're a nefarious lot. Now, on my way to work. Thanks for the sandwich, and I'll let Millie know you loved her keychain."

"At least we can report back to your grandmother and my mom that we spoke more than a few words today. After all, I know your favorite color is turquoise."

"And holiday?" I teased, making my way to the front door.

Beckett followed me to the foyer and handed me my jacket and then leaned against the door, smiling at me. It was like his eyes could swoop me up into some glorious place and make me feel . . . happy.

"Groundhog Day." He grinned, pleased with himself. "And I can't wait for you to tell me why."

It felt like he meant it.

I turned around and made my way down the steps before noticing something off with the snowman.

I burst into laughter as Beckett stepped outside.

"What?" he asked, glancing around the yard. I pointed back toward the porch where a snowman stood proudly. A little too proudly.

"You're kidding me," Beckett said, unable to hide his laughter. "What a dirty old man."

"You're going to blame that on poor old Carter?" I smiled, shaking my head with more laughter. "He wouldn't do such a thing."

"I didn't do that," Beckett explained. "Carter just made the snowman today while he was here with my parents, and when you rang the doorbell, Carter had put the carrot and two grapes exactly where they're supposed to go."

God, I loved teasing Beckett Knox.

But seeing the obscene snowman would make me laugh for days.

"Whatever you say," I chided. "But I'm not sure who the dirty old man really is."

"Payback is going to be something," he joked, shaking his head.

"This gave me just the lift I needed to get to work,

Beckett. Thanks for that."

"I'm telling you, Nina. The snowman wasn't my idea."

I chuckled and turned toward my truck, crunching in the hours-old snow and loving every second of being back in Buttercup Lake.

After he closed the front door, I drew a huge breath and slowly let the air out as I thought about the man who'd been directly placed in front of me by none other than Grandma Millie.

I wasn't mad about it. The thought even made me kind of smile.

Beckett Knox was trouble, possibly my kind of trouble.

But I swore that I would start over here and not repeat my ways. There were far too many obstacles surrounding Beckett. A lot of unknowns.

As I pulled out of his driveway and made my way onto the winding country road leading into town, I thought back to how life had changed so drastically. I'd built my career up from nothing, and this time last year, I had a gallery featuring my artwork, a home that made me proud, a car that had been paid off, and a manager.

Ah, yes. The manager.

Travis Collins. The art dealer turned manager. The creator of all my problems.

I clenched the steering wheel and realized my molars were crushing one another in the back of my mouth. Quickly letting my jaw hang open to relieve the stress, I attempted to hum my breaths to get back to my center.

That was what my therapist said to do.

So far, it hadn't worked.

I drew a deep breath as I turned down the street where Grace's antique store stood on the corner. I was so proud of my sister. Actually, I was proud of both of my sisters. Despite the odds stacked against us, we managed to survive, and I wasn't going to let that streak end.

I found a spot to park my hulk of a beast that nearly died as I turned the key and shook my head. "If it hadn't been for Grandma Millie's boyfriend, I wouldn't even have transportation."

Pushing the aggravation away, I slid out of the truck and slammed the metal door with a thud. The sidewalks and roads had been cleared hours earlier, and a person would never know we'd just encountered a massive blizzard last night. Or that I was dumped into Beckett Knox's universe and couldn't shake the feeling of intrigue. It was as if the universe was determined to get the last laugh.

Or maybe it was Grandma Millie.

I spotted a group of people walking into the antique store and smiled. Grace had really done something good here. As I made my way in, I spotted my sister, rubbing her belly and chatting with one of the customers as I wandered to the back room, where I put my coat and purse down.

The moment I stepped inside, I felt okay again. That was the thing about Buttercup Lake. It made me feel safe and protected from the world. I knew it was kind of a silly dream. Wisconsin wasn't impervious to the outside evils of life, but I certainly enjoyed the change.

For now.

"Hey, Nina," Grace hummed, giving me a quick hug. "Someone came in earlier about your large piece."

"Which one?"

"It's the one that's like forty-eight inches square with all the beautiful glitter."

I chuckled, knowing anything with glitter, my sister loved it. This piece happened to hold a special place in my heart. The sepia-toned photo had been edged with some gold leaf to highlight the beauty of a foal finding its footing in the world for the first time. I'd spotted the scene just as I settled into town this fall, and I had to pull over and take a photo.

"They'll be back around three. He just wanted his

wife to see it before he made the purchase."

I nodded, smiling. I wish Travis had thought a time or two of doing that over the years.

My sister narrowed her eyes at me and smiled. "You look all flushed and happy."

Raising my shoulders up, I smiled back at my sister. "Just happy to be here."

"Are you sure that's all there is to it?"

"Should there be more?"

"Grandma Millie mentioned she gave you something to drop off at Beckett's."

"Now I know how you felt with your Jackson." I chuckled, realizing how difficult it was to have two family members dating someone with the same name. Grandma Millie had a Jackson, and so did my sister. "Constantly having run-ins and people messing with your sense of reality just to ensure you wind up at the same place at the same time."

"At least you know what Grandma Millie is trying to orchestrate. It hit me out of nowhere."

I nodded, wondering if I'd be able to handle much more of this matchmaking adventure while Beckett was here.

"It's a really sweet gesture." I sighed. "But I don't think this is very realistic. He's obviously got a life overseas, and I'm very much confused and rooted here in Buttercup

Lake. He might be a fun tryst, but I can't imagine anything more."

"Maybe that's the only expectation to have. No one said anything about anything more."

I cocked my head at my sister and quirked a brow. "You know as well as I know that Grandma Millie is obsessed with us finding a partner in life."

"I don't know." She shrugged her shoulders. "I think Grandma Millie's broadened her horizons. She might just want you to heal your soul for a few nights."

"Is that some new code word for a no-strings-attached romp around the sack?"

Grace didn't say anything.

"Well? Is that what you're saying? You think Grandma Millie doesn't think I'm the marrying type, so she'll just settle for finding me someone to sleep with to heal my soul? And that someone is Beckett Knox?"

A gravelly voice behind chilled me colder than the blizzard from the night before. "I wouldn't exactly turn down that proposition."

I glared at Grace for not warning me as I slowly spun around to see Beckett Knox holding two cups of coffee, a small bag of pastries, and a set of keys.

My eyes moved to his, and I lifted my brow as my

eyes moved back down to the keys. "Isn't it a little early to be inviting me to move in? I know the book club has a great success rate and all, but . . ."

Beckett let out a low chuckle and handed me the keys, a coffee, and the bag of pastries. "Now, I really don't know what to say."

I chuckled and took the items from Beckett. "Are you telling me this isn't an invitation to move in?"

Beckett glanced at my sister and rolled his eyes.

"Nina is a handful and can rarely be tamed."

My sister's words stung for absolutely no reason. Years ago, I would have taken pride in a statement like that. But after losing everything and feeling like a complete idiot in the process, it felt like a figment of our imagination. Had I truly ever been that woman who'd stuff some items into a vehicle and do an impromptu road trip?

Beckett's smile warmed me through to my core as the quick band of unease released.

"All just stuff of legends. I generally prefer to get in my grandma gown, grab a good book, and eat a grilled cheese sandwich on most nights."

"What about the other nights?"

"I might switch it up to a turkey on rye."

Beckett laughed as I took a sip of the latte and brought

the keys into my vision. "So, what are these for?"

"The new lock on your house. I grabbed a new one at the hardware store and zipped over to Millie's to install it. I didn't want to think about you freezing to death while I was enjoying a croissant in Paris."

"How thoughtful."

Grace clutched her chest with her two hands and made a little *aww* noise while I tried not to laugh. She'd become as bad as Grandma Millie.

But the truth was that I was absolutely touched. I couldn't believe that, of all people, a man I'd only met a couple of times went out of his way to ensure I didn't take my last breath in Wisconsin. It truly touched me beyond belief, but I didn't want to go over the top with it.

"The coffee and pastries were more than I expected." I shoved the keys into my pocket. "But this is really sweet of you."

He put his hands up and laughed. "And no strings attached."

Our eyes connected, and I felt that magical pull to him where every cell swirled itself into a dizzying weakness.

"That's too bad."

Grace left to help some customers, and I nodded.

"I have a confession."

71

"I'm all ears."

I peeked into the bag to see an apple fritter. "These are one of my favorites. Yum. Thank you."

He laughed. "One's for me. Is that your confession? You love Buttercup Java's fritters?"

I closed the bag and drew a breath. "My confession is that I'm a bit of a mess. A little skewed sideways, if it were. Barely holding onto my center."

"Straight lines are boring," he said flatly.

I glanced around the antique store where booths exhibited anything and everything imaginable, from brass bells to jeweled magnifying glasses, old paintings, and reupholstered chairs. And then my little booth. It was hard to believe this time last year, my work filled an entire gallery. Now, my life's work was whittled down to a booth.

Not knowing what to say, I motioned him toward the front. My sister was gracious to put my work front and center, right when customers walked in.

"This is my center," I announced, moving my hands toward the booth of wildlife photography juxtaposed with modern elements and some collage work.

I'd always hated this part of being an artist. The showing it off part was the hardest, especially to people I knew. Would they love it? Would they hate it? Would I be able to handle them hating it or loving it?

Beckett's long stride put him in the center of the booth, his eyes canvassing my work, moving up and down over each piece.

Silently.

My hands turned clammy, and a small ring of sweat formed around my hairline. Never mind that it was twenty degrees outside.

"Nina, your work is exquisite. I'm . . ." He turned to look at me. "Speechless."

Suddenly feeling vulnerable, as if he could see who I really was through the work I exhibited, made my breath catch. I teetered on the edge of wanting to run and hide or stand proud and pretend he hadn't heard everything else I'd said to my sister when he was standing behind me.

Because the one thing that my artwork always seemed to convey was sensuality.

Or at least that was what I'd heard time and again. Being in love with nature and all that.

I looked into his eyes and nodded. "Thank you. I've been lucky with my career . . . until I wasn't."

Beckett cocked his head a little, and I could see the wheels turning.

"How so?"

73

"If you and I ever make it to dinner sometime, I'll fill you in, but I promise to leave out the gory details."

Beckett shook his head, smoothing his hand across his chin as his eyes fell to the work my sister said someone would be returning for.

"This is stunning." He took a step back and knelt to take the images in.

"I think someone is coming back to buy it today."

Beckett stood. "That someone is going to be me."

"Oh, well . . . my sister had mentioned that—" The door opened and in walked a couple. The man waved at Grace and turned his attention toward me once my sister pointed in my direction.

"Are you Nina Bailey?" he asked with his wife next to me.

"I am."

"You have lovely pieces. I'm hoping to include some at our lake home here."

A little stir of excitement mixed in my belly.

"That one in particular. I can just imagine it over our fireplace. Can't you?" He turned to his wife, who nodded enthusiastically.

Beckett cleared his throat. "That one's sold."

The man's gaze flashed to mine. "It was available

earlier."

"Umm . . ." I closed my mouth.

"I secured the work right before you came in," Beckett explained.

I eyed him with an *are you crazy* look, but he pushed on.

"This is a similar piece," Beckett said, directing them to one that still had the sepia tones and size of the one Beckett had unexpectedly claimed.

"I'll pay double the price," the man told me.

Beckett smiled. "I've already paid triple the price."

His wife looped her arm through her husband's and did a little squeeze. "I actually like this one a little better for the rest of our décor."

Softness swept over the man's expression. "Do you? It is beautiful too."

I stood conflicted. I wasn't sure what stunt Beckett was pulling, and I didn't want to turn off a potential client, but if he was truly paying triple the price, I was in no position to get in his way.

"That was taken outside of La Crosse, along the Mississippi River," I explained to the couple. "The fox looked surprised when the first raindrop fell."

"It's astonishing that you captured that," the woman

said. "It's like he's in love with the raindrop."

"Truly astonishing," Beckett said softly.

But when I turned to see him, I realized he wasn't talking about the artwork. His eyes locked on mine, and a force ran between us, and I realized this man didn't like to lose.

Chapter Six

Beckett

"What was that all about?" she asked, eyeing me suspiciously.

The couple had left, and Nina was wrapping the piece up to deliver later today.

I shook my head, finishing the Americano. I pulled out a pack of carrots and hummus from the coffee shop and offered her some. "I don't know what you mean. I told you I wanted to buy that piece before they came back. It was purchased fair and square."

She gave me a playful smile.

"But three times the amount the other man would pay?" Nina laughed. "What is it you do anyway that allows you to make offers like that?"

Without warning, a screech from the front of the store bounced off the walls. The sound of glass chimed, clanged, and pinged as it shattered to the floor. Without thinking, I hugged Nina, hauling her to the floor on top of me. Her leg wrapped around mine as she looped her arms around my neck before we hit the ground.

"What the heck are you doing?" she mumbled into my chest. "You could have just asked for a kiss."

"Didn't hear you that racket?"

"It's probably just somebody clumsy like myself tripping into a China cabinet." She chuckled. "Now, seriously, what are you up to?"

Her eyes locked on mine, and I couldn't help but notice how good she felt in my arms. "Saving you. Be quiet."

Grace came dashing from the back room and eyed us on the floor before seeing the front of the store, where commotion filled the space.

Grace's hands flew to her mouth. "I'm headed out back with my precious cargo. Take care of that thing while I call the police. I don't want any part of this."

"Thing?"

I slid out from under Nina and spun around to see the most beautiful creature I'd ever laid eyes on, thrashing inside the antique store. The albino deer kicked some teacups to the floor, and I jolted with the realization that the Bailey sisters could have their entire store destroyed with each new kick and buck if I didn't stop this.

"Stay under the table," I told Nina.

Grace already went outside to stay safe, and the other customers managed to file out the front door as if this sort of thing happened every day.

A trickle of sweat moved down my neck as I spread my arms in front of me like I was an eagle, definitely an eagle. I had no idea what I was doing other than ensuring Nina would never want to be seen in public with me again.

The doe walked over to a piece of porcelain hanging on the wall and used her pink nose to nudge the plate off the hook. It crashed to the floor, and I swore the deer turned to look at me and smiled with her pink nose.

I heard a snicker and realized Nina was getting a kick out of this a little too much.

"You got this, Beckett. Become one with the deer." She chuckled and shook her head.

I turned my attention to the bucking albino deer making its way deeper into the antique store and crouched, hoping I could make my way to it without startling it into more wild behavior and maybe lure it with my veggie pack.

It didn't help that I had an audience of one behind me, but I couldn't help but look to see Nina silently applauding her hands and nodding me forward. All I needed to do was hand her some popcorn and she'd be set.

"Are you just an instigator?" I whispered with a grin.

Her eyes widened in mischief. "Sometimes."

I smiled to myself as I heard the clopping of the deer's steps an aisle over.

In a normal setting, like, say, in the middle of a field or among pine trees, the pure white deer would be even more magical and majestic. But stuck inside four walls with collectible porcelain and musical instruments, it was a disaster waiting to happen. I was one wrong move from a hoof in the chest.

Nina popped her head out from under the table again as I slowly made my way toward the wild beast.

"What do you think you're doing?" Nina hissed. "You're no deer whisperer. I was only kidding. You shouldn't be doing this. Wait for the professionals."

"Watch me work, Nina. Watch me work."

She chuckled, and I turned my attention back to the deer, who made a sudden U-turn.

The pure-white deer stopped in the middle of the store and stared at me.

Its tongue slid out of its pink mouth and slapped its pink nose as it watched me slip out a pack of carrots from my pocket.

"Here you go, little doe. Tsk. Tsk. Daddy's got you."

Nina snickered. "Daddy?"

I smiled and reached forward with a carrot in my hand.

"It's not Peter Rabbit," Nina whispered with her phone in her hand.

The doe looked around, finally realizing it had made a wrong turn somewhere, and let out a few huffs of impatience. Her ankles got twitchy.

I scanned the animal for any scrapes on her white coat, and there wasn't a drop of blood. Our eyes connected, and she slowly started to back up. But before she did, she charged forward, took the carrot out of my hand, and crunched it.

"Back to your happy place, little lady," I whispered, only three feet away.

As I brought a deep breath in, she turned around and darted through the glassless window, heading down the main road in town.

Nina crawled out from the table and started clapping. "Bravo, Beckett."

Grace heard the commotion from her sister and came back inside.

She looked around the store. "Nate's on his way. He's just a few doors down. How is this place not trashed? How in the world did you do this, Beckett?"

"Apparently, Beckett speaks deer," Nina joked, placing her phone onto the table. "You should have seen him. He became one with the wild beast. He even Tsk Tsked it, fed it a carrot, and looked like an eagle who took martial arts."

"Wow! A man who speaks deer and knows how to make dirty little snowmen?" Grace chuckled. "I knew my CCTV would come in handy."

"You told her I made a happy camper snowman?" I eyed Nina and spun around quickly to stare at Grace. "You're kidding about the video footage of this, right?"

The local policeman walked through the busted glass and looked around before making his way to Grace.

"Hey, Nate," Grace said, shaking her head. "Can you believe it? Only the window was busted. And a few dishes and cups."

"Where'd it go?" he asked, scanning the store.

"Did you miss it running down main street? It was kind of hard to miss, considering it was one of the albino deer. I mean, *really* hard to miss," Nina teased.

Grace flipped her thumb in my direction. "This one tried to reason with the woodland creature, and it worked."

Nate smiled when he realized I was standing next to Nina.

"Well, welcome home, Beckett. It's been a long

time." He looped his thumb through his belt. "You staying long?"

I laughed, shaking my head. We had more dirt on one another than either of us would ever admit.

"Just here for my parents' anniversary party."

Grace and Nina wandered over to the shattered glass while Nate glanced over his shoulder.

"Nina's a great girl," he said, nodding.

I smirked. "I do keep hearing that."

"Well, I'm just glad we didn't have to tranquilize that deer and carry her out. That's a real pain in the ass. When they wake up, it's like they want to declare war even though we just want to help."

I watched Nina taking pictures with her phone as Grace called someone on hers.

"Well, I'm gonna head over to the hardware store to get some plywood until they can get the window fixed."

He shook his head. "I wouldn't bother. I'm sure Tucker will be able to come on over and fix it up."

"On a Sunday?"

Nate laughed like I was crazy. "What else does he have to do?"

I shook my head, forgetting what it was like in a small town. Everyone was always willing to lend an extra hand when it was needed, not according to a schedule.

"I'll be in my car filling out an incident report if you need me. I'll be sure to include the hero of the story," Nate said, wandering over to the Bailey sisters, probably to tell them the same thing.

Nina looked over in my direction and smiled as my mind drifted to getting her to safety underneath me. What did I think? I'd be a human shield for a rampaging doe? Although, I had no idea what the initial crash was. Car? Gun? Lunatic?

All I knew was that thoughts that should not be in my head during a crisis pried their way in as I felt her curves underneath me, her warm breath against my cheek, and her legs wrapped around me.

If I didn't know better, I'd think she'd purposefully crushed her hips against mine.

Nina made her way over. "The glass guy is gonna be here in a few."

"Amazing, considering it's a Sunday."

She nodded. "Apart from it nearly tearing apart my sister's store, that deer was magnificent. I've heard about the pure white deer, but I've never seen them." Nina smiled at me and continued. "You know what the legend is about the white deer, right?"

I shook my head.

"That the person who sees or confronts a white deer has been blessed, and the spirits will bestow a great change in that person's life."

"Makes sense with Grace about to have a baby."

"I was talking about you, Beckett."

I laughed, shaking my head. "I don't see any big changes happening in my life. But it's a sweet thought."

"Sweet thought, huh?" she teased. "I'd better get back to wrapping this up. I need to deliver it soon."

Grace wandered over and glanced at Nina's package. "Thank goodness it didn't get trampled." She patted my back. "And nice moves there, tackling my sister."

I laughed. "Do you have a broom so I can help clean up?"

"Ah, you're just full of good deeds today, Beckett. But no need. Tucker said not to touch anything until he got here. He's got some special techniques to clean up all the shards. I just hung a little sign that we're closed for the rest of the day, which is amazing news because this little one is kicking my butt." She rubbed her belly. "And Jackson should be here any minute."

"Back already?" Nina asked.

"Yup. He just had to show up at an opening of a golf course remodel, so it was a quickie trip."

"Where are my granddaughters?" Grandma Millie charged through the door, stepping over the large chunks of glass as she eyed Grace and Nina. "Are you two okay?"

Grace's smile widened. "We're just fine, Grandma."

Millie looked up at me, and a wicked expression covered her face. "Fancy meeting you here."

Nina chuckled. "Please tell me the Sunshine Breakfast Club didn't force that poor deer into the shop so that Mr. Deer Whisperer could show off his hero skills."

Grandma Millie looked completely puzzled as she shook her head, and the sisters laughed. "We never put wildlife in the way of humans. We do have some scruples."

"If it weren't for Beckett, I think things could have been a lot worse," Grace told Millie.

"Oh, yeah? Why's that?" she asked.

"He somehow convinced the white deer to leave the store before Nate got here."

Millie turned her eyes on me. "Did you say a white deer? As in pure white?"

I nodded.

"Massive change is coming your way, Beckett." She smiled and nodded. "Massive change."

Ah, yes. The small-town legends that shaped the future too. How could I fail to remember so many of the little things that ran through a town waiting in an arsenal for the exact right moment to be revealed?

"I'm just so relieved you both are okay. I was eating dinner at the Buttercup Café and heard the ruckus."

Grace scowled. "It's not even four."

"I was hungry. I can't help when I get hungry." Millie glanced at Nina and then over at me. "Just to set your fears at ease, the Sunshine Breakfast Club hasn't set our sights on you two."

"I don't believe it for a second," Nina said, laughing. "He's everywhere I am, and you tend to be the driving force behind that."

"It's true," Millie confessed. "We're busy with another couple, and it's proving really difficult. But that's all I'm going to say about that. If you'd finally show up to one of our book club meetings, you'd know more."

If I didn't know better, I almost caught a flicker of disappointment running through Nina's eyes.

"That certainly takes the pressure off," I announced.

Nina's eyes rose to mine, and she threw me a brilliant smile. "Doesn't it?"

"Oh, there's Tucker to fix the window," Grace nearly hummed, giving a big old wave toward the man dressed in coveralls.

"Jackson is going to wonder if I went back home without him," Millie said, chuckling. "I'd better get back to the café." She glanced at me and Nina and trundled back the way she came as Nina finished wrapping the last corner of her piece.

"Weren't we the paranoid bunch?" I helped Nina lift the piece of art off the table.

"I don't know if I believe my grandma," she said, taking the package from me. She scowled as she watched Millie dodge the glass and make her way out the door.

"How about dinner tonight? After you drop that off? We could meet at the lodge," I offered.

She drew a deep breath, and a smile broke through her lips. "That sounds wonderful."

Chapter Seven

Nina

When I'd dropped off the artwork, the couple was absolutely lovely. They'd invited me in and showed me where they planned on hanging it. Their home was spectacular, and the view of Buttercup Lake was something special, not quite as exquisite as Beckett's view, but definitely up there. Not to mention, they were both extremely gracious about choosing a different piece than originally planned.

As I pulled into the parking lot in my oversized truck grunting its way to a stall, I shook my head and smiled. There would have been a time when I wouldn't have wanted anyone to see me in a beast like this. The thought made me ashamed. I'd always been lucky when it came to selling my art, and it afforded me a newer car and home with everything in between. But the moment that all got taken away and I had to rent a car just for the trip out to Wisconsin, everything slammed into perspective really quickly.

To say I was grateful for this truck would be an

understatement.

I spotted Beckett's empty car, and my chest strained at the thought. I'd be meeting a man for dinner who was extremely fascinating, good-looking, and leaving town soon. The perfect recipe to get me in trouble.

But maybe I needed a little trouble, a little nudge, so I could remember what it felt like to feel a little. I'd become so numb since everything with Travis went down that the absence of emotion almost felt like a comfort in itself.

Ugh.

Enough.

I unstrapped my belt, opened the door, and hopped out of the hulk of metal that had become my safety net. I'd even named this truck since the blizzard incident—Thor.

Bundling my coat as a blast of frigid air smacked my cheek, I hustled to the lobby of the lodge. It had expanded over the years, but recently, it became the bustling hub of Buttercup Lake. There were a couple of restaurants, a lounge, an espresso shop, and more hotel rooms than I ever imagined for the little town where I grew up enjoying summer visits while pretending my home life was like all the other kids'.

I spotted Beckett immediately in the lobby. He stood and took me in like I was the most anticipated guest in the history of this lodge.

"Good to see you again," he said, sliding an unexpected kiss along my cheek. My heart sputtered before regaining its steady beat.

Awareness zipped through me as his hand lingered on the small of my back as he helped me to take my coat off.

"You're quite the gentleman," I said, smiling.

"Ah, shucks." He winked at me, and I even felt a tingle in my toes.

My toes!

"I chose the steakhouse for tonight, and we managed to secure their last open reservation. Does that sound okay?"

"Absolutely. I could eat a whole cow tonight."

He laughed and shook his head. "We might need to head to a supper club for that type of appetite."

"You know what's crazy?" I asked. His elbow brushed mine as a wave of goosebumps fleshed over my skin.

Not good. I couldn't even bump into the man without my body suddenly becoming hyper-sensitive. Hoping he didn't notice, I continued.

"I've never been to a supper club. Actually, I've barely done anything around this state that makes it Wisconsin."

Beckett smiled and shook his head. "You've never been to a supper club?"

"Nope, and I've never had fresh cheese curds straight from the dairy. I've never been to the Ice Castles over on Lake Geneva or to the Apostle Islands or Crystal Caves. None of it."

The hostess took us to our table overlooking the frozen Buttercup Lake, with snowmobile tracks zipping in several different directions and little ice-fishing huts dotted toward the middle. A person might not even realize it was a lake with the thick sheet of snow and ice covering the water.

As we took our seats, Beckett looked up at me with a smile. "Then I guess I have my work cut out for me these next couple of weeks."

I shook my head, taking the menu from the hostess. She went away, and Beckett smiled at me.

"I'm not following."

"I'll be your tour guide." He grinned over the top of his menu.

"Are you sure that's a good idea, considering you're not really into the place? Are you hoping to get me to hightail it out of here like you did?"

A low grumble of laughter filled the air as the server came over to take our drink orders. We both stuck with iced teas, and I had to wonder if his reason was the same as mine. I was barely able to keep my thoughts squeaky clean around him without a drink. I could only imagine what a glass of wine would do to me.

It didn't help that he tackled me to the ground earlier, and I swore I felt every Godly inch of Beckett pressed against my thigh with the takedown.

"I don't hate Wisconsin. I actually love visiting. Plus, I grew up here, so who better to show you around than me?"

I nodded, feeling my pulse pick up speed. "We'll see if you still want to extend the invitation after our meal. We've had a crazy few hours. You might just be high on the adrenaline from the deer incident."

Beckett smiled and nodded. "I won't push you to let me be your host."

"You're not. I'm just . . ." I scrunched my face at the emotion attempting to knock on my heart of stone. "I'm confused."

He steepled his hands together and nodded. "Is there anything I can do or say to clear things up?"

My chest lurched when I realized he thought he was the issue. "No, it's not you. I've just had to swallow the bitter pill, and I don't want to infect anyone else."

"Doubtful." He eyed me closely, which gave way to a wave of surfboarding butterflies in my belly, gliding to safety only when I ripped my gaze away. "And you seem absolutely full of light, happiness, and everything in between."

I let out a grunt of a laugh. "Are you sure you're not talking about Grace or Maya?"

"Positive."

I brought my eyes back to the menu and landed on a full pound of prime rib. Food was one of the closest things I felt to satiety, emotionally. Before, I never cared when my next meal was, but since I crossed the line to Wisconsin, it was top of mind.

"Tell me what really made you leave everything behind in New Mexico."

His request seized my motor, and I became unable to function. Formulating a simple thought was out of the question, speaking even more so.

"Tell me what you do over in Paris to keep yourself busy," I blurted out.

He took the hint and did a quick nod. "I work, eat, sleep, and wander the streets at night."

I leaned into the table. "You just described Jack the Ripper."

Beckett laughed and shook his head. "Honestly, I just take in the sights. I've been living there forever, and yet I find things all the time that strike me as beautiful. Even their cemeteries are breathtaking, and they're nestled right in with the rest of the city. One minute, you're grabbing a croissant from a bakery, and the next, you're walking along a beautiful hedge lining a wrought-iron fence with the most intricate metalwork, and then boom. There's a gate leading into a park, only it's not a park. There are statues and headstones and family chapels, all along winding cobblestone pathways which dip over rolling hills."

His description of something I may never see in person dug at my heart a little, but it also created a stir in my belly from the way he so eloquently painted a beautiful picture of something many find frightening.

"So you've never bumped into your perfect match while roaming the cemeteries of Paris?"

He chuckled. "Not living."

"Is this something I should be concerned about?" I teased.

Beckett's dimple resurfaced, and I let out a weightless sigh. "So, this work thing you mentioned you do a lot of . . . what is it, exactly?"

"It's an app used for farming."

My brows rose in surprise. As buttoned up as Beckett appeared, I thought he'd tell me he was a hedge fund guy or had a windfall playing stocks on his personal time.

"Farming? Well, this would be a great place for that. But you don't live here. How in the world did you come up with an app for an industry that thrives in a place you don't want to be?"

"Way to get to the point." He took a sip of his tea and cocked his head ever so slightly as he returned my stare. "You're really pretty, you know."

I shook my head. "I've heard that now and again, but I also know when a man is trying to change the subject."

His shoulders dropped, but his smile remained. "Fine. I came up with the idea when I gave online dating a go."

"What? How in the world do you go from online dating to developing farm equipment?"

Beckett grinned. "I didn't develop farm equipment. Just an extremely helpful app."

"Based on hooking up with the opposite sex online? Do tell." I arched my brows, and Beckett's eyes didn't stray from mine.

"Ever heard of the app that promises something like a ninety-five percent success rate?"

I scooted my chair in. "Don't they all?"

"Well, this online dating experience was a doozy." He blew out some air and shook his head as he reflected on it, which made me giggle.

"Must have made a mark."

"This company developed an app that is based on a mathematical equation for love, and it's on a global scale. No pictures are involved. No couple meetings. Just math shoving two people together to see if they fit, and so far, their success rate has allegedly been at about ninety-five percent.

I snickered. "Allegedly."

"Anyway, they take all sorts of data sets and squish possibilities together, and when some kind of tabulation is completed, there are two outcomes. Either it's matched you with someone, or the algorithm decided you need work."

"Need work?" I asked, surprised. "Like a new personality or what?"

Beckett laughed. "No, like they have all this online counseling you have to go through and more tests to take before they try to match you again. And that's only if the professionals give the go-ahead and let you back into their dating pool."

I grinned wickedly as my mind filled up with so many questions. The server came over and took our orders. Beckett looked like he was going to fall over when I ordered.

"Just know if you plan on inviting me out again, I don't hold back on food consumption."

"Noted."

I waved my hands briskly in the air to get us back on topic. "Okay, so you have got to fill in the blanks for me how matchmaking, counseling recommendations, and happily-ever-afters led you to concentrate on the agricultural field."

"After I got my results, there was a tiny map with all of these little red dots bleeping away with characteristics, actions, and goals listed."

"And?"

"Those bleeps represented all the fish in the sea that I couldn't have because the algo didn't like me."

"Oh, don't take it personally." I shook my head.

Beckett laughed. "I didn't give it a second thought, but what intrigued me was how precise these little dots filled with information were, and it got me thinking. What if farmers could examine their crops like this over hundreds and even thousands of acres?"

"Wow. That is incredible. How did you do it, and what does it tell the farmer?"

"They can manage nutrient levels, moisture levels, overall health of the plants, and they can make adjustments right from their phone. Initially, we used satellites to get the data over, but now that cell towers are all over the place, things really fell into place. The setup is easy with different soil readers and sensors for the crops, and the app handles the rest. The business took on a mind of its own, really. At first, I mainly sold the concept in France for the vineyards, and word spread globally."

I sat stunned, staring at the man in front of me. He wasn't even aware of his own brilliance.

"Once the States got ahold of the app, business just . . ."

"Grew like the cornfields surrounding us?"

"Yeah."

"Well, I'm impressed." I had some iced tea and churned my thoughts over and over again about his online dating. "Here you start trying to find a match online, and the next thing you know, you're building an empire."

He smiled. "Just lucky."

"When it comes to business," I added, and he grinned.

"Just not when it comes to love, I'm afraid."

"Do you think you'll ever get it?" I asked.

"Love?"

I nodded and let out a slow breath, almost fearing what his answer might be.

Beckett grinned. "I've always been fascinated with my parents. They've always just been so complementary to one another, and I wondered how things that drive some people apart never touched my parents."

"And yet you've managed to stay single."

He nodded. "Yup."

"Did you ever take the tests and complete the counseling?"

"Nope." He cupped his hands together. "Remember when I said the algorithms hated me? I meant it. I fell into this pool of undateables."

I busted into laughter. "That's a thing? Oh, no. I wonder what that makes me?"

"You're very dateable."

Our dinner arrived, and Beckett eyed my tall slab of meat.

"You think you can finish that?" he prompted.

"Oh, please. Without question." I waggled my finger. "But no changing the subject on me. I'm completely fascinated by your results."

"I don't think the app was ready for my answers."

"Okay, give me an example of a question and your answer."

Beckett smiled. "First of all, I realized the app didn't have a sense of humor."

"Okay . . ."

"Here's one for you. What would you do if your significant other hated the meal that you spent hours cooking?"

"And your answer?" I cringed internally, worrying he might have said something really, really bad for the robot to kick him out of the program.

"I wouldn't spend that long cooking."

I frowned. "That's all you said?"

He nodded.

"Well, even though the algorithms feel you're too screwed up to date, I'm glad you seized such a great opportunity. It's pretty incredible."

"And I actually just got an offer."

"A match?" My heart sank.

Beckett laughed. "No, for my company. My attorneys are working on it as we speak."

"Wow. And then what? You just stay in Paris, waltzing down the sidewalks while looking at the River Seine?"

Beckett shook his head and took a sip of the iced tea the server brought. "I'm actually taking after Cash. I don't think I'd do very well sitting alone in my place, staring at the river."

"How so?" I asked, intrigued. Everything I knew about Cash had to do with flipping properties or collecting them so he could turn around and rent them out.

"I've found some pretty incredible deals in really obscure places, and I'm thinking of redoing them here and there. It would keep me busy."

I nodded. "That's really cool."

"I haven't even told my family about the offer."

"Your secret is safe with me." I tapped my chest and smiled, feeling an odd sense of anticipation wash over me.

"I believe that."

"And you've never done the online dating thing before?"

I shook my head. "No, I get myself in enough trouble in the real world. I don't need AI shenanigans and algorithms telling me who else will screw me over."

Beckett laughed, tipping his head back slightly, which only highlighted his broad shoulders, and all I could think about was the idea of no-strings-attached.

"That's the spirit."

"I guess we all have our stuff." I looked around the restaurant, taking in the tall ceilings painted a light color that matched the Wisconsin sky in the winter and the dark timbers hoisted on the walls with chandeliers hanging above. I drew a deep and steady breath as I matched my eyes to Beckett's. "But, I'm pretty sure I take the cake in the screwed-up department. I foolishly trusted my heart, business, and life to a conman and lost everything. All I had when I came out here were the clothes on my back and my cameras. I even had to give the rental car back."

Beckett jolted in his seat as horror washed over his features. "Oh, my God, Nina. I'm so sorry. What happened?"

My heart rate climbed as I swallowed down a thick lump of something in my throat, possibly regret or embarrassment.

"A man named Travis Collins came rolling into my town several years ago. No one knew much about him, but that wasn't too unusual, especially since he had some great stories about what led him to our little town in New Mexico."

Beckett nodded, waiting for more.

"When I look back at everything now, I can see the signs as plain as day, but in the moment of it all, I totally fell for his spiel, and he had a good one." I pushed a smile onto my face so I wouldn't look as mortified as I felt. "At first, things started casual. He mentioned he'd been this famous guy's dealer."

"Art dealer," Beckett clarified.

I nodded, laughing. "Might have been better if were something else."

Beckett grinned.

"Anyway, he sounded so credible and was telling me

about all the amazing things he could do for my career and getting my work more exposure if he became my manager." I sighed. "And I have to confess that my heart might have gotten a little involved, and before I knew it, I signed an agreement with him. The next few years were incredible. He put his money where his mouth was, and my work became more recognized, my gallery grew to solo exhibitions, and my income multiplied with licensing deals. Things were good." I shrugged. "Until they weren't."

"I'm so sorry." Beckett's voice was tender, along with his expression.

I hadn't let anyone, not even my sisters, see the open wounds I did so well at concealing. Everything about Travis clung to me every day, not about the man, but what he'd done to me. Everything I'd lost.

I'd always heard it was easier to never have everything than to have everything ripped away from you. Whoever said that knew what they were talking about.

"Anyway, enough about that. I'm here, and I'm enjoying this fabulous evening out with the Deer Whisperer."

Chapter Eight

Beckett

Nina's eyes met mine with embarrassment, and she had absolutely no reason to be embarrassed. The man she met was a scumbag, and it was no reflection of her. Yet, I could see her worries written all over her face. She didn't want to be thought of as a fool, and she never could be.

"I have a confession," I told her, hoping to lift her spirits.

"Please tell me you're not an art dealer on the side," she pleaded.

"No side hustles." I laughed, shaking my head and seeing the sparkle in Nina's gaze. "Not in the slightest. I just know what I like and buy it."

"Then what have you been keeping from me?"

I pressed my lips together and studied this enigma of a woman. She was carefree, intelligent, creative, and everything in between.

But in this very moment, she looked as fragile as an already shattered porcelain dish.

"I'm not an actual Deer Whisperer. In fact, the thing did the exact opposite of what I told it to do."

Nina let out a happy sigh as our dinner arrived. "I'm sorry to hear that about you, Beckett. I almost thought you were too close to perfection to be in my orbit."

I laughed and shook my head. "I think you're talking about my brother Cash. He's got it all going on. Always has."

Her brows arched in surprise. "Oh, yeah? You seem pretty put together to me."

I smiled, watching Nina saw into her piece of meat like a lumberjack, and thought about how good she felt against me earlier today.

It also came to my attention from the same set of circumstances how skewed my priorities were in a crisis. The fact that I'd actually stopped in the middle of an emergency to feel her hips under my fingers and the curve of her ass backing into my body while a deer thrashed around an antique store seemed off. Maybe the app had been right.

I shrugged. "You know how it goes. Sibling rivalry and all that."

She nodded and looked down at her plate.

"Or is that something the Bailey sisters never encountered?"

Nina grinned, meeting her eyes with mine. "I

wouldn't say never. I'm lucky because from the moment I could express myself, everyone just figured I was the flighty one who couldn't be contained. Poor Grace got labeled as the mature and responsible one and did a great job of delivering there."

"And Maya?"

"Ah, she's just the sweetest, most inner-reflective person I've ever met. She's always been like that. I got off easy. Expectations were low once I went to art school."

I laughed, knowing exactly what she meant. My youngest brother Hunter kind of paved the way for going against whatever my parents had set their sights on for him.

"You're coming to my mom and dad's anniversary party, right?"

"I wouldn't miss it for the world," she said, tilting her chin slightly as the light from the chandelier bounced off her eyes, turning the color into melted caramel. I knew I could be lost in them forever. "Apart from after-church potlucks, before-church potlucks, holiday dinners, and the like, I'm missing a bit of entertaining or getting entertained."

"Did you do a lot of that in New Mexico?"

"I did. Since I had the gallery, every Thursday evening, we did a cocktail hour where we'd have a guest artist exhibit work or demonstrate their technique, and just about every Saturday night, either I was hosting a dinner or someone else did with the local college's resident artists."

My chest tightened when I saw the strain in Nina's expression. She really did leave a full life behind. When I think back to Paris or any of the places I lived, I wouldn't be leaving much. Sure, I'd meet a client for dinner now and again, but I spent most of my time there, alone with my thoughts, taking in the art, food, and scenery by myself. Nina gave up everything to come to Wisconsin.

Or had it stolen.

"I have a proposition for you."

Nina's smile widened. "Should I be worried?"

"Depends." I took a sip of my drink. "Would you be my date for my parents' party so that I'm not there alone and don't give the family a reason to set me up?"

Nina chuckled and nodded. "I like the way you think. We'll beat them to the punch."

"Exactly."

The server took our plates away, and Nina declined dessert, which kind of bummed me out since I wanted to spend more time with her.

But I was getting ahead of myself.

Way ahead of myself.

"It's been an amazing evening with you, Beckett."

Nina's eyes flashed to mine.

The server brought the check as Nina pulled out her reading glasses and nudged them on her nose. She reached for the bill, but I slapped my card down right when the server went to leave.

"You didn't have to buy my dinner," Nina said, shaking her head.

"I wouldn't invite you out to dinner and then ask you to pay."

Nina wet her lips and pressed them into a thin line. "I'm going to be honest with you, Beckett Knox. I'm in no way, shape, or form mentally available for any kind of romantic interlude."

"You mean a relationship, sex, or both?"

Nina's gaze pinned me in place. "Relationship."

"That makes it easy."

Heat and heaviness pooled deep in my abdomen, stretching to my groin.

"Does it?"

I nodded, glancing around the restaurant that had thinned out substantially. Something had told me Nina and I had sat here a lot longer than either of us realized.

"If we got a room here, the town would be talking by tomorrow," I said, laughing.

"And if we were better planners, we'd have one by now. The hotel is sold out for the weekend." The heat in her gaze made every single inch of my body feel like I'd been tossed in front of a flame thrower.

"You checked?"

She nodded with a naughty grin. "I called on my way over."

I stared at Nina Bailey and tried to take in every feature of her. It was like I thought at any minute, she was just going to go *poof*. And maybe on some level, I felt she didn't really want to be in Buttercup Lake either, and if she left, would I ever see her again?

Would it matter?

"I should probably head home," she said, standing from the table.

I immediately followed, nodding my head while trying to adjust myself in a quick twist that nobody would notice.

"We're still on for my parents' party?" I asked.

"I wouldn't miss it for the world."

"And what about letting me plan a few Wisconsin-themed events?"

She grinned, nodding. "You're on."

"Good. It will give me something to do with myself

while I'm here."

"I know this might sound crazy, but it was really nice to talk to someone about what happened back in New Mexico. I've been holding it all in, and I feel a lot better."

I knew she'd barely touched on it, but it was a start.

"Anytime. I'm always a phone call away." I smiled. "Or a text."

We slowly made our way to the lobby, and I suddenly felt like I was saying goodbye forever, which was ridiculous because we'd already made plans.

"Okay, Beckett Knox." Nina breathed my name, and there was something so sexy about it as she turned around to face me and I nearly walked into her.

Our lips were so close together from the near collision that I wondered what would happen if I bent down and kissed her. By the fire in her eyes, I didn't imagine she'd do much other than kiss me back.

"Drive safely, and try not to get into too much trouble by the next time I see you."

"Same could be said for you," I teased. "Oh, and can I come pick up my artwork tomorrow?"

She smiled a little wider and shook her head. "Free local delivery is always included with every purchase."

"Yeah?"

If she were to come home with me tonight, I knew what would happen. I could feel the chemistry ripping between us, and by the look in her eyes, she knew it too.

"I'm certainly not someone who turns down free delivery."

She gave a quick pat to my chest. "Good. I'll see you tomorrow after seven."

"I'll have dinner ready," I told her.

Surprise washed over her features.

"Yeah?"

"For your trouble."

She smirked. "Of course. I'll bring dessert. Have a good night, Beckett."

I kissed the top of her head, taking in the smell of vanilla, and smiled as she stepped away.

A dreamy look in her eyes told me I was right about tonight, but I was dying to know if the hotel was actually booked.

Nina gave a quick wave and pivoted out of the way from some guests. I watched her walk outside, and my heart finally started to beat normally as I went up to the check-in counter.

The innkeeper looked up from his screen and smiled.

"Is the hotel fully booked for the weekend?"

He nodded. "I'm sorry, Sir. We are. But we do have some availability on Wednesday."

"Great. Thanks. Good to know."

"Anytime, Sir."

Damn. Nina really did call. As I made my way into the frigid temps, I wondered what more Nina didn't tell me. When she brushed everything off about what had happened to her in New Mexico, I could see an endless pit of despair, and for some crazy reason, I wanted to make it all better.

Chapter Nine

Nina

"There is something around here that smells like rotten cheese." Grandma Millie peeked her head into the room of the community center where the Sunshine Breakfast Club was about to start their book club session. "It's driving me nuts."

Grandma Millie spotted me across the room, and her silver brows rose in surprise.

"Nina, what in the world brought you in this early morning? I've been trying to drag you here for months."

Grace snickered next to me and elbowed me in the ribs.

"Grace told me the book you were about to start might be a fun escape for me," I told her as she continued sniffing the air.

"I even brought some blueberry muffins," I added as Grace peeled one of the muffin wraps from the giant buttery mess.

I held my book up, and Grandma Millie smiled just as

Maya walked in with a glass dish full of something yellow. My guess was a frittata.

Abby, who owned the coffee shop in town, trudged into the room with a giant box of coffee with a little brown spigot waiting for people like me to drain the liquid gold.

"My hero," I said, standing up and glancing at Grace. "Want some?"

"Are you just trying to be cruel?" She chuckled with an instinctive belly rub.

"Oh, right. Sorry. I'll grab you a juice."

As Abby set the giant box of coffee down, I glanced around the room to see a variety of women here, ranging from twenties to nineties, and many faces I recognized from town.

No wonder this club had so much pull when it came to making love connections. I spotted the librarian munching on a cinnamon roll, a couple of checkers from the hardware store gabbing in the corner with their books tucked in between their arms as they balanced a plate of food, our postal lady who always made sure to leave our packages under the porch so they wouldn't get wet, and the owner of Buttercup Café. Not to mention countless others. If it were true that they didn't have their sights on us, I'd find out today.

I felt somewhat guilty since I'd been avoiding my grandma's invitations for so long and suddenly appeared when I was worried that I'd become the next target, but hey. At least I made it. The book promised to be good too. And I needed a distraction. This morning, I was woken up to another prank call, no words, just silence. I shivered thinking about it.

"It's so good to see you," Abby said, giving me a quick wave. "I actually wanted to talk with you about purchasing a couple of pieces for our coffee shop."

A flutter of excitement buzzed through me. "Really? That's amazing. Thank you."

She nodded, taking a sip of coffee before filling up her plate with an amazing assortment of breakfast goodies.

"I spotted a black and white photo of a monarch butterfly over at Grace's. It wasn't in your area, but Grace said it was yours. It would be wonderful to feature a local artist." She took a bite of a mini waffle from her plate and chewed quickly as her words dinged me. I had to wrap my head around the fact that I was now a local artist in Wisconsin, not New Mexico.

"The detail is magnificent, and I just love how you managed to make the edges of the wings translucent and sparkly. Ah, it's just incredible," she continued.

I'd managed to capture a butterfly flapping its wings toward a patch of milkweed, and when I'd blown it up on the canvas, I'd added some pearlized paint, etching the shape of the wings, and plastered Ogura lace paper along the body of the monarch.

"Thank you so much. I got really lucky with that shot."

"Well, I hope to be over to purchase it later."

"You've made my day. I'm just so happy you like the piece."

She put her coffee down and touched my shoulder. "Loved it."

"I found the culprit," Grandma Millie yelled from a closet in the corner of the spacious room. She spun around with a Ziploc bag of cheese in various shades of green. "Something tells me the teenagers had a little fun over the weekend."

I chuckled, thinking how innocent a prank that was compared to the rest of the world at the moment.

Grandma Millie wandered out of the room. Moments later, we saw her walking by the window to toss it in the outside bin.

I returned to Grace with her juice, my coffee, and two plates of food stacked precariously as Abby sat across from us in the circle of chairs.

"Since Mandy is out from the flu, I'll be starting off our discussion. We'll wrap up last week's book and talk about our expectations for the new one."

Grandma Millie came in and cleared her throat and shook her head. "How about we skip over the wrap-up from last week's book?"

Abby cocked her head and smiled. "Why's that?"

"No reason." Grandma Millie cleared her throat again.

I turned my attention to my grandma and chuckled. "Something about it makes you uncomfortable with me here?"

Grandma laughed. "Not at all. I'm no snollygoster. I have principles. What I'll say behind a person's back, I'll say to their front."

It was cute to see my grandma getting all fired up.

My grandma took a seat next to Maya and sighed. "Ah, what the heck. We can go over it."

"Well, I just love that the ending was set in Paris," Abby said wistfully. She touched her heart and raised her shoulders. "And the way he was willing to give everything up for her . . . ooh, I could just eat it up."

Maya chuckled and nodded. "Especially because he didn't have to do that. Everything just kind of lined up the way it was supposed to be."

My right brow arched at the mention of Paris. I gave

my grandma some side eye as she shifted uncomfortably in her seat.

"But the fact that the main female protagonist was an artist and could live out her dreams . . . Scrumptious." Jenna, the postal worker, beamed. "To know a man would move mountains for you. Oh, I wish for love like that someday. Made me swoon all over the place."

I scowled. Artist. Paris. Long-distance relationship.

Beckett popped into my head. Oh, who was I kidding? He'd never left my mind since the dinner the other night. He'd even sent some really cute texts, which wasn't what I needed if I were to stand firmly with my convictions.

One of the checkers I'd recognized from the hardware store nodded. "And to think, all they really wanted was each other, and it didn't matter where they lived as long as they had that."

I leaned over to Grace. "Don't you find this a little odd?"

"What's odd?" she whispered back.

"Beckett lives in Paris. I'm an artist. Just like the main characters of the story? Don't you see the similarities? The book club is at it again."

Her eyes connected with mine. "It's just a book, Nina. I'm not sure I'm following. Are you planning on falling in love with a man who can move mountains for you?"

I scowled at her as only a sister could and chuckled, feeling completely paranoid. "No, you're right."

"Maybe on some subconscious level, it's something you've thought about." She quirked her brows. "You know, with Beckett."

"No, I don't know." I pressed my lips together and huffed before adding, "Not on my best day and most certainly not on my worst."

"What are you two gabbing about?" Grandma Millie strained her body toward us.

"My sister seems to think that the book we finished last week resembles her love life," Grace explained.

Grandma Millie shook her head. "Don't be a ninnyhammer. Grace is right. We didn't pick that book because of your love life."

The entire room went silent, and all eyes turned to me.

"Thank you for that, Grandma." I laughed, shaking my head. "To set the record straight. I don't have a love life."

Jenna laughed. "Join the club. It's nearly impossible to find a man in a town this size."

The single women nodded while the married women shook their heads.

I looked around the room, taking in all the women and

their love for reading, and I felt guilty. Maybe this was merely a book club, truly a place for book lovers with no side of shenanigans.

"So, does anyone want to add any final thoughts about the last read before we delve into the new one?" Abby asked the group.

Everyone looked pretty interested in their breakfasts, so Abby cracked open the new book.

"Okay, so this story is about what?" She flipped it over and glanced at the back.

"I picked it out," Grandma Millie explained, "Because it's got a little mystery and intrigue. It's about a bar owner, and a woman who comes to work for him strikes his fancy, but she's only there temporarily, but something big goes down. Maybe a heist? I don't know. But it sounded good."

Okay, I should have stuck with my first thought.

"Doesn't Hunter own a bar down in Madison?" I knew Beckett's brother did, and it was a super popular one. I really just wanted to highlight that I knew that I was onto them.

Grandma Millie's brows pulled together. "Yeah. So?"

"And isn't Daisy working down there for the winter?"

Daisy just so happened to be the sweetest girl I'd met

in a long time. She works as a bartender over at the hotel bar here in Buttercup Lake, but she was looking for a change for the winter where she might make a little more than the lodge and unwind from taking care of her great uncle. So, she wound up in Madison, working for Hunter until April or so.

"What do you want me to say, Nina?" My grandma had a twinkle in her eye. "Art imitates life."

"I've been dying to read a mystery," Grace said, nodding. "I can't wait to dig in."

Abby went on to explain some of the questions we were supposed to think about while reading the first six chapters. She also mentioned that the next book club would be at the coffee shop because the community center was rented out for the arts and crafts fair for the week.

As the discussion ended and everyone divvied up the leftover food, I glanced at my grandma. Maybe, the book they'd all just finished had been about my circumstances, and maybe after seeing me with Beckett, she gave up and decided to focus on some other poor victim. I was almost insulted.

But I was more annoyed than anything because I couldn't get Beckett Knox out of my brain. When I'd push him out of one quadrant, he'd sneak up in another. It was infuriating.

The little dimple.

His sense of humor.

His incredible listening skills.

And I'd done a pretty good job of imagining him undressed.

Completely.

I was a hopeless case . . .

But hopefully, when I dropped off the artwork at his house later, he'd be super crabby or maybe hooking up with another woman, or even better, he left for Paris unexpectedly.

My family and I wandered into the hall of the community center with our plates piled high and books tucked underneath to act like a table.

"I'm so glad you're joining the book club," Maya gushed. "It's so much fun, and the food is phenomenal."

Jackson pulled up to the door, and Grace spun with the brightest smile on her face as she gave us a quick wave and nearly skipped to the car with her man inside.

"That is so adorable." I sighed.

Maya nodded in agreement as Jackson helped Grace buckle the seatbelt over her expanded belly before they drove off.

"Abby wants to buy a piece of mine for the coffee shop, thanks to Grace."

Maya nodded and shivered as the door opened and let

in a giant gust of Arctic air. "Absolutely. I'm so proud of you, Nina. People are just loving your artwork."

"I think I also happen to have an amazing saleswoman as a sister."

"Ah, baloney." Grandma Millie shook her head. "Nina, your art sells itself. This is what got you in trouble in the first place. You need to believe in yourself. You didn't need that Travis conman to sell your art. You already had an amazing career. He knew it, seized the opportunity, and took complete advantage of you. Your photos and their embellishments speak to people." She drew a breath and teared up suddenly.

I reached out for her, along with Maya. "What's wrong?"

She waved us away and dabbed her tears from her cheeks. "Just . . . your dad had the gift as well. I think that's why all of you girls are so creative. It's just a shame he never had the opportunity to try. He squandered everything."

Out of nowhere, a lump lodged deep into my throat, like I was choking on a golf ball.

My dad . . .

What my sisters and grandma didn't know was that I had sent him money when my mom overdosed, right before he disappeared this summer.

I knew instinctively not to, but he begged, and I was in the middle of all my stuff, and I just sent it.

Just sent the money to a known addict.

These were the secrets that ate away at me. My bad decisions in life, like trusting Travis or believing my dad when he said he wanted to get clean. That this time was different.

Grandma straightened and wiped away the last of the tears. "So silly of me to be crying over something I can't control."

"You're human, Grandma." I gave her a hug, realizing how small she'd become even though she was a giant of a person to us.

Chapter Ten

Beckett

Trying to play it cool seemed impossible around Nina. She was far cooler. She couldn't be contained, and I had absolutely no idea what she was thinking or what she might say.

Which was completely fascinating.

But I hoped to keep her on her toes too. The sun had long since set, and I knew she'd be over here with the piece of art I'd purchased over the weekend.

I knew I didn't have many chances with Nina since I was only in town for a short while, but the enormous pull to her couldn't be ignored. And I'd tried.

But it didn't matter if I were picking grapes out at the grocery store or whether I was brushing my teeth, Nina flashing her brilliant grin always popped into my head.

And I didn't mind one bit.

Tonight, I was kind of running a gamble. I wanted to show her a bit of the Wisconsin I loved growing up here, and this evening, that included snowmobiling after a homecooked meal. Never mind that by the time I made it to senior year of high school, I was ready to jet from small-town living

The oven beeped, and I went over to pull out dinner I'd picked up from the grocery store. The fact that Buttercup Lake had a grocery store that wasn't hooked to the gas station any longer amazed me, and their gourmet deli area completely threw me for a loop.

Earlier today, I'd driven around town and hardly recognized the place. Between the gift stores, restaurants, and bustling sidewalks in the dead of winter, I was baffled.

My family kept telling me how much our little town had changed, but I couldn't wrap my head around it. To me, Buttercup Lake would always be the one-road town with a gas station for a grocery store, a bait shop, a laundromat, and a bank. And if you were lucky on a Saturday morning, the diner might be open unless the owner was out hunting during deer season . . . or turkey season.

I smiled at the thought and shook my head as the doorbell rang. I glanced at the chicken Kiev and took a deep breath as I suddenly felt on edge.

"Get a grip." I made my way to the door and opened it to see Nina dressed in a pair of jeans, an oversized grey sweatshirt, and a matching knit cap. Her puffy jacket almost swallowed her as she came inside and shook it off her shoulders with my help before setting the large artwork down and peeling off some grey gloves.

Her knuckles grazed my arm, and I felt electricity charge through me.

Nina's eyes caught mine, and I smiled, pretending I didn't just feel the sparks.

"I keep telling myself I'll get used to the cold, but I'm not sure whether I'm lying to myself or just being hopeful." She lifted one shoulder. "Any idea?"

I chuckled as I hung up her coat and turned to look at her. "Surprisingly, I'm starting to acclimate, but I didn't nearly freeze to death in a blizzard, so there's that."

She smiled, which made the world okay. It didn't matter where I was as long as I got to see that smile. I dropped my gaze and cleared my throat as if she could read my mind.

"Thanks for putting that new lock on Grandma Millie's place. It has been giving me trouble for weeks."

"No sweat." My eyes met hers. "Thanks for bringing this over tonight."

She winked at me. "Like I said, all part of the deal. What smells so amazing?"

"I picked up some chicken Kiev from the market. I just pulled it out of the oven. You're staying for dinner, I hope?"

Her eyes lit up, and she gave a quick nod.

"If you're game, I'd love to take you out after dinner."

Surprise washed over her expression. "What in the world is open on a Monday night?"

"Other than a million local dive bars?" I laughed as we walked into the kitchen. "Although, Cash told me there's a good one down the road that does Karaoke."

"Seriously? I love Karaoke."

I smiled. "Then we'll have to add it to the list."

"The list?"

I plated our meals and took them to the dining table.

"You know . . . remember I made it my mission to show you around my home state since you haven't even had a fresh-from-the-dairy cheese curd."

Nina laughed and nodded as she took a seat across from me at the table.

"Ah, right. A tour guide from the man who loathes this small town. Good times."

I chuckled and took a sip of water. "I'm still in shock that there is a real grocery store in town. The place has really changed."

She smiled, glancing around my home. "It really has. I remember in the summers, we'd come to Buttercup Lake to escape everything back home. Yet, there wasn't much here aside from my grandparents, but between the town and Millie and Renny, it was enough. It gave us the strength to go back home for the school year."

"You didn't have a great upbringing?" I didn't expect to hear this from Nina. The Bailey sisters were always so happy, and Grandma Millie was incredible. It was hard to fathom how things could go so wrong with their parents.

Nina ignored my question and forged on. "Our big thing was grabbing ice cream on the beach. Now, there are ice cream stores all over, and espresso on demand."

I laughed. "Mind-blowing."

"Right?" Her eyes settled back on mine, and the familiar pull to her started up again. "So, what do you have planned for after dinner? Should I be worried?"

She dipped her chicken in the butter sauce and took a bite, closing her eyes in the process.

"Snowmobiling."

She choked out a laugh and shook her head. "At night? I've never driven one of those things in the day, let alone in the dark. I'd probably drive right into the lake."

"Good thing they're all frozen over. We can just drive over the lakes."

"It's completely dark out, Beckett." She took another bite of chicken. "Yum."

"Believe it or not, driving at night is easier to see with the snow and everything. The headlights reflect."

"If you say so."

"Says the woman who has been to Burning Man six times."

She giggled. "We aren't flying across the desert in the middle of the night at Burning Man."

My brows quirked in amusement.

Nina laughed and smiled. "Well, maybe some people were, but I wasn't one of them."

"So no to snowmobiling, then."

"I didn't say that." She smiled. "But is there one big enough for two riders?"

I nodded. "Mine is a two-seater."

"Good. And helmets?"

"Absolutely. I even have some warm snow coveralls you can put on. They might be a little big, but they should work."

"Who knew when I pulled on my flannel-lined jeans this morning, I'd actually need them?"

"The world is a wondrous place."

I took a bite of dinner and watched Nina eat her chicken while keeping her eyes averted from mine. The little nagging feeling ate away at me as I wondered what she meant about her childhood. Growing up in Buttercup Lake, I always knew Millie and Renny. We'd bump into them at the gas station or the lake, but I never thought anything was off with them.

"Is everything okay?" I asked.

Nina's eyes met mine. "I have to tell you something."

I nodded as the nagging feeling crept into my blood.

"I went to the Sunshine Breakfast Club's meeting this morning. Your mom wasn't there," she added. "But I think my grandma is telling the truth. They don't have a bullseye on our backs."

"Really?"

Nina nodded. "But I think they do have your brother on their radar."

Surprise ran through me. "Hunter? He doesn't even live here."

"It seems like they want to set him up with Daisy."

"Who is . . .?"

"A bartender here at the lodge, but she's working for your brother down in Madison right now." Nina let out a few breaths. "So, I'm completely relieved. No prying eyes in our direction."

I laughed. "Do you think there's something coming up they shouldn't see?"

"Who knows?" She lifted her shoulders up to her ears. "But it takes the pressure off."

She finished her meal, and I realized I'd barely touched mine. I took a sip of water.

"Sometimes I wonder, with everything I've been through and my trust detector completely malfunctioning, if maybe I should only do meaningless encounters." She pursed her lips while I choked on my drink.

"Is that a rhetorical question, or . . . you want my two cents?" I asked after noticing her studying me.

"Two cents."

"I would love to have a meaningful relationship with someone, but I've only mastered the meaningless encounter "

Nina nodded as her lip quirked, eyeing some brownies on the table. "I've apparently mastered neither."

She reached for a brownie. "May I?"

"Absolutely." I took one too and polished it off in two bites.

Nina devoured the brownie, and I couldn't help but wish I'd been that chocolate.

I smiled. "You ready to suit up and get on the snowmobile?"

She stood and stretched toward the ceiling. "It's now or never."

The chemistry running between us could bubble over any minute. If I got too close, I'd slide a kiss on those luscious lips, and I knew she'd kiss me back.

But we were both keeping our distance.

"Suits are in the mudroom on the way to the garage." I motioned for her to follow me and made my way down the hall.

The bedrooms were down this direction as well, along with the stairs to the basement, where I'd completely outdone myself. A bar, a game room, a couple of extra guest bedrooms, and a bathroom made it feel like an entirely different home.

"What's down there?" Nina asked as we walked by the stairs. "Is that just like fancy concrete walls and lots of storage boxes nobody ever sorts through like most of the basements around here?"

"Since I rent the place out, I made it like party central down there."

"That sounds fun. You'll have to show me sometime."

"Totally." I spun around to nod in agreement when she smacked right into me.

I looped my arms around her waist to steady her, and Nina's gaze locked on mine. Our mouths were so close to one another's.

"This is nice," she said in an overly chipper voice that sounded nothing like Nina.

I didn't let go.

"It is."

She twisted her lips to moisten them, and my entire body craved her instantly.

"Would this be a meaningless encounter or . . . ?" she teased as I loosened my embrace.

I took a step back, but she caught my hand in hers.

"Nina, I have to tell you that I don't think anything with you would be meaningless."

"Okay," she tried again. "How about a no-strings-attached encounter?"

I pulled her into me and felt her body crush into mine, molding against me like we'd been built for each other. My fingers rested on her hips as she looked into my eyes. Her hazel eyes smoldered with something more than no-strings.

Nina's eyes fell to my lips, and I knew I had to kiss her.

Chapter Eleven

Nina

Oh, please kiss me.

Beckett's eyes darkened into a fiery need before his mouth pressed against mine. His lips made mine tingle as I parted my lips and our kiss deepened. He tasted incredible, like chocolate, and all the desire I'd been trying to tuck away came roaring out of me as I kissed him back.

Goosebumps rolled over my flesh with each twist of Beckett's tongue or nip from his lips as his fingers glided up my body and twisted in my hair.

A rough growl fell from Beckett's lips as he smiled against my mouth, our bodies pressing into one another.

"You fit just right," he whispered as I broke my mouth from his.

I opened my eyes to see him studying me, taking me in like I was some sort of goddess.

"Nina, everything about you is perfect," he said, his arms lowering to my waist.

"There's no such thing." I kept my eyes on his as the tension between us tightened like a string about to snap.

"Perfect for me," he corrected.

My knees felt wobbly as I drew a shaky breath.

"I'm a mess, Beckett. Mentally, physically, emotionally. I don't know what I want or what I need or where I should be or what I should do." I shook my head, noticing the tenderness in his gaze.

"That will come in time."

I rested my hands on his chest and kept my eyes on him. "I sure hope so, Beckett, or my life might become very lonely."

"I won't let that happen."

"In just a week and a half, you're going back to your world, and I'm going back to mine."

He nodded, keeping his smoldering gaze on me. My heart pounded so hard I swore he could see my chest rising and falling with each beat.

Every part of me wanted to pretend that I could start something with Beckett Knox that could last, but the reality of our situation told me otherwise.

I'd finally started to scrape my life back together, collecting payments from the new sales of my artwork to create the new version of Nina. I'd managed to pay most of the debt that Travis had accumulated under my business. It left me with nothing, and worse yet, it left me confused. My mind was all over the place with paranoia and distrust.

To protect my heart, I knew all I should muster was a no-strings-attached romp. But the look in his eyes made me wonder if that was possible.

I laughed, shaking my head. "Let's get riding. See if you can top that kiss with your driving skills."

He let go of me and nodded with a smile. "My pleasure."

When he turned around to head to the mudroom, I finally caught my breath.

I didn't even know if I'd be able to survive a night with Beckett, let alone the moment he flew away.

As I stewed on that last thought, Beckett turned around and handed me a dark navy snow bib, which I quickly stepped into and zipped up. The more fabric between Beckett and me, the better.

"Here, wear this jacket. It's warmer than the one you brought, and I've got these insulated gloves, and this scarf and hat should work." Beckett handed me everything before he put on his own ensemble, and I wondered if everything that happened down the hall had even happened.

Maybe it hadn't happened at all, and I was already

losing my mind.

By the time I'd zipped up the bib and jacket, put on the gloves, scarf, and hat, and pulled up the hood, I felt like a mummy dressed as the Stay-Puft Marshmallow Man.

"I can't move," I mumbled through all the layers of fabric.

He smiled and touched my nose with his gloved fingers. "At least you'll be warm."

I rolled my eyes as I waddled after him into the garage. The large garage door lifted, and he pushed out the snowmobile, guiding it onto the snow.

"Does it have gas?" I asked.

His brows lifted. "Yeah. Why?"

"I don't know." I chuckled. "Just asking from personal experience. I tend to let Thor run to the empty line."

Beckett tilted his head slightly as he handed me a helmet. "Who's Thor?"

"My truck. I named him after the night of the blizzard. If it weren't for him, I don't know what would have happened."

"He reminds me more of a Rusty or an Ol' Blue or something."

"It's Thor."

Beckett laughed and handed me a helmet. "You can

pull your hood off, and I'll help you tighten it."

I nodded and adjusted the helmet until it felt right while Beckett clicked the straps. "Not many people are into helmets around here. It's nice to see you are."

"I've never understood that." He shook his head. "I have a buddy who's an ER doctor down in Madison, and he says that so many injuries and deaths could be prevented if people just put one on. It stuck with me."

"Well, you've won my trust already."

Beckett snapped his helmet in place and climbed on the snowmobile, motioning for me to slide on behind him.

I hadn't really thought this through when I agreed to do this adventure. Not that being straddled around Beckett for an hour or two would be a bad thing, but it certainly wouldn't help calm my raging libido. I placed my hands on his shoulders and swung my leg over the snowmobile, sliding into the seat.

My thighs wrapped around the back of his hips, and I felt him tense.

"Only a few rules," Beckett said.

"Okay, shoot."

"No tickling."

I laughed. "What? Who would tickle someone while they're driving a snowmobile?"

"I've asked Hunter that same question a million times, and he still does it."

I snickered and shook my head.

"Second rule is lean into the turns. Basically, follow my motions as I drive. If I'm moving forward, let your body do the same. If I'm leaning back, you do that too."

"I can handle that."

"Lastly, if you have to pee, please tell me. Don't pee on the machine." The moment my imagination pictured pee all over the snowmobile from Hunter, I bolted from the machine and dove into the snowbank.

He cut the machine off and sprang next to me.

When I tried to unbury myself, my body only fell deeper.

Beckett smiled and took his helmet. "And never do that," he said, trying to extract me from the driveway's snowbank.

"Sorry. I was just imagining Hunter's pee all over the seat, and I freaked."

Beckett laughed, scooping me out of the rigid snow, and set me upright.

"This is a new machine. There's been no peeing."

He dusted my jacket off and laughed. "You've got really quick reactions."

141

"I don't do well with most bodily fluids."

Beckett was trying to hold it together. "Right. Okay. So, let's try this again."

I nodded as he turned on the machine, and I slid back into the seat, feeling the strong build of his body underneath the layers of protective clothing between us.

"I could get used to this," I muttered as Beckett slipped his helmet back on.

"What was that?" he asked.

"Nothing."

He steered the snowmobile down the drive at a slow pace and stopped at the end. He looked both ways and turned onto the road that led to some trails. I'd always noticed the snowmobile crossing signs but never imagined I'd be on one.

As we continued down the road, I heard the familiar buzz of the snowmobiles as I spotted several more riders congregating near one of the trails.

They took off in front of us, and Beckett slowed down to give some space between us.

The snowmobile took off slowly with Beckett driving us gracefully over small hills and dips. The moon's glow blanketed over the fresh snow. Pine trees clung to puffs of white like cotton balls. Beckett spotted a marked clearing and slowed the snowmobile down to a stop.

"Over there," he said, pointing toward the full moon.

The empty farmland covered in brilliant white stretched as far as I could see with the glowing disc in the sky.

"Do you hear that?" he asked.

I removed my helmet to hear faint howls from what sounded like wolves in the distance. "Are those what I think they are?"

He smiled and nodded as I slipped my helmet back on.

"Wolves."

"Have you ever seen any?" I asked.

"Many times, but I guess there's even more now since the reintroduction."

"So I've heard. I've actually never seen one in Wisconsin." I smiled, thinking about how incredible it would be.

"You got your phone?" he asked.

"Yeah. Why?"

"I'll get you some photos. Hold on. We're going off trail."

"Won't we get in trouble?"

"I won't tell if you won't." Beckett drove the snowmobile over the field as I held on tight, and I wondered if the night could get any better.

Chapter Twelve

Beckett

"I got a call from the Sveltzes last night," Nate told me over the phone.

I cleared my throat and smiled, thinking about how incredible it was to show Nina the pack of wolves that frequent my yard. She'd taken so many photos using her phone. I had no idea if any of them would turn out, but it was an incredible experience.

"They mentioned they saw one of the Knox brothers riding toward the bluff on their property."

I didn't say anything.

"Any idea which one?" he prodded with a tease in his voice.

"Well, Hunter is still in Madison until the weekend," I explained, kicking my feet out in front of me on the couch. "But I have no idea what Cash was up to last night."

Nate laughed. "I do. He was with me."

"I see. Officer, what do you intend to do?"

"Mr. Sveltz didn't seem too put off because you're a man pushing forty and not some teenager doing donuts on his acreage."

"I'll have to drop by with an apology gift."

Nate laughed. "I doubt that's necessary, but I'm curious. What were you doing out there?"

"Showing a woman some wolves."

"Is that what the kids call it these days?" Nate joked.

"Nina hasn't seen any wolves in Wisconsin, so I thought I'd show her. They run back between the Sveltzes' property at the bluff and mine near the lake's edge. Luck was on my side."

Nate groaned. "Isn't it always?"

"Not lately, but thanks for the heads up. I'll make amends."

"Nina's an interesting soul." He laughed. "A little complex."

"Turned you down a few times, I see?"

Nate laughed. "Too many to count."

"If it makes you feel any better, I think she's only hanging out with me because I'm heading out of town."

"Sounds about right. Well, off to crack down on a rooster violation."

"Is that cop lingo for something about to go down?" I asked, flipping on my fireplace with a remote.

"No. It's an actual rooster. In town, we can only have chickens, no roosters."

I laughed, realizing I should have known it was an actual rooster predicament. "Go get 'em, tiger."

"I plan on it."

A thought occurred to me.

"What do you actually do with them? You don't . . . ?" I let my voice trail off.

"No way. I usually take them, to be honest. I have three right now. Since I don't live in the city limits, I might as well. Why? Do you want this one, at least until you leave?"

I laughed, wondering why I felt a sudden kinship with this rooster.

"You know what? I do. Bring him on by. I need the company."

"Will do."

Nate hung up, and I stretched, feeling every muscle in my body ache from last night's ride. It had been a long time since I'd ridden a snowmobile.

I stared at my phone, writing down notes and things to mention at my parents' party. There was so much I wanted to say about my mom and dad. They'd shown us kids how to do it right. How to make a relationship seem effortless.

But it was also rather intimidating. I wasn't sure if I'd ever find a partner who was so in synch with me.

On that note, I climbed off the couch with a grunt and wandered over to Nina's canvas. Her piece was beautiful, and I had just the place for it. I'd moved the painting on my brick fireplace to the entryway and planned on hanging hers over the mantel. It fit the space better than the other one, and it did a fantastic job of reminding me of something I'd never have.

As I put her piece up, my doorbell rang.

"That was fast, Nate," I muttered to myself with a quick step toward the front door.

When I swung it open, I was shocked to see Nina. Her rosy cheeks matched the pink in her sweater as she handed over a pair of my gloves.

"I stole these and realized I'd better give them back." She grinned, handing me the gloves.

"You borrowed them," I corrected, taking the gloves from her. "I just finished hanging your artwork. Would you like to see?"

Her eyes brightened, and she nodded. "Sure."

"Come on in."

"Is it in the bedroom?" she asked as I closed the door behind her.

"Uh, no. But that would have been really smooth had I thought about it."

She chuckled. "Better luck next time."

"Let's hope so."

Nina shook off her jacket and draped it over the arm of a side chair before turning to look at me.

"I got busted last night."

"For what?" Her brows knitted together.

"Trespassing. But the good news is that I have a rooster coming to visit."

Nina laughed so hard that tears ran down her cheeks. "Please tell me you're kidding."

"Which part?"

"The rooster part. Is that your retribution for trespassing? You have to babysit a rooster?"

"No. Just coincidental. The poor fella needed a place to be, so I volunteered." I lifted my arms up. "How hard could it be?"

Nina grinned and eyed me. "Good thing you don't have any neighbors close by. They wouldn't be thrilled."

"How early could they possibly get up?"

Her brows rose. "You're kidding, right?"

"What? Seven?"

"The butt crack of dawn, Beckett." She threw her

head back in more laughter. "You don't have to worry about me staying the night. That was the one downside to staying at Grandma Millie's in the summers."

I grinned. "Like I had a chance."

"How have you lived in farm country and not hung around roosters? Now, let's see where you hung my favorite piece."

"Just one thing," I told her.

She spun around. "Yeah?"

I scooped her into my arms and planted a tender kiss on her lips. "I've wanted to do that since you got here."

Nina looked into my eyes and let out a wistful moan. "Yeah? It's been on your mind?"

I let out a low rumble and nodded. "A lot more than that has been on my mind."

"The whole no-strings-attached romp?" she teased, stepping away.

I could see the walls going up again, and I knew I needed to find out what really happened in New Mexico.

"Maybe." I reached for her hand as we made our way toward the great room.

Her hand moved to her mouth when she saw her art. "Wow, Beckett. This looks sensational."

"It really fits."

She turned around, moving her hand lower. "It speaks to me all over again."

"You're extremely talented, Nina. I hope you know that."

A flicker of some emotion I didn't recognize flew across her face. "Thank you. I have to keep reminding myself of that."

"You want some coffee?"

"I'd love some."

I nodded as she took a seat on the couch, and I went to the kitchen and poured us each a cup. "Do you take anything in it?"

"Nope. I like it plain."

I brought the coffee to Nina, and she took it with both hands and gulped the first sip. "Ah, I needed that. I'm used to a latte a day to keep the doctor at bay, but with things recently, I've had to abstain. It's more like a latte a week or two."

A zing of anger darted through me unexpectedly from what the bastard conman did to her.

"I realize you probably only want to share so much, but I really don't know many of the details. I'm always here to lend an ear."

Nina set the mug on the coffee table and brought her eyes to mine. "Thanks, Beckett. There are days where I want to scream at the top of my lungs about the injustice of it all, and others, I have my head on straight and realize it could be worse. I have my health."

"A lot of people might not be able to see it that way."

She pointed at a throw. "Do you mind?"

"Go ahead."

Nina pulled the blanket over her lap and reached for her coffee, but she didn't take another sip.

"I had the perfect home. It was around a thousand square feet with an indoor/outdoor patio. The wall looking to my back yard was a panel of glass doors, so on nice days, I could just open them up and paint or work on my photos on the patio. My bedroom was exactly how I wanted it, with a chaise by the window and an amazing bathroom. The second bedroom was tiny, but I didn't care about that. I stored all my art supplies there. It was my sanctuary, even when things with Travis went south. It might have looked like the Easter Bunny threw up inside with all the pastels, but I loved it."

I laughed, feeling the strain in my chest tighten. "It's hard to lose things that represent who you are and your achievements."

She let out a sigh and brushed her hand over her forehead. "It is, and then I have to snap back to reality and remind myself that I can do it again, and how lucky I am to have a place in which to bounce back."

Her overwhelming positivity struck a nerve. It was something our family always had growing up, and even with it, I still felt like I didn't belong in Buttercup Lake.

"It's crazy. When my Maya started dating your brother, I was planning on flying out here and visiting, and nothing much had unraveled at home. By the time they really started hot and heavy, my life was imploding, and I could barely afford a rental car to get out here. It's so embarrassing, and yet here I am telling you."

"Do your sisters know the extent of everything?" I asked.

She shook her head. "No. In fact, there's something I've been meaning to tell them. It's so bad that I don't even know how to put it into words."

My heart stilled as she pushed her lips into a frown. "Our mom died this summer from an overdose, and the funeral home sent the ashes to me. I'd planned on bringing them with me when I visited in the fall, but I'd put them in a really beautiful urn, and one day, when I returned from the grocery store, it was missing, along with a lot of my jewelry and artwork from some of my favorite artists."

The color drained from my face. It was a physical reaction. I could literally feel the blood pooling at the bottom of my feet. What kind of evil does that?

"I have no words."

She nodded and brought her hands to her head with the lift of her shoulders. "Pretty much how I've felt."

"To be burglarized and have that taken." I shook my head in disgust, but I caught a fleeting something behind her gaze. "And your sisters don't know?"

Nina shook her head. "No. The relationship with our parents is—was—beyond complicated. I think they're grateful I haven't brought up her ashes because none of us, truthfully, even know what we want to do with them." She cleared her throat and took a sip of the coffee that had become her hand warmer. "And my dad basically went AWOL after my mom's death."

"And he's still into . . ."

Nina let out a deep breath. "Yeah. As far as I know. They both were in really deep . . . homeless, living under bridges or in tent cities out in Seattle."

She set her coffee cup down and brought her gaze to mine. "So, there's lots of messy bits just floating around my aura, and I feel really bad about even exposing you to a fraction of them."

"Don't say that, Nina. I know you don't want to start anything, and I get that. I really get that now, but if nothing else, I want you to know that you can always talk to me. I'll drop everything I'm doing to be there for you."

"Even if you're happily eating a croissant while wandering the cemeteries of Paris?"

I laughed softly. "Even then."

Chapter Thirteen

Nina

Apparently, my new dating motto was to scare them off in the beginning so there's no chance of an ending. I'd say I stuck to it fairly well.

But Beckett was polite enough not to run. Instead, he refilled my coffee and told me how much more enjoyable the trip back to Wisconsin was because of me. There was no judgment or unsolicited advice. It was nice.

"Are we still on for our date on Saturday?" he asked, smiling.

My heart skipped a beat. "Yeah. For sure." I glanced at the clock in the kitchen and drew a silent breath. "I should probably get going. I need to pick up a couple of things at the hardware store before I make my way to Grace's store."

I almost thought I saw a wave of disappointment surface behind Beckett's gaze, but I was probably only imagining it.

Wishful thinking and all that.

"It was amazing spending time with you last night and

this morning." His smile warmed me up. "Did any of those photos come out?"

He remembered. Wow.

I nodded with a huge smile. "Yeah. Believe it or not, the place you found to spot the pack of wolves was amazing. The photos came out with this eerie quality."

"Not too grainy?"

I smiled and stood. "I'll work my magic."

Beckett laughed. "I believe it."

The doorbell rang just as I turned to get a glimpse of my art over his fireplace again. It was so pretty, and for some crazy, unrelated reason, it made me want to tell him more about what happened to me in New Mexico and everything with Travis.

But, saved by the bell.

"I'll think of you every time I look at it."

I chuckled. "Is that a good thing?"

"The best. Now, I think I have a rooster to meet."

"This ought to be great." I smiled, glancing at Beckett as we made our way to the door.

"Okay." He drew a deep breath in as his chest expanded.

Opening the door, there stood Nate and a rooster.

I giggled as the rooster's eyes snapped to Beckett's

and his neck stuck out.

"It's a really pretty rooster," I told them, and it was. The body was black with a plume of long, white feathers erupting from the tail and ankles. "That's a really impressive comb and wattle. Really brilliant red."

Beckett threw me a strange look, and I shrugged.

"What? It's true. You don't see a wattle like that every day," I informed him.

"Or a comb," Nate snickered.

"Do you have a leash or something?" Beckett asked.

Nate scowled. "It's a rooster. Has Paris softened you?"

Without warning, the rooster's right wing flew up. We all looked at one another before the rooster jetted his neck out and started pecking at the air in circles. The rooster was dancing.

"What the heck is going on?" Beckett asked, glancing at me.

I threw my hands in the air and shook my head. "It's all you."

Nate snorted as the rooster kept spinning. "He hasn't done that all morning."

"Should I be worried?" Beckett asked as the rooster stopped and pointed his beak toward Beckett.

"He's either trying to court you." Nate coughed. "Or he's about to attack."

The rooster's wings suddenly flapped back as he darted toward Beckett, who jumped straight up in the air.

I swore it was ten feet high as Nate cracked up.

The rooster stopped charging and glared at Beckett.

Nate grinned. "Well, whether he loves you or not, we've all seen who's the alpha."

I snorted in laughter as Beckett glared at the bird when suddenly, the rooster started chortling, which turned into a trill like no other.

"I feel like I'm witnessing something I shouldn't be," I whispered to no one in particular as the rooster slowly waltzed to Beckett and nuzzled his ankle with his beak.

"Yeah, he's definitely courting you," Nate muttered.

Nate pointed his two index fingers at Beckett with raised brows. "And that is my cue to exit. I dropped some food off under your porch. Let me know if you need anything."

The giggling wouldn't stop. I tried, but I couldn't rein it in when I realized the rooster was flirting with Beckett.

"I think I'm going to follow Nate's lead," I said, scooting by the pair while still snorting in laughter.

"You're gonna leave me alone with this thing?"

Unable to stop my giggles, I nodded as tears rolled

down my cheeks.

"This isn't what I had in mind." Beckett shook his head, shaking his foot to get the rooster to leave him alone, which suddenly worked.

The rooster stood straight and turned his neck to see me in his range. I swore if the bird had hands, he would have shut the door in my face.

"Don't leave me," Beckett joked as I laughed my way off the porch to the sound of the rooster chortling his love for the same man I couldn't stop admiring.

When I got to Thor, I saw Beckett still shaking the rooster away when his eyes connected with mine.

"If you have second thoughts about our date on Saturday, I understand. The rooster is way more forward than I'll ever be."

Beckett laughed as I turned Thor on and blasted the heater. I wondered if it had occurred to Beckett that his rooster wasn't going anywhere. He'd probably be curled up in front of the fire the next time I swung by, and the thought tickled me.

And I didn't know if it was the rooster or Beckett whom I got a kick out of most.

As I made my way down the windy country road to town, I thought about how I just word vomited so much to

Beckett, and I hadn't even told him everything. I shivered at the thought and reprimanded myself. I didn't need to bury complete strangers in my muck. It was mine and mine alone.

Beckett had an amazing family, a life in Paris he seemed to enjoy, and no misgivings about where he planned on living in the future. I didn't need to confuse him, or myself, for that matter.

When town appeared in front of me, a little twinge of excitement erupted. Seeing the little town of Buttercup Lake somehow made me instantly happy. There were families and couples wandering down the shoveled sidewalks with snow piled everywhere else. Christmas decorations remained up all over town because why not? And the stores and restaurants looked lively with people. It was amazing what a thirty-degree day could do for the spirits around here.

I laughed, thinking back to New Mexico and how anything lower than fifty degrees, and we all thought the end was near. Here, it felt like spring was almost a reality.

I found a spot quickly and parked in front of the hardware store. Grace asked if I could buy some more picture frame wire, hooks, and double-sided tape, but with Beckett's new addition, I thought maybe I could look in their chicken section.

The door opened in front of me, and one of the

checkers I recognized from the book club waved. "Hi, Nina. What do you think of the book so far?"

"Oh, shoot. Busted. I haven't read it yet. But I plan to before Friday's meeting." I grabbed a red basket to load up.

"It's sooo good," she gushed. "Is there anything I can help you find?"

"Well, I need to get some things to hang up stuff. How's that for specific?"

She chuckled and nodded. "Aisle four."

"And what about chicken supplies?"

"Are you planning on raising some this spring?" she asked.

"No. Beckett is watching a rooster while he's here, and I think he's got his hands full. In fact, I think the rooster has a crush on him."

The woman laughed. "Who wouldn't? Aisle nine is where you'll find most of that kind of thing. Where's he keeping him?"

"I'm not actually sure." But I had a hunch if the rooster got his way, it would be his family room.

Wandering the aisle of the hardware store was cathartic. I felt normal and so close to feeling settled here at Buttercup Lake that I could almost imagine my life here.

Almost.

And it was intriguing.

Also a little scary.

I loved being around my sisters and grandma, and I was slowly making friends here, and I felt a kinship with the work I could produce in this new setting. But I was worried the novelty would wear off. The residents would get tired of seeing my art, or the tourists' tastes would change.

Not that where I lived in New Mexico was exactly a bustling metropolis, but I'd been there so long that I'd kind of made a name for myself. I was concerned that might not happen here.

When I looked down at my basket, I was surprised to see everything and more piled in it. I must have just been dumping things inside as my brain worked overtime.

I rifled through everything and made sure I got what Grace needed and made my way to the chicken aisle. I was definitely in Wisconsin if they had an entire aisle related to chicken paraphernalia.

And boy, did they.

By the looks of it, Beckett had no idea what he was in for.

Bedding, heat lamps, nesting boxes, chicken feed, and toys that looked like they belonged in the dog and cat aisle filled the shelves.

Since Beckett had a rooster, he wouldn't be needing most of the items laid out in front of me. Unless, of course, it was a miracle rooster, and that opened a whole other can of worms.

I reached for a tiny, furry pig the size of my hand and an oversized strawberry for the rooster and tossed them in my basket before making my way to the checkout counter, where I grabbed a Snickers candy bar. The checker from earlier was nowhere to be seen, so an older woman scanned me through.

By the time I walked out of the hardware store and to my truck, I was a certified icicle. My spine did a little shiver as I started Thor's engine, blasted the heat, and made my way to the antique store.

The window had already been repaired at Grace's shop, and there was no sign that a deer had decided to dance its way into the building full of antiques. I chuckled, thinking back to the scene and Beckett. The entire fiasco could have ended very differently, but thank goodness for his ability to calm things down a bit. It's a characteristic that might come in handy.

I turned off Thor and slid out of the truck with the bags for Grace. As I walked into the store, the familiar smell of apple cider drifted over me. Ever since Grace hit the second trimester, she'd been craving anything apples.

"Oh, thank you," Grace said from the booth near the window. It was across from mine and happened to be where she displayed a lot of the crafts and repurposed items she made.

I handed her the bag of goodies as her eyes skimmed my pants leg. I looked down to see what she was eyeing. "What?"

"You have a huge white feather stuck to the back of your pants." She brought her eyes to mine.

I laughed, bending over to pick up the beautiful plume. "Beckett is babysitting a rooster before he leaves."

"Must be Cindy's again."

"Huh?"

She shook her head. "The woman is nearing seventy and doesn't want to be told what to do by the authorities of Buttercup Lake. She had roosters all her life and doesn't understand why she can't have them now. It's an ongoing battle. Every time Nate takes one away, she goes out and gets another one."

I grimaced. "That's kind of irresponsible."

"She's a bit . . . grumpy."

"Hopefully, everyone out of the town limits will keep offering to take them," I said, shaking my head.

Grace laughed. "Well, so far, that somebody has been

Nate."

I chuckled, thinking about our local policeman. "I never would have thought he would have been into roosters."

"I don't think he is, but he just doesn't want to think about what would happen to them in the middle of farm country."

I trembled at the thought. "Good point."

"Anyway, what do you think about this?" She showed me a mosaic of a deer with pieces of porcelain.

"That is gorgeous."

She nodded. "I thought so too. I used all the broken pieces of porcelain to make this replica of the deer."

"I love it, and what a great way to make lemonade out of a bunch of lemons."

Grace set it down. "It's kind of heavy. Do you mind hanging it for me?"

"Of course."

She handed me a hammer as I fished around in the bag for the perfect hook.

"I'm going to get some cider. Want any?"

"Sounds great."

Grace wandered off as I stood on a chair I'd pulled from a corner and stretched toward the middle of the wall.

With a nail in my mouth, I muttered a quick,

"Perfect."

"That is an understatement." Beckett's voice surprised me, and before I had a chance to pound the nail into the wall, my foot slipped off the chair, and I spat out the nail and yelped as my world turned into slow motion.

Two strong arms caught me before I hit the ground, and Grace giggled as she stood over Beckett and me toppled on the floor.

"That could have hurt," Grace said with a smirk as I attempted to roll off my savior-slash-instigator. "Good thing he was there to catch you."

I scowled as he stood, and I reached for the cider from my sister. "I wouldn't have fallen if he hadn't snuck up behind me and said something."

Beckett grinned. "You can't be sure of that."

I spun around to face him. "Yes, I can. You surprised me out of nowhere."

"A good surprise or a bad surprise?"

Grace's eyes bounced between us, and I let out a huff of annoyance before taking a sip of cider.

"Admit it. You're happy I'm here."

I scowled deeper. "Where's your rooster?"

"Blackheart is at home."

I choked on my cider. "That's a little intense, don't

you think?"

Beckett laughed and shook his head. "Believe me. It fits."

I smiled. "You named your rooster after a Marvel character who is considered to be filled with colossal evil and massive superpowers?"

"How in the world did you know the name was from a comic?"

"Okay, this is my time to back away, my little nerds," Grace teased, and I rolled my eyes.

"Why wouldn't I know my Marvel characters?"

Beckett shook his head, scratching his jaw. "No, I'm pretty sure the question is, why would you know that? The character is pretty obscure, and you'd need to be in pretty deep to understand the significance."

I smiled even wider. "Maybe I am. Maybe I'm not. But I did buy a couple of things for Blackheart."

He looked surprised and glanced at my failed handyman attempt. "How about I finish this up for you?"

I chuckled and nodded, picking the nail off the floor. "I thought you'd never ask, and then I'll show you what I bought for your rooster. It's out in the truck."

Beckett grabbed the nail from me, and all it took was his fingers brushing against mine to remind me of how much he made me feel.

Sparks. Happiness. Hope.

All the things I'd buried along with my ego back in New Mexico.

Chapter Fourteen

Beckett

It wasn't like I was searching for signs when it came to Nina, but the fact that she knew where Blackheart's name came from threw me for a loop.

Grace wandered over and looked at the mosaic. "That looks fantastic."

Nina nodded. "Grace made that out of the porcelain the deer broke over the weekend. Isn't it fabulous?"

I saw the pride overflowing from Nina, and I couldn't help but wonder if she would ever leave Buttercup Lake now that she was here.

"It's really awesome. The Bailey sisters are all so talented."

Nina flashed her big hazel eyes at me, and I was sure Grace caught how I looked at Nina. It was getting to the point where I couldn't hide it any longer.

"Hey, how about you two go over and grab some lunch?" Grace offered. "It's slow right now."

Nina shook her head. "No, I couldn't leave you."

Grace laughed. "I insist, or I won't get to eat my peanut butter and pickle sandwich in peace."

Nina eyed her sister and didn't object to the accusation. "Fine. If you say so."

"Would you actually eat a pickle and peanut butter sandwich?" I asked Nina.

"Oh, yeah. My favorite is pickle and mustard."

"With meat, or . . . ?"

"Nope." She shook her head. "Just pickles and mustard."

"See you later, you two," Grace said, waving as we walked outside.

"It's warmed up," Nina said with a shiver.

"Nothing like hitting mid-thirties in the middle of January to get a person toasty." I smiled and looked down the sidewalk. "Want to brave it or drive the block?"

"I'm no pansy. We can walk." She pulled some gloves out of her pockets and pulled them on as we made our way to Buttercup Café. "Oh, but here." She darted toward her truck and opened the passenger door and handed me a bag. "For Blackheart."

I laughed, opening the bag to see a strawberry and a pig. "He's a rooster, not a dog."

She lifted her shoulders and raised her hands up.

"Beats me. They were in the aisle."

"Where'd you put him?"

"He's in the garage. I threw some sheets and towels in there, turned on the radio, and gave him his food and water."

"Well, hopefully, he doesn't peck a hole into your wall or something."

I glanced at her. "He wouldn't do that. We have an understanding."

Nina laughed as we made it to the door of the café. The moment I opened it, the smell of sizzling bacon permeated the air. A big sign written in chalk with sprawling cursive letters spelled out the day's special. The walls were a crisp light blue, and there were booths with dark grey vinyl surrounding the main eating area with several tables in the center with cobalt-blue chairs. The atmosphere was funky and eclectic, the exact opposite of what I was imagining.

"BLT?" I nodded, reading the sign. "Nice."

"And the homemade fries are amazing." The door closed behind us when Nina froze. I scanned the café and chuckled.

"Your grandma is here with her boyfriend," I pointed out.

"I know."

"Nina, my favorite granddaughter," she called, waving frantically. They were seated at a large table with several other people from around town. "Good to see you, Beckett."

"It's not what it looks like," Nina muttered.

"No. Of course not, dear." Grandma Millie gave me a wink when Nina turned to sit in a booth near the window and out of the view of her grandma. I gave a wave back as I slid into the booth.

"Gotta love a small town." I grinned.

"Do you, though?" She shook her head with a teasing smile. "The scary part is that it's feeling more and more like home."

"That doesn't have to be scary," I pointed out. "But it's easy for me to say that since Buttercup Lake has never felt like home."

She pushed her chest into the table. "Ever?"

I shook my head, refusing the urge to tell her that it hadn't felt like home until recently.

Until I met her.

But I was pretty confident that slinging that line in Nina's direction would send her running out of town.

"My brother's coming to town tonight."

Nina smiled and glanced at the menu before sliding it

back into its holder at the end of the table. "That's going to be nice for your parents. Finally, having you all together at once I'm sure it's difficult having you live so far away."

"I'm sure it is," I confessed, knowing that the first five years of my living abroad made my mom nuts. They visited me twice a year without fail. "But they know I'm just not comfortable here."

The server came over and took our orders, a BLT for me and French onion soup for Nina.

"Why do you think that is? You seem to fit in just fine to me." She laughed. "At least you didn't come to town looking like a Gypsy, and I mean no offense to Gypsies anywhere, but I certainly felt out of my element. My hair, my clothes, my jewelry . . ."

Nina smiled, and her vivid red lipstick outlined her plump mouth. She slipped off her coat and underneath wore a pair of slouchy pants in bright yellow and a bright blue top that fit her body tremendously. A large belt cinched everything in, showing off the curves of her body.

But I could see what she meant about making a statement when coming to town. Buttercup Lake had a more casual look, and Nina was anything but casual when you looked at her. Whether it was her huge stone earrings or enormous necklaces, she was always decked out.

Except for that first night.

And I couldn't help but think that her showing up in a white flannel nightgown was the closest thing to who Nina actually was.

An angel dressed in artist's clothing.

I groaned at the cheesy thoughts dashing through my head, and Nina's gaze slid to mine.

"What's up?" Nina laughed, glancing behind her. "Are they holding up *Nina Hearts Beckett* signs behind me or something?"

Laughing, I shook my head. "No, but I'm thinking I was doing enough of my own cheerleading inside for all of us."

Nina reached over and touched my hand. "Ah, and you should, Beckett. You keep up with those self-affirmations. You're a great guy, and someday, there will be an exquisite Parisian woman who falls head over heels for you."

"Great," I said flatly.

"Isn't that what you want?"

Looking into Nina's eyes, I didn't know what I wanted. I knew what I didn't want.

I didn't want to leave next week.

I knew I didn't want to stop seeing Nina.

"What I'd love is if you'd let me take you to the best place for cheese curds."

The server brought my sandwich and Nina's soup over.

"When?"

"What time do you go to the store tomorrow?"

Nina shook her head and took a sip of soup from her spoon. "I don't."

Excitement bolted through me. "Then how about I pick you up at noon?"

She thought about the offer for a second, and it felt like I was about to fall off a cliff at any moment.

"Okay. I'd like that."

I drew a slow breath and nodded. "And what about Sunday?"

"You mean the day after your parents' party?"

I nodded. "Yeah. The last Sunday I'm here."

A flicker of panic bounced across Nina's features, and a guilty amount of relief spread through me. She was feeling this too.

"Can you be free?" I asked.

"Yeah. Why?"

"I've got a lot to show you around Wisconsin before I leave again." I took a bite of my sandwich and set it down on the plate. "This is the best BLT I've ever had in my life. My life, Nina."

She chuckled and nodded. "I'm telling you, there are a lot of perks to living here."

"I'm beginning to realize that."

"What do you have cooking for Sunday?"

"A trip to the ice castles on Lake Geneva."

"You think we can make that happen in one day?"

I nodded. "We'll just start early."

"You don't think the celebrating might go deep into the evening on Saturday?"

"Not if I know I get to spend the next day with you."

Nina's lip curled up on the left. "Nice. Very smooth, Beckett."

I grinned, shaking my head. "I'm not trying to be smooth. I'm just really . . ."

"Yeah?" she prompted.

"Into you."

She glanced toward her grandma's table and smiled, ducking her head a little lower as if there were prying ears all around.

And there were.

I'd noticed Millie had flashed more looks this way than anyone not eavesdropping since we'd sat down.

"I'm pretty into you, Beckett." Her eyes locked on mine, and I felt every cellular part of me react in a fiery warmth of desire . . . and something more. "Which scares the crap out of me."

"What are you doing Friday night?" I asked softly.

"Won't your brother be in town? Shouldn't you spend time with him?"

I smiled at her thoughtfulness. "I'll make it work."

"Then my evening is free."

A teenage girl came bounding into the café and beelined toward Millie. She had an uncanny familiarity about her as she bent over and kissed Millie.

"I need fries." Her voice rang out like a typical melodramatic teenager. I glanced at Nina. "She sounds like you."

"Hey, now." Nina grinned. "Give my niece more credit than that."

Nina peeked her head around the corner and waved at the young girl as a teenage boy burst into the café next. He scooped her into his arms, and I waited for World War III to transpire, but Millie just rested her head on Jackson's shoulder and looked on.

The girl pulled the boy toward us and stopped at our table.

"Hey, Izzie." Nina smiled as Izzie reached for a fry. "This is Beckett."

She grinned, chomping on a fry. "I know who he is. He's Cash's brother."

"You do?" I asked, surprised.

She flashed a wry smile that reminded me so much of Nina that I had to push away a laugh. "Yeah. Your picture is on the gallery wall at your parents' house."

"Oh, right." I laughed. "The wall of shame."

Izzy nodded. "Indeed."

Nina followed her niece's stare and cocked her head slightly. "Is the picture of Beckett that good?"

Izzy chuckled. "Oh, it's good. It's good."

The guy standing next to Izzie looked confused.

"This is Caleb. My boyfriend."

I nodded. "Nice to meet you."

And then it hit me. This was the son of one of the few friends I'd had back in high school.

Izzie stole another fry before kissing her aunt and heading off to a booth with Caleb.

"Wow. I know that kid's dad."

Nina's brows rose. "Really?"

"I don't know why I'm always shocked when I realize what it means to be in a small town."

"It's not all bad, you know." She winked at me, and my heart skipped a beat.

Damn. This was bad. I was having hormonal heart issues as a grown man at forty.

"When you're in need, the community rallies. When you're trying to hide, they find you . . ." Her voice trailed off.

"Is that a good thing?"

She chuckled. "Depends on which Friday night I'm trying to hide from people."

I laughed, knowing precisely how she felt. More nights than not, I enjoyed nothing more than staying in my flat in Paris with nothing but a good book or comic, a glass of wine or two, and the curtains pulled shut.

"That's how I spend many Friday nights too," I confessed.

Her eyes got huge. "In Paris? How could you stay in?"

"I've been there a while."

"Interesting." She smiled and finished her soup. "Maybe you need a change."

Chapter Fifteen

Nina

I stared at the envelope from a creditor I hadn't heard of before and sighed. Sliding my finger through the envelope, I drew a deep breath and held it while I pulled out the piece of paper. Maybe this was who was making the calls to me. They were just checking to make sure a female lived at this address.

I'd been receiving so many of these bills since my world imploded several months ago that one would think I'd be ready for whatever was in print waiting for me. It would be just one more thing to send to the police department back home.

I clenched my eyes shut when I realized what I'd thought.

"Not home, Nina. Here is home." I opened the folded piece of paper to see a credit agency I hadn't heard of before demanding nine hundred dollars before the end of the month, or it would blemish my credit.

Fury rose through me as I tossed the page onto the counter. It was never-ending, and I had absolutely no fight left in me.

When things like this happened, the truth of the matter seemed to be that the victim often got screwed over more than once. But I had to take some of the blame. I'd blithely handed things over to him that I never should have. I could have fought it in the courts and kept all the bills unpaid, but by the end of it, I'd have awful credit because all the collection agencies would have dinged my credit, and I'd probably owe more in attorney fees than if I just swallowed my pride and did what I did.

I had nothing to my name, but I'd cleared the debt attached to it, at least. Or so I thought. Until this lovely envelope arrived.

It was a good thing I'd just had three sales in the last week so I could send the money off again.

But not today.

Today, I was too tired to pick up the phone in embarrassment and explain the situation and then hand over my card info and watch the money zip out of my account as fast as it came in.

That was my one saving grace. By selling my house, car, and most everything else, I'd managed to keep ahead of the looming threat.

The restitution that Travis was ordered to pay me

someday might help recoup some costs, but I certainly wasn't counting on ever seeing a nickel. He'd probably figure out a way to go MIA or something once he got out of jail. Currently, he was sitting there awaiting his trial since he couldn't afford bail. He'd already pled guilty to some of the charges, but the biggies made him clam up.

I slid the paperwork on the kitchen counter and made my way upstairs. I'd been working on a fun surprise for Beckett all day. During the deer fiasco, I'd somehow managed to snap a photo of him becoming one with the deer. Or at least that was what I saw when I looked really hard. At first glance, he looked more terrified than anything. The thought made me smile as I thought about the image I'd retouched, his arm stretched toward the deer, a knowing look in the snowflake deer's gaze, and the bend in Beckett's knee in case the deer jumped on him.

Hopefully, it would bring a smile to his lips as it did mine. Part of me wanted to keep it for myself.

When I made it to my bedroom, I laid back on the bed, wrapped myself in a blue throw, and stared at the ceiling. No matter how torn up I felt inside, I would not cry over what Travis did to me. He was a bad man, and as my grandma always said, life would catch up with him.

Right then, the phone rang and my spine stiffened. I

rolled over and reached for the house phone and answered.

Silence.

Breathing.

Click.

My thoughts went back to my grandma's tears the other day about her son, my dad. She rarely ever showed emotion about how things turned out. I think it was a coping mechanism. She'd spent her life trying to help her son and his now-deceased wife get clean, to no avail. So, Grandma Millie did the next best thing and tried to make our summers with my grandparents full of bliss. When August ended, I never wanted to go back home, but my sisters and I never told our grandparents how truly awful it was growing up with our parents. We wrongly felt it was somehow a reflection on us when it was nothing more than addiction robbing us of our parents. With everything that happened in New Mexico, and my mom's death and my dad AWOL, I needed Buttercup Lake more than ever.

But then having something like this follow me here and invade my sacred space? I shook my head as anger tipped me over the brink. I pushed my fingertips into my forehead, hoping to ward off a building headache. Tonight was a date with Beckett, and I didn't want to bring him down too. Blowing out a gust of air, I wiggled my wrists and sat upright, glancing at the closet.

Everything would sort itself out.

Beckett had already introduced me to the best cheese curds in the state of Wisconsin in an afternoon out with him, and I couldn't wait for what was next.

A set of headlights appeared down the drive, and I panicked. Too much wallowing for one night.

"Right on time, and I'm late. Great."

I pulled a pair of navy wool pants out of the closet, traded them out for my sweatpants, and yanked my sweatshirt over my head while simultaneously pulling an ivory cashmere turtleneck sweater off a shelf. Quickly tugging the turtleneck over my head, I glanced in the mirror and tucked in the top. With the wide-leg, high-waisted pants, the tight top really accentuated my curves.

I smiled at my reflection and chuckled. For someone who wasn't trying very hard, I certainly tried hard enough to look good in front of the man leaving for Paris next week.

I dotted some red lipstick on my mouth, reached for a chunky sterling necklace and bangles, and dashed out of the room.

By the time I reached the front door and flung it open, he was standing there with a huge grin.

Beckett's gaze ran up and down me, sending a thrill

through me.

"You look spectacular."

He stood in a pair of jeans that snugly wrapped his thick thighs and hips, leading to a trim waist. The charcoal sweater pulled slightly over his broad shoulders, but what impressed me most was his smile.

And that little dimple.

"Wanna warm up for a second?" I motioned for him to come inside, and he nodded, stepping over the threshold to Grandma Millie's house. Snow had started to fall again. "It's pretty fripply out there."

He laughed and shook his head. "Did you just say fripply? What does that even mean?"

I thought back to the saying my grandpa always said and realized I never really thought about it in detail. I cocked my head and shrugged. "I don't know. Maybe a frozen nipple that's chilly?"

"I'll have to take that back to France with me." Beckett laughed.

"Yes. Definitely show them some culture, courtesy of my Grandpa Renny." Boy, I missed him.

I took Beckett's jacket and hung it on a coat peg in the entryway.

"When Hunter was a kid, he always used to say he

had a nippy noodle, and it mortified my mom."

"That sounds like something you'd say."

Beckett flashed a huge grin. "Where do you think he learned it?"

"Boys are crazy." I rolled my eyes with a smile.

"Girls are crazier."

"Probably true. Want some tea before we head out to this mysterious outing?"

Beckett nodded.

He wouldn't tell me what he had planned for tonight, but I knew it had to do with Wisconsin. That seemed to be the general theme.

I poured some hot water into two cups with mint tea sachets and studied him.

"Are you going to give me a hint?" I asked.

"Frank Lloyd Wright," he said simply.

My eyes widened. "You're not telling me he's going to make an appearance, right? Because I might be a free spirit, but I'm definitely not up for a séance."

Beckett looked puzzled as a smile crept over his expression. "Uh, no. No getting in contact with the other side tonight."

I handed him his tea. "Then what are we talking?"

"That was the only clue I'm giving."

186

"Well, he was born in Wisconsin." I pursed my lips together and thought hard. "How did you know I was into him?"

"I saw the book tucked in between you and the couch the first night we met."

My pulse sped up at the thought of someone like Beckett noticing anything about me, let alone my interests. "Wow. I'm impressed. You're really observant."

He finished his tea and nodded. "To a fault."

I put our cups in the sink and turned to him. "Ready to brave the cold weather?"

Beckett smiled and nodded, and I suddenly didn't care where we were going or what we were doing. I just wanted to spend time with him.

And there was only so much of it before he was heading back to France.

We suited up for the outdoors, even though it was only ten feet to the car, but the winter weather was turning again.

By the time we pulled up to a Frank Lloyd Wright home that I never knew existed less than an hour from Buttercup Lake, excitement was boiling over. The soft glow of the interior bounced off the glistening snow surrounding the structure. I felt like I was in another world. I wasn't merely tucked in between farmland and quaint towns. I was seeing another side of Wisconsin, one with creativity bursting at the seams and potential just waiting to be uncovered.

"Beckett, I'm speechless." I glanced at him to see a smile slide onto his mouth in the shadows as he found a place to park under a tree in the driveway.

The long and low structure of the home, with its horizontal lines and heavy brick and natural wood, fit into the wooded surroundings in a surreal way. The overhanging eaves and long window designs created a sleek look to match the rest of the home.

"I figured with your love of art and design, you might be interested in seeing this home."

I turned to him and smiled. "Like we get to go in?"

Beckett laughed and turned off the car. "Well, I hadn't planned that we just park in the driveway."

"What in the world did you do to get us to be able to go inside?"

Beckett zipped up his coat, and I did the same. "It's available as a rental. Dinner is being prepared as we speak."

"I'm at a loss, Beckett. I don't know how I could ever repay you."

Concern flicked through his gaze. "Why would you ever need to do that? I'm enjoying every second of this, just like you. Now, let's go eat and explore this incredible house."

Beckett came around to my side of the car and helped me out, guiding me toward the front of the home. It felt like decades of happiness flooded the energy around this space, and I only hoped to soak up as much as I could to take with me.

As we got to the door, it opened to a chef wearing a tall white hat and a black- and white-checkered apron.

"Welcome," he said. "Your first course is awaiting you."

Beckett squeezed my hand as we followed the chef to the dining area. The floor plan was open and spacious, with exposed brick from the outside and wood wrapped around so much of the interior it almost felt like we were in a treehouse. Built-in seating wrapped around an eating area tucked next to the kitchen. The tweed cushions were rectangular and low.

"Frank Lloyd Wright really did see these creations as a family home, didn't he? Trying to solve problems with modernizing answers."

Beckett smiled and nodded, but I realized he was taking me in more than the house. "Absolutely."

I blushed and laughed.

The chef brought out the first course. "*Le hors-d'oeuvre*, or in Wisconsin, appetizer."

He set down a little tray of mousse on top of toasted bread.

"*Mousse de Saumon Canapés*," he told us in French. "Salmon mousse on lightly toasted bread with a brine-washed double-cream that is semi-soft and folded into the mousse. Beckett wanted to add a little Wisconsin to each of the French dishes tonight."

My eyes connected with Beckett's as the chef left, and a flutter of butterflies danced away in my belly.

"You've really thought of everything to introduce me to my new state."

I took two canapés and set them on my plate.

"My motives aren't pure," he confessed as I took my first bite.

My eyes flashed to his as the delicious taste sent me to another orbit. "This is incredible. Keep feeding me like this, and I don't care what your intentions are."

Beckett laughed. "I hope tonight's meal will convince you to visit me in Paris."

My heart stopped as my mind raced to the latest bill that showed up and the simple fact that I had nothing to my name. "I don't . . . I can't . . ."

"No rush. No pressure," Beckett said, keeping his eyes locked on mine. "But I hope I can persuade you to move the trip up on your bucket list."

I swallowed down all the worries and let my mind drift to a simpler time when I was younger and didn't have a care in the world. When I would just pack my things in my car and travel the country and sell my art along the way. Why did things have to get so complicated as I got older?

Nodding, I polished off the appetizer and smiled. "I'll definitely think about it."

The chef brought out the next course and set a bowl of soup in front of each of us.

"*Le Potage*. Soup." The chef smiled, refilling our champagne glasses. "Garlic and sausage soup."

The tiny bowl was the size of a shot glass, and Beckett knew what I was thinking.

I was a hungry woman.

The chef left us to our two-bite soup.

"Pretty funny." I winked at him. "Very Wisconsin of us to have champagne and sausage."

"Very."

I took a bite and closed my eyes with satisfaction. "I could eat an entire pot of this," I told Beckett.

"Ditto."

I thought about Beckett's invitation and smiled at him. "I would love to visit you in Paris."

He sat back and grinned. "That's all I needed to hear."

The chef brought out the main course, which was a Wisconsin twist on *Le Gratin Dauphinois* or, as the chef translated for us, Au Gratin potatoes with local cheese, cream, and potatoes. Soon after, a salad came out with micro greens, chopped bacon, and a maple vinaigrette. When I thought I could eat no more, he brought out a cheese board with all Wisconsin cheese.

As I reached for one of the last crumbles, I looked up at Beckett. "I can't let any of this go to waste."

"I'm glad you're enjoying it. I forgot how incredible our food can be here."

"Are you saying you're not always into the tater tot casseroles?"

Beckett laughed. "I love me a good casserole as much as the next person, but this has been fun."

I chuckled, feeling lighter than I had in months, maybe years. Because the truth of it was that things weren't always smooth sailing with Travis, even before his criminal escapades.

"And to end our meal." The chef appeared with two small cakes topped with whipped cream. Even though I was stuffed, my mouth started watering as he placed one in front of me.

"*Baba au Rhum*. Cake soaked in rum with freshly-whipped cream and caramel sauce." He smiled. "And on that note, I'll be leaving. I hope you two have a wonderful night."

We thanked him but didn't say a word until we heard the front door shut. As I looked at the beautiful dessert in front of me, I suddenly didn't want to pick up my fork. I didn't want the night to end.

"When do we need to vacate?" I asked Beckett as I reluctantly picked up my fork.

He dabbed his mouth with a napkin, and a little twinkle of something gathered behind his gaze as he reached for his glass of champagne.

"Tomorrow at noon."

Chapter Sixteen

Beckett

Nina looked stunned. "I hadn't really planned on telling you that. My main goal was to enjoy this dinner here and head back to Buttercup Lake."

An impish smile touched her lips as she glanced around the dining area. "Who's going to watch Blackheart?"

"Nate is watching him while we're out." I stood, wishing I knew what was going through Nina's mind. I hadn't intended to tell her I had to reserve it the whole night, or I would have just framed it as a pack-a-bag trip.

"I like that you're a responsible rooster owner."

"Well, I don't think I'd have anything left if I left Blackheart by himself. He managed to peck right through some of my plastic storage containers in the garage, so I brought him into the family room. He likes it there, but he can only be there when I am."

She chuckled. "It's good that he's training you well."

I laughed, shaking my head and standing.

Nina put down her napkin and stood next to me. "I

have to tell you that I have never had anyone do something this thoughtful for me."

"You deserve it and more." I eyed her for a split second, feeling a trill of electricity running between us. My mind went back to the kiss.

And she'd kissed me back.

The thing that screwed my brain up the most was that I wasn't used to any of this. Nina got under my skin and stayed there in a way that made me wonder about the future, and my future had been just fine and very secure before running into her.

Nina drew in a breath as my fingers interlaced with hers. I pulled her with a gentle tug as we started toward the great room. "Let's explore."

"I wonder how big it is?" Nina mused and then snickered. "The house, I mean."

I stopped in my tracks, and she walked into me.

"It's pretty big," I said flatly, trying not to crack up. "So I was told."

Her hazel eyes got huge.

"It's around twenty-three hundred square feet," I told her.

"That is big."

"I totally thought you were going to tell me that you'd

seen bigger."

She stomped her foot. "I am not that immature."

I eyed her.

"At least on a date, I'm not."

I chuckled as we wandered into the great room that had built-in seating with more built-in shelves completely wrapping the room from the waist up, with exposed brick below.

"It's pretty cool, but it doesn't look very comfortable." She shrugged, eyeing more rectangular tweed cushions for the couch. "The fireplace is pretty."

I nodded as we started down a hall full of floor-to-ceiling windows.

"I wonder if the bed is comfortable," she mused, and my heart skipped a beat.

"Were you planning on testing it out?" I asked, glancing at her.

She playfully scowled as we walked the narrow corridor wrapped in more of the dark wood until we found the first bedroom. The bed was low to the ground and the décor was minimalist at best. She poked her head in and nodded. "Stunning. Look at the closet and all the shelves."

I smiled and nodded. It was fun getting to hear what popped into her head with each new revelation. We found the primary room, which was larger than the other two.

She sheepishly grinned and wandered over to the bed and put two fingers on it and bounced the mattress up and down. "Nice and firm."

"Firm is always good."

"Rock hard is even better."

My jaw hung open, and I glanced at the mattress before returning my gaze back to Nina.

She fell backward on the bed and moved her arms over her head like she was in the middle of making snow angels. "If I could sleep on concrete, I would."

Nina came in a spritely package full of mischief and Trouble, the capital T intended. Her curvy body wiggled on the bed as she let out a deep breath, and the heave of her breasts fell with the exhale.

It felt like someone had been in my mind and had ripped out every fantasy I'd ever had and wrapped it all up into a colorful Nina package and hand-delivered it to me with a note that read, *Do not touch.*

Wonderful.

She sat back up. "What do you think this is? A king?"

I stood there, smiling. "Yeah."

Nina patted the empty space next to her, ruffling the ivory comforter under her fingers. "Wanna try it out?" She glanced out the window and turned her gaze back to mine. "It looks like the storm is getting worse."

"We should probably head out then." I stared at her, refusing to let my lips curl into a smile.

Nina blinked in surprise at me and frowned. "Really?"

I walked over to her and stared down at the bed, wishing she were sprawled out and completely naked.

"You really want a no-strings-attached fling." It wasn't really a question. Just confirmation.

I didn't know all the details that led her to come back to Buttercup Lake. She'd only given me bits and pieces. I didn't want to add to her pile, but the desire pulsing through me made it hard to think straight. I needed to go into this with the right intentions.

Nina flicked a rebellious wave in my direction in an obvious dare I undoubtedly wanted to accept.

I came closer.

"More than you know." Her eyes locked on mine, and I felt the familiar longing building inside.

I leaned over, and she skimmed her fingers along my arm. Every part of me felt a crazy pull to be with her, feel her in my arms, and taste every part of her.

A possessive shiver ran through me.

I caged her with my arms and leaned over her, running my mouth along her neck.

"Mm," she moaned, and I smiled, helping to undress her.

After a few seconds of struggling with the clothes, she laughed. "Gotta love all the Wisconsin layers."

I smiled, loving that we didn't have to take everything so seriously. "Wait until February."

Nina laughed, stretching her arms over her head as I gave one last pull, but her hands immediately went to the bottom of my sweater and lifted it over my shoulders. Her gaze ran over my body as her mouth curled into a beautiful smile of acceptance.

Quickly kicking and pulling the rest of my clothes off, I slid my hands under her head and brought her mouth to mine. Skin-to-skin contact sent me to a place I never wanted to leave.

"Tell me, Beckett. Did you plan on a Wisconsin rendezvous?" she teased, curling her fingers through my hair.

I laughed, looking deep into her eyes. "Never."

Nina's smile deepened as her eyes smoldered with the same need pulsing through me.

"Ever since you tackled me at the antique store, I've wanted this." Nina's eyes fell to my mouth. Within an instant,

I pressed my mouth to hers.

The taste of her only exploded the craving inside. I wanted to lick every part of her and feel her around me.

Slipping my fingers along her thighs and finding her warmth and wetness, I placed an open-mouthed kiss on her belly as her eyes closed in bliss.

"Beckett," she whispered as my fingers worked her into a frenzy.

"Yes, love." I raised my head to watch her reach the brink.

"Don't stop." I smiled as my pace quickened and she clenched around my fingers as her breathing turned ragged.

I wanted her so badly, the ache turned to pure pain as her naked body lay underneath me. With labored breathing, she fluttered her eyes open and smiled.

Nina looped her arms around my neck, and we rolled over with her on top of me. She straddled me and took in my body with a smile.

Every rational thought escaped me as she sat on top of me and slid her thighs over me, grinding her hips into me. Her breasts bounced with every breath as she sheathed me inside her. My breath caught as I slid into her tightness. I ran my hands along her back, cupping her cheeks, and she smiled as I spun her over.

Nina smiled as I nudged her knee open and thrust into her again. She bit her bottom lip and moaned as her eyes closed, finding our groove.

And I realized our night wasn't about no-strings because she'd tied me to her heart in ways I never thought possible.

Chapter Seventeen

Nina

I did not know that worlds could be rocked like that. Every muscle in my body ached from last night, and yet I couldn't wait to do it again. Thanks to the overload of windows in every room of this house, including the primary bedroom, we were blinded by the early morning light.

"We didn't even need Blackheart to wake us up so dang early," I muttered, pulling up a sheet to my chin.

Beckett laughed, rolling over to look at me. "We probably should have figured out how to work the blinds. But I have to admit that it's nice turning over to see you next to me."

My heart hammered in my chest as he reached over to slip another kiss along my cheek. Spending last night with him felt amazing, both spiritually and physically.

"I just thought of something," I groaned.

"What's that?"

"Since Nate babysat the rooster, the entire town is going to know we spent the night away together."

"Nah," Beckett said, laughing. "I texted him that the snow was coming down too hard. As an officer of the law, he totally understood. Said as much."

My brows quirked. "Did he now?"

Beckett nodded. "Told me he'd seen enough of what could happen if a person didn't respect the weather."

I giggled and put the sheet over my head. "I bet he did."

"Okay. You're right. The entire town will know, won't they?" Beckett tugged the sheet away from me and peppered kisses across my bare breasts.

"At least you're headed back to Paris and won't have to hear the whispers," I teased.

He sat up, and tenderness filled his gaze. "Leaving isn't as appealing as it once was."

I grinned, pulling the sheet back up.

Beckett cradled my head in his hands and softly kissed me. Tingles erupted from my lips to my toes, and I couldn't help but smile.

He pulled away slowly.

"Can I ask you something?"

"What's that?" My eyes met his, and my heart fluttered.

"Would you think I'm crazy for wanting to spend

every second with you until I leave?"

The thrill of the question lingered as my mind rolled his question around, and my heart clung to it.

"Your family might not be very happy with me." My body stretched with his as we both laid on our sides.

"Something tells me they'd be extremely happy."

"You have less than a week here. By the time you board your plane, you might be glad to be rid of me."

He propped himself on his elbow. "I know that's impossible."

"Why's that?"

"You tickle my brain."

I let out a happy sigh and smiled. "I know myself pretty well, and I can be exhausting, stubborn, and ditzy."

Beckett let out a low growl, which made my entire body heat up as he studied me quietly for a few seconds. "I happen to love being exhausted by you. Your stubbornness is actually discipline."

"What about forgetting where I put my keys or losing my cell all the time?" I reminded him.

"It's adorable."

"For now," I warned.

Part of me wanted to believe everything coming out of Beckett's mouth made sense, but it didn't. My quirks might be cute now, but when I lose his keys and phone, he might not think it's charming.

"You might be right about the discipline being disguised as stubbornness or vice-versa, but there are times when I'm working on one of my pieces when I don't want to be bothered for hours."

Beckett smiled. "I can understand that."

"As in twelve."

Beckett's smile widened. "And I'd respect that."

"You say that now . . ." My words trailed off, and I saw the look of determination in his eyes. "I guess time will tell."

"And with that, I'm going to make us some coffee before we head back." Beckett stood, and my eyes took in his lean, muscular body. He looked absolutely incredible, and it was impossible to imagine he didn't have blocks full of women following him through the cemeteries he visited.

I chuckled at the thought and then laughed even harder when I focused on his boxers.

He spun around and shrugged. "I wouldn't have worn my donkey-at-a-disco boxers had I known we were going to be . . ."

"I love them. Just like I love hearing that you tromp through cemeteries and see the beauty in something so underrated."

Beckett nodded slowly and drew a breath. "And most would just call it weird."

"As I've told you before. I'm not most people."

"No, you're not." He turned around and started toward the door. "I'll have coffee ready in a jiffy."

"You can take the boy out of Wisconsin, but you can't take Wisconsin out of the boy," I muttered.

He glanced over his shoulder with a grin. "What was that?"

"Nothing," I teased, knowing he heard every word.

I rolled over in the bed, resting my arm across my forehead, and thought about last night. Everything about it was so thoughtful . . . so Beckett.

For hating Wisconsin, he certainly seemed to enjoy himself here. I wondered what really made him want to leave. There had to be more to it than just wanting to see the world.

I blew out all the air I'd been holding in and stretched my arms toward the wood ceiling.

It was still hard to fathom that I was waking up in a Frank Lloyd Wright home after a night of amazing sex. A nagging feeling surfaced about that word. Last night, it didn't just feel like sex. It felt like a truly deep connection. But I knew that was absolutely impossible. We hadn't known one another for that long.

Yet, I knew there was something going on here that I couldn't understand. I kicked off the covers and took a quick shower before meeting Beckett in the kitchen.

"That's not fair," he laughed, glancing at me fully dressed in yesterday's clothes but with a head of wet hair.

Beckett walked toward me and slid his arm around my waist, pulling me into him as he kissed me slowly.

Every part of me lit up again. It was like I was on a carnival ride with him. I couldn't get enough.

He slowly parted his mouth from mine and ran his fingers through my wet hair. "Sorry about not thinking things through."

I laughed and shook my head. "You couldn't have possibly known that I've wanted to do that since I met you."

Beckett's brows rose. "You're right about that."

His hand lingered on my back, and he studied me for a few seconds.

"What are you thinking?" I prodded.

"It's going to sound cheesy," he said softly.

"Isn't that what happens when you live in Wisconsin?" I joked.

"Ah, the whole Dairyland thing. Good one." Beckett walked to the coffee pot and poured us each a cup. "Seriously, though."

We took a seat at the built-in table, sliding onto the bench.

"I feel like I really click with you." The genuine look behind his gaze made me fall a little harder for him, and that worried me. He was leaving town in less than a week. Last night was meant to be a no-strings-attached romp to be used as a reminder that I was indeed human.

I sucked in a deep breath but didn't let it out. "I feel the same."

Beckett smiled and nodded. "That's nice to hear."

Sipping my coffee, I looked over the cup and watched him stare out the windows overlooking the latest round of snow.

"What really made you want to leave Wisconsin so badly?" I asked, setting my cup down.

His lips quirked at the corners. "I don't know that it's relevant any longer."

I cocked my head slightly. "What do you mean?"

"I've never been that guy who had a massive number of friends. I have my brothers and about three other really dependable guys I can count on."

"I'm more of a quality over quantity gal myself." I laughed. "Or at least I was until I moved here. Somehow, nice people just flock to the newbies, and I have a whole gaggle of meddling folks."

Beckett nodded. "Yeah. I didn't really experience that growing up in a small town. There were very few kids my age in town, and the school I went to had kids from all the surrounding towns." He shrugged. "I just never connected with anyone here. I'd listen to conversations about what the other kids were doing over the weekend, and not only was I not invited, but I also really didn't want to go, anyway."

"No cow tipping for you?" I joked.

"Believe it or not, that seriously was a thing for a few kids. But for the others it was drinking all night at bonfires." He shrugged. "It just wasn't my thing."

I tried picturing Beckett as a teenager. By looking at him now, I could tell he would have been considered hot. Maybe the other guys were jealous.

"I totally get that." I nodded. "I avoided high school parties like the plague, but that was mainly because I saw what drugs and alcohol could do to people beyond that first try. Plus, I was busy taking care of my sisters as best I could. I didn't have time for high school friends."

Beckett leaned back. "You know how some people are reliving their high school years decades later?"

I nodded, laughing. "Oh, yeah."

"Definitely not me. In high school, I was dreaming of being an adult and all that afforded me. Granted, I was fortunate enough to have parents who showed us the world beyond this state, and that piqued my interest. I wanted to experience things on my terms, and I was tired of being lonely. Whenever I came back to Buttercup Lake to visit for college breaks, apart from my family, I just didn't feel . . . accepted. I didn't have any of those shared experiences when I'd bump into an old classmate." His eyes stayed on mine. "So, it's not like I had one major event that chased me from town. I just didn't fit."

I reached for his hand and squeezed it. "I totally understand that."

Beckett's eyes remained on me. "You want to hear something kind of funny?"

I nodded. "Totally."

"As I got older, I realized I don't fit in where I'm at, either." He bit his bottom lip briefly before turning it into a smile. "So, all these years, I've been searching for something that didn't exist. I've grown accustomed to being numb."

"That's really interesting." I put my hands together. "And extremely sad."

Beckett laughed. "I thought so. It was a rather big revelation when I was sitting under an awning at a café in

Paris with it raining like it planned on flooding the city. It was beautiful, but I had no one to share it with. The city suddenly felt really isolating."

I sighed and nodded. "I was worried that's how coming to Buttercup Lake would feel after leaving New Mexico. My whole life had been there for decades. I wasn't sure if my family would be enough."

I wanted to tell him everything. But we didn't have enough time for that, and going down the rabbit hole certainly wasn't appropriate before his parents' anniversary party.

"And?"

"They're enough for now. Exactly what I needed." I shook my head. "It's funny. I just assumed you'd be the popular guy in high school with tons of girls and even more guy friends."

He laughed. "Well, I did get voted Most Likely to Succeed and Homecoming King."

I smacked the table softly. "Nice. Okay, so my people detector isn't failing me. You were just miserable underneath the cloak of popularity."

"Precisely." He smiled wider. "But what is this about a people detector?"

I laughed. "Well, up until my encounter with Travis, I'd always prided myself at having a perfect people detector to protect me."

Beckett raised his brows. "Oh, yeah? Is that like a B.S. detector?"

I nodded. "Kind of. But after Travis, I felt like maybe I'd lost my sixth sense somehow. Like my intuition had failed me."

"Sometimes, we do a very good job of ignoring red flags because we want to believe in the good." Beckett touched my hand.

"Thank you for that." I glanced at the clock. "I guess we should probably get going so we aren't late to your parents' party tonight."

"Good call."

I breathed a sigh of relief because I suddenly felt foolish about my dalliance with a conman, and I wasn't sure Beckett would think the same of me.

Chapter Eighteen

Beckett

I rang the doorbell at Nina's house and waited. I'd dropped her off earlier today so she could get ready and I could attend to some stuff back at my house, like plowing the drive and shoveling the walkways before the next snow hits.

The door opened, and my tongue about hung out of my mouth.

"Nina, I suddenly want to skip the fiesta."

"What? This old thing?" she teased, inviting me in.

"Are you going to be warm enough?" I closed the door behind me and kissed her cheek.

The pull to take her into my arms and carry her upstairs was nearly overwhelming. She was wearing a fully fitted long, red dress that didn't leave one inch to the imagination. A black belt cinched her waist, and her hips screamed to me. I wanted to take them between my hands and tug her into me. Spending last night with her didn't satisfy anything in me. It only made me want to have more of her.

"It's a wool sweater dress." She smiled.

213

"I have never seen wool look so damn sexy."

She laughed. "Thank Ralph Lauren."

I followed her down the hall to the kitchen, where she grabbed something off the table.

"Just one sec. I have to put my earring on, or I'll look like a pirate." A large, dangling earring in silver with bright red gemstones hung from her fingers.

I laughed, realizing she only had one earring on, and I hadn't even noticed because I was so taken with Nina.

After she secured the jewelry, she raised her hands. "All set, I think."

"I'm pretty sure all eyes will be on you," I teased, cupping her hands in mine. Without another thought, I pulled her into me and brushed my lips over hers. She parted her lips, and we kissed gently, careful not to ask for too much. I felt her smile as our kiss slowed.

Nina patted my chest. "You're just a little smitten from last night."

She had no idea.

Nina reached for a small bag. "I just have a little something for your parents."

The thoughtfulness surprised me. I was pretty certain that most of the town was showing up just to have some free beer and food, and of course, congratulate my parents on an impressive span of matrimony.

"I'll take it," I offered as we approached the front door, and she slid her feet into a tall pair of boots.

"Are those going to be slippery?" I asked, glancing at the black over-the knee boots.

"That's what I have you for." She grinned, slipping on the second one.

I loved my parents, but the thought of skipping the party and spending all night with Nina again was starting to rank right up there as the best worst idea I'd had in a long time.

"What's that silly look for?" she joked.

"Honestly want to know?"

"Sure do."

"I can't stop thinking about last night."

She flashed a wry smile and pulled her coat on. "I'm kind of hoping for a repeat before you leave town."

The thought created a burning ache deep in my groin, and I shook my head. "Tonight is going to be quite the night."

"Is Blackheart upset with you for leaving him again?" she joked.

"I got the neighbor kid from down the road to babysit him tonight."

Nina looked at me as if she wasn't sure whether I was

serious or not.

The ride over to the lodge wasn't long enough. Everything about Nina just made the minutes zip by. By the time we made it into Buttercup Lake Lodge, the party was in full swing in a ballroom overlooking the lake.

"You want a beer?" I asked Nina. "It's from a local brewery here. My parents' friends."

Nina smiled, spotting Maya. "Sure. I'll take one."

Maya made her way over as I gave a quick hi before starting toward the bar where my brother Hunter was standing.

"Hey, man," I said, slapping his shoulder.

Hunter turned around and held up a beer. "I was beginning to wonder if you were going to make it."

I laughed and shook my head. "The party only started five minutes ago."

"Didn't you get mom's text last night about coming early?"

I scratched my head and ordered two beers. "No. I was a little occupied."

Hunter caught the slight upturn of my mouth. "Occupied with what? Or should I say who?"

He followed my gaze to Nina and beamed. "Ah, you're forgiven. She's a great girl."

"You've met her?"

Hunter nodded.

"Are you here with someone?"

He let out a grunt and shrugged. "I got ghosted a month ago by my girlfriend, if you can call it that. I've kind of been out of sorts since."

"I'm sorry, Hunter."

"Nah." He shrugged. "Don't be. I think it's for the best. I just need to let my ego heal."

Millie and her boyfriend, Jackson, came over to the bar.

"Have you seen Nina tonight?" Millie asked with a suspicious look in her eyes.

"Yeah. She's talking over there with Maya. She came as my date." I thought I'd just set the record straight.

Jackson handed Millie a glass of wine. "Did you, now?"

I nodded, glancing over her shoulder to see Nina looking this way.

The thought of leaving this week was hard. Her gorgeous smile splashed across her features, and I knew it was going to be tough to get on that plane.

"So, did she enjoy the Frank Lloyd Wright house?"

My gaze flicked back to Millie's. "Pardon me?"

Millie smiled. "Didn't you two spend the night there

to weather the storm?"

I nodded. "Oh, right. Yeah. It was a beautiful home."

Nina made her way over to us with Maya right behind.

"I thought I'd better rescue Beckett, and I was thirsty," Nina said.

Millie smirked. "Why would he need rescuing?"

"Oh, I don't know. Just a hunch." She winked at her grandma, who eyed Hunter next. "Where's your girlfriend?"

"You mean Brielle?" he asked.

Millie nodded.

"She ghosted me. I have no idea where she went or who she's with."

My mom and dad made their way over. They looked incredible. My mom had her hair swept up in a barrette with pearls that matched her ivory dress. She was positively beaming.

"Oh, no. Are we talking about Brielle again?" My mom snickered and shuddered. "She wasn't a very nice person."

Grace walked over with Jackson. "She's not coming, is she?"

Maya and Grace traded a horrified look.

"No, she's not coming." Hunter sounded vaguely

annoyed, but not like someone who'd lost his soulmate.

I clapped his back. "This woman must have left quite an impression."

"She's the most pompous, egotistical, unkind woman I think I've ever met." My mom pressed her lips into a thin line. "And that's on a good day."

My mom rarely said an unkind word about anyone, so I took note.

"Sounds like it's for the better," I said, nodding as Nina eyed me curiously.

"Well, we can all breathe a sigh of relief that she's not coming, but what about Daisy?" Millie asked, sounding particularly chipper. Nina eyed me with an I-told-you-so look, which I returned with a grin as I slid my arm around her waist.

"She took an extra shift down at the bar." Hunter shook his head. "She's trying to save up money for a down payment."

Panic filled Millie's gaze as well as my mom's. "Why? Where's she planning on buying a house?"

Hunter shook his head. "Not sure."

"Please tell Daisy she was definitely missed. She's always a ball of sunshine."

"You missed our book club meeting yesterday morning," Millie pointed out to Nina.

Nina's hand flew to her open mouth. "I can't believe I did. I've just been so busy and kind of scatterbrained."

"Is that so, honey?" Millie's eyes jetted to me before landing on her granddaughter with Maya and Grace chuckling behind her.

Without missing a beat, Nina handed over the small bag to my parents. "Just a little something for your celebration."

"Thank you, honey. That's really sweet of you." My mom nodded at Nina and then looked over at me.

I kept my arm looped around Nina, but I could tell what my mom was thinking.

See? Isn't she perfect?

"Should we open it now?"

"If you'd like," Nina said softly.

My mom and dad nodded as my mom opened the small gift bag. My mom tugged out a small item about eight inches square and gasped as my dad's gaze flicked to the woman standing beside me.

"Nina, this is more than I could . . ." Tears pricked my mom's eyes, and my dad's too. "Just incredible, Nina. Thank you."

Millie was looking at us all and spun around to see what my mom had clutched between her fingers.

It even left Millie speechless, and that was a feat.

My mom turned around the square canvas to reveal a picture of all of us kids. Photos of my brothers Hunter and Cash, my sister Evie, and myself had been put into a collage. We each had our baby photo, teen photo, and current photo splashed onto the canvas. It was so understated yet spoke volumes. She'd outlined each of the photos so they transitioned seamlessly from one age to the next.

"I will always treasure this, Nina. Really," my mom said as my dad came over to give her a hug. I let go of her as my parents embraced her.

When my mom stepped away, she looked at me and shook her head slowly. "It's really a shame you have to fly back to Paris this week."

Millie nodded in agreement. "Isn't that the truth?"

Nina chuckled. The Sunshine Breakfast Club might have their focus turned to Hunter and Daisy right now, but two of the members were obviously always scheming.

But the truth of it was that they were right. It was a shame.

"Maybe it's my sign to explore the country again," Nina offered. "You know, without a care in the world. Just me and my camera."

My heart stopped, but I saw Millie beat me to the

punch.

"Not in the dead of winter. Hold onto your tights a little longer."

Her sisters chuckled.

"Are you already getting antsy here?" Grace asked.

"No. I love it here, and I have an expert tour guide." She glanced at me.

"Hopefully, tomorrow's little excursion to Lake Geneva will make up for heading out of town," I told Millie.

"Oooh, to see the ice castles and all the sculptures?" Millie's eyes lit up as she elbowed her senior Jackson. "This is the kind of stuff we should be doing. We're still in the honeymoon phase, Jackson. But I fear we're turning into old fuddy-duddies."

The older man chuckled and looked completely tickled with her.

My dad laughed and shook his head. "Millie, there's not a chance in Wisconsin that you could ever turn into a fuddy-duddy."

Maya nodded as my brother brought her into his side.

The music turned up slightly behind us, and my mom chuckled. "The party must be getting into full swing. You boys had better not fill up on too much beer until after you say lots of wonderful things about your dad and me."

Hunter shook his head and smiled. "We'll be fine. Mom. Now go enjoy your night."

My dad grabbed my mom's hand and led her to the dance floor where they were the first two to start dancing.

"This is going to be a great night," Millie said as Jackson reached for her hand. "Dancing before dinner."

We all watched them on the dance floor, and I could see Nina eyeing her sisters in between. Was she wondering the same thing as me? Would that ever happen to us?

"That sounds so fun tomorrow, you two." Grace grinned at Nina.

Nina nodded as I slipped my arm around her again. She was like a living magnet for me.

I drew a breath. "I actually hope to fit in one more spot."

Nina turned and looked up at me in surprise.

"The Northern Lights are supposed to be happening on Tuesday night, and I found this great place up near the Apostle Islands. We should be able to get a good look at them." I looked at Nina. "If you're interested."

She drew in a sharp breath with eyes as big as saucers. "Are you serious?"

"Completely." I glanced at Grace and Maya. "The place is big enough for everyone."

Maya squeezed Cash's arm. "What do you think?"

Cash smiled and nodded. "Sounds great."

Grace nodded but rubbed her belly. "I think I might sit this one out." She looked at her fiancé, Jackson, and beamed. "But you can go."

Jackson scowled. "No way. And miss getting you pickle and peanut butter sandwiches at three am? Not a chance."

She giggled as he squeezed her, and a dull ache surfaced behind my ribs.

What was happening to me? Why did I suddenly crave a love like that?

Nina touched her hand on mine, and I wondered if she felt it too.

Chapter Nineteen

Nina

Life felt good. Really good.

But it also felt extremely temporary. In a matter of days, Beckett would be headed out of town for the foreseeable future. There hadn't been any discussion of his return back to Wisconsin, and if history repeated itself with him, it sounded like it could be years.

I pushed that thought away and shook my head before popping in a sausage-stuffed mushroom.

"So good," I told Grace.

She chuckled. "They're addicting."

I reached for a fried cheese curd on my plate and popped it in my mouth. "Is it bad that I'm just standing by the buffet table?"

Grace grinned. "Nah. That's what you've got me for. You'd be amazed at how much leeway people give me now that I'm plus one."

I looked at my sister fondly and nodded. "I'm so happy for you, Grace. I really am . . . and so proud."

225

She smiled, taking a bite of cheese curd. "Thank you. I feel the same way about you and Maya. We've certainly been through a lot, but we've made it to the other side."

I laughed. "Is this the other side? It's been exhausting lately."

Grace rubbed my upper arm. "I know it hasn't been easy, but I'm so proud of you. Starting over is hard."

My sister knew exactly how that felt. Her entire life had been shattered, and Buttercup Lake had only been meant as a retreat for her teenage daughter and her, then life showed her the way. I kept hoping life would show me the way too. But so far, I just kept getting mail I dreaded opening. At least Travis was sitting in jail and not enjoying his freedom until the trial. My dad popped into my head, but I tried to push the thought away. We'd become experts at that.

"What's wrong?" Grace asked, her expression changing as quickly as my thoughts.

"Just . . . do you ever think about Dad?"

Grace nodded. "All the time. You want to hear something completely pathetic?"

"Kind of."

She laughed and let out a sigh. "There was a part of me that wanted to believe Dad was the good guy. Like our mom had just led him astray, and when she passed away, he'd try to get his life back in order. Ridiculous, right?"

I shook my head. "Not ridiculous at all. Just full of the same hope we've all carried for years."

"I suppose you're right." She eyed her plate. "Have you heard from him?"

I froze. I hadn't mentioned to anyone that I had sent money to him after my mom's death. I didn't want to make my sisters angry or have them think I was enabling him.

Guilt clung deeply as I thought about it.

I was just trying to buy peace.

"I take that as a yes," Grace said softly. "When?"

"Right after Mom died. He asked for money." Telling the secret felt freeing.

Grace let out a heavy sigh as our eyes met. "I understand. I probably would have done the same."

"Done the same?" I asked.

"Sent him money."

"How'd you know I did?"

She smiled the same comforting smile I'd gotten so used to seeing growing up, even though I was the older sister.

"Because you never told me."

I laughed. "You know me too well."

"It's a sister thing."

"But I haven't heard from him since I sent the

227

money," I confessed. "It happened at the same time everything in my life was imploding, and I just sent it to make things go away." I shook my head. "I shouldn't have, but I did. I just hope—"

"Don't let the guilt drown you, Nina. We've all been through it with our parents. We tried our best over the years, and all we can do is live the best lives we can for Grandma Millie."

She was right. If it weren't for our grandparents, I doubted any of us would have made it out of the living conditions as unscathed as we had.

Grace hugged me as Maya walked over. "Everything okay?"

I groaned and laughed as Grace nodded. "I'll fill you in later. Nina looks like she's about to pass out from the conversation."

Maya shrugged and turned to me. "Okay. Sounds good. But I am so excited to go see the Northern Lights. How romantic is that?"

I grinned. "Yes, nothing like being merely a wall away from your siblings for a romantic getaway."

"Cash said that Beckett is like a new person since he's met you."

"It's barely been a week."

Maya nodded. "I know, but I guess his other visits usually incorporate lots of grumpiness, a few grunts, and hiding out at his house."

The thought tickled me inside.

"Well, I'm sure it will wear off before he heads back to Paris."

"Maybe." Maya nodded.

"What?" I joked. "You're not supposed to say that. You're supposed to tell me that he'll figure out it was the worst decision of his life as he sits in the airplane seat and all that junk."

"Oh, right. I mean, no. Not at all. I'm sure he'll be pining for you the moment he touches down in France." Her robotic tone made me laugh.

I smiled, feeling the sense of calm I'd become accustomed to since coming back to Buttercup Lake with my sisters. We could love, hug, and flip crap with the best of them.

"In all seriousness." Maya lowered her voice. "He is into you. Maybe he wouldn't mind postponing his return date."

I shook my head and glanced over at Beckett chatting with his brothers and Nate. Beckett's eyes connected with mine, and I felt heat run through my body.

"It's probably better this way. We won't get to the part where we learn about one another's ugly truths."

Grace tilted her head and gave an eye roll. "You don't have any ugly truths."

My niece Izzy wandered over with Caleb's hand entangled with hers. They looked inseparable, and Caleb looked like a happy puppy dog just lapping up anything Izzy would give him.

"Hello, Aunties," Izzy hummed, stealing a cheese curd off my plate. "Mom, Caleb and I were hoping we could go to the game room."

Grace scrunched her nose. "Game room?"

"You know, an arcade?" I prompted.

"Oh, right. Sure. I don't see why not."

Maya folded her arms over her chest. "Well, I could think of a couple of good ones why not."

"Aunt Maya," Izzy scolded my sister playfully. "It's not like that."

Maya smiled and glanced at Grace, who was lovingly looking at her daughter.

"Just check in every so often," Grace told her daughter as the teenage duo wandered out of the room.

"Does that scare you?" I asked, genuinely curious.

"Yes, but I can't keep her in a cocoon, and Caleb is a

great guy. If they happen to sneak some kisses while playing Pac-Man, the end of the world won't happen."

I knew Maya was thinking the same thing as me about it not ending with kisses, but we kept our mouths shut. Grace was an amazing mom, and we didn't need to raise her blood pressure and have her become a mom too soon to the second one on the way.

An announcer's voice boomed over the speakers, and the crowd hushed as Nancy and Harold moved to the front of the ballroom hand in hand.

"We want to invite Evie, Hunter, Cash, and Beckett up here to say a few words."

The room clapped, and my heart skipped a beat as I watched Beckett wander toward his parents with his brothers and sister. He looked good, really good. Which made my mind wander in the direction of later this evening.

Would Beckett just drop me off? Would I invite him to stay?

But he had the rooster. And he probably had to let the rooster sitter go home.

So maybe we should go back to his place?

My cheeks warmed when my sister looked at me oddly.

"What?" I whispered.

"You were talking to yourself," Grace whispered back. "And I'd go with option two."

I snickered as the music lowered, and my eyes fell to Beckett, who took the microphone first.

"Mom and Dad, there are so many things that you've taught us throughout your marriage. First, never argue with Mom. You won't win."

The crowd chuckled, and Beckett smiled.

"In all honesty, you've taught us that it's wonderful to be loved, but it's even better to give it. Whenever I think about my parents, I'm in awe at how easy they make marriage look. They excel at compromise, and they're great communicators. But above all, they never forget what ties them together." He paused. "Love. Love is what bound them all those decades ago. When times get tough, being united in love is what saw them through to the easy again. To the effortless." Beckett put the microphone to his side and looked at his parents and smiled before bringing it back up again. "But what your love has taught me most was that when you know, you know." Beckett's gaze landed on me. My sister's breathing quickened while mine stopped. "And don't make love more complicated than it needs to be." He didn't remove his eyes from mine. "So, I hope I can make you two proud someday. I hope I can walk in your footsteps and experience the love that you two share for one another with my own person because isn't imitation the best form of flattery? We love you, Mom."

Nancy dabbed her eyes as Beckett handed the microphone to Hunter.

"Maybe we should stop with Beckett," his dad teased, and we all laughed.

Hunter smiled and shook his head. "What can I say? You've set the bar extremely high. In fact, I think Beckett and I are scared of screwing up your amazing track record."

I glanced at Beckett and noticed him watching me as his words still ran through me. Could I have made it up? Maybe his looking at me when he said it was all a coincidence.

Hunter handed the microphone to Evie. "Mom and Dad, you two are my heroes. You never put pressure on me to find the perfect human, to date a man to take care of me. None of that. You showed me that I have to love myself first, really know myself, and the other things will fall into place. I appreciate that about you both so much. We might tease one another about our lack of partners, aside from Cash." She glanced at him. "But that was a very sudden turn of events. I'm talking to you, Maya."

Everyone chuckled as Maya gave a quick wave.

"But he was ready to receive that love and to give it.

233

I know someday, I will be too. But I'm so grateful to have such an amazing family unit who supported me and who I can look to as a role model. It means everything." Nancy sniffled again as Cash took over.

I snuck a look at Beckett and wondered if our no-strings-attached session might have sewn in a few threads. As Cash finished up, the lights lowered, the music volume increased, and Beckett made his way over to me.

Beckett brought me into his arms and dropped his mouth to my ear. "Yes, I was talking about you."

A flutter of excitement ran through me like a herd of gypsy moths.

He straightened, and I looked into his eyes.

"I want to kiss you," he said softly. "But not here."

We glanced around the room, and he lowered his hand into mine, directing me out of the room, leaving the beat of the music behind.

Beckett found a corridor down the hall from us as my pulse raced. I didn't know that I'd be able to stop at just one kiss. He twirled me into his arms and quickly pressed me up against the wall. Pinning my hands above my head turned the heat up as his breath hovered against my skin. Beckett cupped my face with his free hand.

"You're so damn incredible, Nina."

His broody eyes read my wants with the skill of someone experienced. He brought his mouth to mine and kissed me.

A little moan escaped my lips as I parted my mouth. Feeling his body pressed up against mine made every single fiber running through me ignite with serious passion.

"You taste incredible," he whispered between kisses.

"It's the chocolate decadent," I whispered back.

His body shuddered with laughter, and I felt his mouth curl into a smile.

"It's going to be so bloody hard leaving you," he said, kissing me again.

"Aunt Nina? Is that you?" Izzy's voice shattered whatever planet Beckett and I thought we were on.

I looked at my niece and cocked my head slightly when I realized her sweater was on backward.

"Where did you come from?" I asked. "I thought you were at the arcade?"

"We got lost," she mumbled with flame-red cheeks.

I chuckled. "I bet you did."

"I won't tell if you won't tell." Izzy's toothy grin made me smile, and I realized I didn't want to be anywhere else.

Chapter Twenty

Beckett

It was almost six in the morning, and I was wondering why in the world I thought making a day trip to the Ice Castles was a good idea. As I rang Nina's doorbell, she swung open the door all bundled up like a marshmallow.

Nina quickly shut the door behind her and followed me to my already running SUV without a word. It was too cold to speak.

When she climbed in, she spotted the hot latte waiting for her from Buttercup Java.

"You are the freaking best," she said, eyeing the drink.

"I'm just glad they open at five."

She nodded, happily taking her gloves, hat, and coat off since the SUV was super toasty.

"I can't believe we decided to do this the day after your parents' party." She took a sip of coffee. "But I'm grateful I get to see this before you head back to France."

The way her tone changed on the word *France* made

me laugh. "I hope you visit."

She nodded but kept her gaze in front of her, drinking the latte. "Me too."

"I highly doubt I'll let so much time go by before I come back."

Nina looked over at me and smiled. "Time will tell."

I let out a deep breath and nodded. She was right. I wasn't going to give her empty promises. It sounded like she'd had enough of those, but there was still so much I didn't know about why she really came back to Buttercup Lake. Sure. There were messy breakups, and then there were catastrophic breakups, and by the sounds of it, Nina's fell into the latter.

"We should be there in about four hours." I glanced at her as I followed the country road in the pitch black, keeping my eyes open for leaping deer in every direction.

"Awesome." she said, taking another sip. "I am so pooped."

"You can sleep on the way there," I offered.

"And miss out on Beckett time? No way." She giggled and raised her shoulders, glancing at me. "Your parents looked so happy last night."

"They're like that all the time. I think it's a disease."

Nina playfully swatted at my arm. "You do not."

"You're right." I nodded with a smile, eyeing her. "But I'm not sure that kind of love exists for everyone."

"Why do you say that?" Nina slid her leg under her as she adjusted the recline on the seat.

"I don't know." I laughed. "I guess because I haven't experienced it."

Nina laughed and nodded. "Yeah. I get it."

"You do?"

She grinned, turning to me. "You're one of *those* people who don't believe things unless they happen to you."

"What? It's not like that."

"Oh, yeah? Prove me wrong. Tell me one thing you think is possible that hasn't happened to you."

I shifted in my seat and nodded. "I've never fallen in love, but I think it's possible."

"That's nice to hear." Her voice softened, and she drew a breath. "I have to confess to being a little gun-shy with the possibility."

"Whatever you went through sounds brutal."

She clutched her hands together and stretched them in front of her as I turned onto a highway.

"Yeah. For sure." She looked out the window. "But I think it was more of a burn to my ego after all was said and done."

When I realized she wasn't going to say anything else, I decided to press a little.

"I know it's absolutely none of my business, but . . ."

Nina laughed and looked over at me. "But what happened?"

I grinned. "Exactly."

"You said we have four hours? That might be enough time."

I wasn't nervous before I pressed, but now my nerves were on fire. Would she tell me the man was the love of her life and she was scarred forever? That I had no chance?

"So, I told you he portrayed himself as a big-time art dealer, and I let him help manage the business side of things." She twisted her lips into a pout and shook her head. "That was all true, but he was actually stealing from me, using my name for credit and purchases I didn't know about. The whole thing lasted for years, but it went off the rails this fall. My saving grace was that we never married. We didn't even live together. He was over a lot, but he didn't move in."

Nina's words smacked me in the face like a cement wall. "You lost everything to him?"

She let out a big sigh carrying more weight than I could understand. "And more."

"He was skimming money off the top for years, and

when I didn't notice, he got greedier. He'd wine me and dine me, and little did I know, it was all with my own money." She laughed with the first bitter edge I'd ever heard leave her lips. "I was a fool. No doubt about it. He was good-looking and charming."

"You loved one another," I said flatly.

"I know he didn't love me at all. Did I love him? I thought I did, but I realize now that it was more infatuation." She shook her head and took a sip of her latte. "You know those people who always have to figure things out the hard way?" Nina pointed at her chest. "That's me. I'm that person."

"What made you realize it was infatuation and not love?"

Her cheeks blushed. She stretched her legs in front of her. "Because I never got to know the man behind the curtain. I was content with flattery and really shallow definitions of sweet platitudes. He didn't provide any bumps in the road, so I went with it."

"Wow. That's honest."

She laughed. "Too honest, probably."

I slid my hand to her knee and felt that intense pull again to her. Just feeling the warmth under the fabric of her pants brought out a need to uncover everything about her. It reminded me that the woman I was falling for was right next to me, opening up, being vulnerable.

"In your defense, people always say love shouldn't be hard."

She chuckled. "But I don't think it's supposed to be *that* easy. I could have told the man that the sky was green and the ocean was yellow, and he'd be like, 'Yeah, you're right. You see color like no one else. Now let me skim a little more off the top here.'" Nina touched her forehead and shook her head. "Honestly, I was just an idiot, and for some crazy reason, my ego needed to be filled up."

"You're human. I know most of the wrong relationships I tested out had to do with my ego."

"Really?" Relief spread through her gaze.

"For sure."

"But the silver lining for you is that you weren't blinded enough to lose everything you'd worked for."

I laughed. "Fair point."

Nina snickered and curled her fingers through mine as I kept my hand on her knee. "He's in jail now."

Shock rattled through me. "Seriously?"

"Oh, yeah. He's awaiting trial in the slammer since he couldn't afford to post bail and pled guilty to some charges and not others."

"That has to feel kind of good."

Nina nodded. "Whenever a new envelope arrives in my mailbox from an unknown debt collector, I remind myself that he will get his."

"You're still getting bills?"

Nina squeezed my hand. "Yeah. I just got one a few days ago."

"What do you do with them? Forward them to the police?"

"I pay them and then I send a copy to the attorney in charge of the case."

"You pay them?" Why on earth would she pay them?

"Because until everything is settled, it's my name and brand that get dragged through the mud. I won't let him take that from me too. I'd rather sell everything—as I did—and pay it all off and start over than give him the satisfaction of also destroying my future. I've kept my credit intact so far. If I just threw up my hands and assumed the criminal courts would have my back, I'd be in a really tough place for the next ten years. The way I did it, I've got maybe a few bumpy years ahead as I reestablish things."

"Nina, I had no idea." I shook my head. "You've been so positive and . . ."

"Thank you." She leaned her head against the seat. "My family doesn't even know everything. It's just . . .

embarrassing."

"My God, Nina. You have nothing to be embarrassed about. You did nothing wrong. This guy is a criminal. You are the victim."

"I don't like thinking of myself as a victim." She looked at me, and I nodded.

"I understand that."

"I refuse to let him define me like that. I felt the same way about my parents. I had a crappy childhood, but I knew I would never let it define me the way it could have."

And with that, I knew I was falling in love with Nina Bailey. I just didn't know whether she could ever love me back.

Chapter Twenty-One

Nina

"Beckett, this is so magical." I looped my arm through his as the brilliant colors splashed behind walls of ice. We'd spent the day at the resort, eating lunch, wandering the property, and viewing the white mounds of ice and snow. But with the sun setting, the scene turned into a mystical land of rainbows and sparkles igniting the night sky.

Blues, reds, and purples danced behind the thick ice walls of the first castle we walked into. By day, it looked like an interesting ice sculpture, but by night, it lived.

I squeezed his arm and squealed. "I feel like I'm a magical fairy flying to my home in some far-off land."

Beckett laughed. "What would that make me?"

I put my finger to my lips and thought about it for a second. "How about Fairy King?"

"I was thinking like a Night Elf or something."

"Yeah? You fancy yourself more of an elf?"

"They have wicked powers." He laughed. "Or so I've been told."

244

We stood in the middle of the ice sculpture with ice pouring from the ceiling and down the walls in dramatic pillars. It was something I couldn't have imagined to be this pretty.

Beckett and I were the only two in this structure, and calm surrounded us.

"For the first time in a really long time, I feel at peace." I smiled, looking into Beckett's eyes. "Like everything is going to be okay."

He tightened his embrace around me and looked deeply into my eyes. "It's going to be more than okay, Nina. No matter what life brings you, you're a survivor. You don't just turn out *okay*. You thrive when adversity strikes."

"You think so?"

Beckett's lips lifted into a wide smile. "I know so, Nina Bailey. You're a fighter."

I rested my hands on his chest as he held me in his arms. "Sometimes, I don't feel like a fighter. I feel like an idiot."

Beckett chuckled. "Maybe you just need someone to remind you how amazing you are with no strings attached."

I smiled and nodded, letting my head lie on his chest. "That's when feelings start happening."

And they already had. I told myself I could handle a

romp in the sack with Beckett. After all, he was a short-timer in Wisconsin. I knew the game before I slid under the covers with him, but the more we got to uncover about one another, the more I needed to share and learn.

With Travis, I didn't really have that interest to know. Granted, I'd been shut down the first few times I asked questions, but it didn't scare me away. It selfishly made me relieved.

"Is that a bad thing?" he asked. "You know, feelings?"

I lifted my head, and Beckett locked his gaze on mine. I didn't say a word.

"Is it?" he repeated.

"I don't know," I whispered. "But I'm afraid it's already happening."

Beckett slid his hands from my waist, up my spine, to my head, and without wasting another second, he kissed me.

He wasn't holding back. His mouth tasted like hot cocoa, and his tongue coaxed me into a dance far away. My breathing sped up with each passing second, and I let myself dream a little as I stood in the middle of an ice castle with a man who believed I was a fighter when sometimes, I felt like quitting.

Our kisses slowed when we heard feet shuffling

outside the castle.

I smiled, taking a step back.

"Nothing to see here." I lifted my brows, and he laughed.

We laced our gloved fingers as best we could and walked outside to a colorful ice city filled with a surreal sense of the present. I glanced at Beckett and realized he was right. I was a fighter. I fought for my sisters to have as normal of a childhood as they could. I fought for my parents' sobriety before realizing it wasn't my fight. I fought for my education, and I fought for my career.

I looked up at Beckett and realized that this was worth fighting for too. I had to at least give this a chance.

"Wow." Beckett pointed at a glowing green dragon guarding a large castle with blue and green blazing through the ice walls.

"I think that dragon could crush your elf self," I whispered.

"What the hell?" He shook his head. "Not on its best day." He raised his arm and pretended to flex his muscle as I clung to it, and he pulled me into him.

By the time we'd drunk our weight in hot chocolate, we decided to head back to Buttercup Lake. At this rate, we'd pull into the driveway by ten or eleven.

As we climbed into the SUV, Beckett blasted the heater. "Want some Culvers?"

I laughed, nodding. "Absolutely."

Beckett looked at his phone, trying to locate the nearest one and set the directions. "Are you having the fish fry dinner or the butter burger?" he asked.

Things suddenly turned serious.

"I'm going with a double butter burger with cheese."

"Good call." He slid his hand onto my knee again, and we drove where directed in blissful silence. As he placed the order at the drive-thru, he looked over at me and smiled. "And a vanilla concrete mixer with wild cherries."

As he pulled forward, I glanced at him. "Is that for you or me?"

"That depends."

I scowled playfully. "On what?"

"Do you promise you won't forget me when I leave Wisconsin?"

I groaned and slid my hands to my eyes. "Don't say it. I hate the thought of you leaving."

"I do too."

My eyes blinked open as he pulled up to the window and handed over cash. "And no. I won't ever forget you, Beckett Knox, but I believe the question is more for you."

Beckett shook his head and handed me the delicious frozen custard blend. "Forgetting you would be like forgetting the address where I grew up."

The cashier gave us a number we stuck on our side mirror and pulled forward for the food to be delivered.

I took a sip and moaned. "You have some competition, Beckett. This is extremely satisfying."

He laughed and took the frozen concoction from me and sipped. "You're right. I need to up my game. But don't forget I have Blackheart back at home, and he's very fond of me."

One of the workers brought out our food and handed Beckett the bag, removing the sticker from our mirror. I set the cup down and searched for our meals.

"How do you do it?" I asked.

"What's that, hon?"

It felt like I suddenly had the case of the collywobbles, but I knew I wasn't sick. I was . . .

I was falling deeply for Beckett Knox.

And it hit me. I'd never had any man call me a term of endearment. Never. Not once.

I smiled fondly at Beckett and unwrapped my burger. "They don't have this in Paris."

He smiled and watched me take a bite. "And they

don't have you."

"No, but I bet they have a lot of beautiful women with sexy accents."

Beckett shook his head. "It's not about that for me."

I nodded, realizing he was probably telling the truth or he'd have a ring on his finger. Beckett was extremely attractive, intelligent, sensitive, and did I say sexy? He could have his pick. There had to be more to it than what he'd told me so far.

"I can actually relate to starting all over, Nina." He took a bite of the cheeseburger and closed his eyes. I wasn't sure whether he was truly enjoying his food or debating what next to say.

"I'd imagine it would feel like starting from scratch, moving out of the country and to a new one."

He nodded. "It did, but I knew what I was getting into then. The time I'm talking about was unexpected and really brutal."

I turned in my seat and took another bite. "Really? What happened?"

"My first business failed." He took a sip of soda. "Not like it just didn't make money. It epically failed. I lost everything because I'd tied my personal assets to my business ones, and I had zilch when all was said and done. I couldn't even afford a plane ticket back to the States. I refused to tell my family. I didn't want any of that *I told you so* energy."

"What did you do?"

"I thought about finding a sugar mama, but it didn't pan out. That's when I came up with the idea for farming."

I laughed and shook my head. "Wait a second. You were swiping left and right for a sugar mama, and that's when the location and sensor ideas came to you?"

Beckett's smile turned into laughter as he held his sides and tears flooded his cheeks. "No. Please tell me you didn't believe the sugar mama thing."

The worry I didn't know I suddenly had drained instantly.

He squeezed my hand.

"Wow. Becket, I never would have guessed any of this. I just thought everything kind of came easy to you."

He let out a deep breath. "Not at all. I fought for everything I have now, but I'm at the point where I want to step out of the ring a little."

"I get that." I drew a deep breath and wondered just how much more in common Beckett and I had because every day seemed to bring us closer together at the same time it was moving us apart.

Chapter Twenty-Two

Beckett

It felt good coming clean to Nina about my failed business. I'd been hanging onto that piece of information far too long, but I didn't know if she'd just think I was trying to get too personal in the beginning.

I reached over to Blackheart, who bobbed his head toward me and pushed a toy at me like a dog.

"You're so weird," I muttered, picking it up and dangling it in front of him.

"Yeah, but he's the not the one talking to a rooster," Cash said, coming up behind me.

"Hey, how'd you get in?" I laughed, giving him a hug.

"Last I checked, when you don't lock your door, it makes it easy."

I groaned and shook my head. "Man, the old habits come right back."

"I take it you have to lock your door in Paris?"

"Absolutely."

"The girls are in the car," Cash explained. "You ready?"

Blackheart stopped playing with his toy and stretched his neck, glaring at my brother.

"Uh-oh," I muttered.

"What's that?" Cash asked, and before I had a chance to answer, Blackheart charged at Cash.

My brother let out a yelp as he jumped into the air, landing on the couch as Blackheart pushed his one wing out and started to do the circular dance. I wasn't exactly sure what it meant, but I was pretty certain it wasn't good.

"Tell that bird to stand down, man." Cash shook his head with his knees tucked under his large body.

I laughed. "I don't know. This is kind of fun."

"Beckett."

Blackheart stopped his dance and lunged at my brother, trying to peck his boots, halfway jumping onto the couch and sprawling his wings to get at him.

I snickered as Cash shooed him away.

"That's enough, Blackheart." I pointed in front of the fireplace, and the rooster complied but still glared at my brother.

Cash hopped off the couch and scowled. "One word of that to the girls, and I'll—"

I held up my hand. "My lips are sealed. Nate's going to pick up Blackheart in a little bit. I'll just leave the door unlocked."

"Maybe you ought to leave it open," he joked.

I glanced at Cash. "Thanks again for driving. That's nice after eight hours in the car on Sunday."

"Totally." My brother stopped and smiled. "You know, if you weren't set on leaving, you wouldn't have to try to push every possible scenic attraction of Wisconsin into a short visit."

I knew he was right, but I didn't . . . I wasn't ready to think in those terms, so I did what I do best and changed the subject.

"You seem so happy with Maya."

"Happy isn't even the right word. She makes me feel alive, Beckett. It's something I can't even describe."

I nodded, smiling.

"Tell me the truth. Why do you keep dragging Nina to all these places?"

I'd thought a lot about this myself, but I didn't feel like sharing it with my brother.

"Since it's her new home, I just want her to know she chose well."

"But not good enough for you to stay?"

"I've built a life in Europe. You've seen it. You've even stayed at my place in Portugal. Should I give all that up?"

"The houses?" Cash asked as we went outside, and I shut the door behind me. "Yeah. In a heartbeat. You're in the front. Maya and Nina are in the back."

As we made our way up north, the sisters were chatting behind us, every once in a while asking for our opinion on things but mostly keeping themselves amused as I took in the beautiful ride.

By the time we made our way to the rental on the lake shore, it was nearing dark. The towering trees outlined in ice and snow along with rugged cliffs harboring chunks of ice and water drips frozen in place for the rest of the winter were stunning. The lake effect snow cast a sheen of white across the landscape, but the skies had been clear.

We parked in front of a small log cabin with snow drifts piled high.

"Cozy," Nina said, tapping my shoulder from behind. "I love it."

"The back looks out over Lake Superior, so we should get an amazing view of the Northern Lights."

Nina squealed and squeezed my shoulder as Cash gave me a funny look.

"I brought my camera. I cannot wait."

I helped Nina and Maya out of the back of the compact Jeep before they wandered up to the cabin. I gave them the code to get inside, and they quickly left us at the SUV.

Cash and I pulled the small bags out of the back of his Jeep that had been crammed inside.

"She really likes you, Beckett. You're not going to find that in Paris." Cash shook his head. "You're making a big mistake by leaving."

"We've only spent a couple of weeks together," I told my brother as if he didn't already know that.

"I'm just saying."

"Duly noted."

Cash and I brought our bags inside the small cabin where a sitting room, dining area, and kitchen could all be seen from the front entryway. A loft upstairs had a ladder from the sitting room, and a small bedroom and bathroom were located behind the kitchen.

"I thought you said it had two bedrooms." Cash laughed.

Nina grinned. "We'll take the loft."

"We will?" I choked out, and she beamed.

Yeah, pretty much anything she wanted, I'd do.

I smiled and nodded. "Yeah. We will."

"Are you sure?" Maya asked.

"Totally," Nina assured her. "It will be like sleeping in a treehouse."

I slung my backpack over my shoulder and climbed the ladder to see a queen-size bed, two pine side tables, and a green beanbag in the corner. It matched the green comforter. The place looked cute. I tossed my backpack on the wooden floor in the loft and climbed back down to do the same for Nina.

"I'm just glad the roads weren't as nuts as sometimes." Cash crashed on the couch with Maya as Nina wandered to the kitchen to put some of the items I'd picked up at the store into the fridge.

I came into the kitchen to help, and she smiled at me.

"It just hit me that you're leaving the day after tomorrow." She inhaled. "It snuck up fast."

"It did." I put a pack of bacon in the fridge. "Imagine how Blackheart must feel."

She giggled, and it made my world right.

"You're pretty much abandoning him."

Nina leaned against the counter and opened up a beer. "But I've been thinking a lot about things."

My heart hammered in my chest. Was this where she let me down gently?

"I think I'd like to adopt Blackheart. I know I won't be at Millie's house for much longer, maybe just another six months or so, but I also know I won't be in the city limits of Buttercup Lake, so he'd be fine with me wherever I landed. And I feel like on some level, we're kindred spirits. Neither of us wants to be anyone's charity case, so I think I'll eventually be able to persuade him that we're on the same team. I'd like him as my guard rooster," she said emphatically.

"You'd take Blackheart for me?"

She nodded, taking a sip. "Totally."

I didn't want to bring up the elephant in the room, but I knew I needed to do it.

"I'm worried about the safety issue."

Nina scowled. "What safety issue? Do I need baby gates or something for him?"

I laughed and opened the fridge, reaching for a beer too. "No. I'm worried about *your* safety."

"What in the world are you talking about?" She laughed as I swept her into my arms.

"I don't think Blackheart likes you."

"That rooster is totally jealous of you, Nina," Cash added from the family room. "He only has eyes for my brother."

I nodded in agreement. "I think my brother is right."

Nina chuckled and shook her head. "I can win him over. I know it."

"If you say so," Cash muttered. "But he wanted to peck my eyes out earlier."

Nina and Maya burst into laughter.

"We'll talk more about it," Nina said, patting my arm. "Now let me cook you all dinner."

She clapped her hands and waved me toward the sitting area with Maya and Cash.

Maya grinned as she watched her sister pull things out of the fridge and happily chop away. Nina was humming some tune I didn't recognize and looked so carefree. It was hard to believe that she'd been through so much. To be robbed of everything by a person you thought cared for you was brutal. I wasn't sure she'd ever be able to trust again, and I wasn't sure I blamed her.

"I still can't believe you're hopping on that plane," Cash said with his voice lowered. Maya nodded in agreement.

"There's something special happening between you two," Maya said softly. "We can all see it."

"And you're just going to fly back to Paris and act as if nothing happened back home that could change the trajectory of your life." Cash frowned. "It's a shame."

I felt it too. Every single word Cash said, I knew deep

down. But what could I do? Nina wanted no strings, which I promised, and I had several of my lawyers from the States meeting me on Friday in Paris to go over the sale of my business. They'd used me as an excuse to fly to France with their families, I was sure, but I certainly couldn't ditch them.

"You know it too," Cash said. "I can see it."

I looked over at Nina, and the pull to stay hurt.

"No matter what, I have to get on that plane," I said quietly.

Cash scowled deeper. "Why?"

"I haven't told the family yet, but I'm selling my business."

Cash looked shocked. "You haven't even told Dad?"

I shook my head. "You know how he is. He'll think I'm being ridiculous to sell my business."

My brother nodded. "He always thinks idle hands and all that."

I laughed, nodding. "Exactly. But it's not like I'm selling and then just kicking back to do nothing."

"Anyway, I have to review and sign the papers my lawyers have for me." I cupped my hands together. "They're already over there."

"That does complicate things." Maya twisted her lips in disappointment. "You could always just fly back."

I laughed and nodded. "True, but I don't know that your sister wants that. I look intriguing to her because she knows I'm leaving. She doesn't need anything complicated, especially right now."

Maya sighed and nodded. "I suppose I've just turned into a hopeless romantic like my grandmother."

"Millie does rub off on people," I agreed.

"What are you all secretly planning over there?" Nina asked, smiling as she dried her hands off on a towel.

"How to keep Beckett from leaving," Maya chipped in.

My insides tensed as I tried to read every little thing from Nina. Her gaze moved between her sister and me.

Nina saluted me with a wink, and I couldn't help but smile.

"Well, we knew this was a short-term thing we had going." Nina winked at me, and the tension turned into nausea. "Plus, I have a place to visit with a built-in tour guide, and the way he's showing me around Wisconsin tells me Paris will be a real treat."

Maya laughed and glanced at me. I was certain she could read the disappointment as I stayed stuck on Nina's description of our relationship, but it was true. That was what we'd agreed to, and now I regretted pretending like I could do that with Nina.

"Super-easy salmon quinoa bowls are done," Nina announced.

"Sounds delicious," Cash said, helping Maya off the couch.

"It does."

We wandered over to the eating area, set the table, and scarfed down dinner.

"So good," I said, shaking my head.

Nina smiled and nodded. "Glad you like it."

"There's about three hours before the light show," Cash announced, glancing at his phone. "Theoretically, and the night sky is still showing as clear."

We played board games the host had left and enjoyed the rest of the night inside, laughing and keeping conversation light.

When it was time to go outside, Nina grabbed her camera equipment and set it up out back. I helped where I could while Maya brought us all hot drinks.

And then it happened. A brilliant light show took over the sky. Nina quickly hopped to her equipment with a yip of glee as she worked her magic, taking photos, changing settings, kissing me in between. Cash and Maya wandered away from the house hand in hand, giving Nina and me some privacy.

"Look at that purple and bright green," she gushed, pointing north.

"Beautiful," I whispered in awe.

She turned to face me and drew a deep breath. "Thank you for this, Beckett. All of this. I doubt I would have done this for myself, and it's . . . magnificent."

I nodded as the night's sky swirled in brilliant green with blue auras, leading into purple crowns of light.

Nina took another photo and turned away from her camera. "You've shown me another side of Wisconsin, Beckett. I'll never be able to thank you for introducing me to my new home for now."

I smiled as she closed the gap between us. "I've enjoyed every second."

She looked into my eyes and smiled. "You have? For a guy who doesn't like Wisconsin, you've certainly shown me a lot of things to like about it."

"It's just never felt like home . . . until recently." My gaze stayed on Nina's.

"What changed?" she asked softly.

"Meeting you," I whispered, cradling her head between my hands as we kissed.

Chapter Twenty-Three

Nina

We'd decided to hang out at Beckett's house for his remaining time in town, mainly so Blackheart could get used to me. After all, I wasn't exactly kidding about his being my guard rooster, and with a name like Blackheart, I felt like he could live up to my expectations. The calls hadn't stopped. In fact, they'd become more frequent.

But the rooster experiment wasn't going quite like I'd imagined.

When I'd open the fridge, Blackheart would curl his neck around the door and stare at me like I was stealing food straight from his beak.

When I'd lie on the couch, his red comb would slowly raise until two little beady eyes and a red wattle rested on the cushion.

And he'd stare.

Just stare long enough until I got off the couch.

When I used the restroom, he'd be waiting for me when I opened the door.

It was unnerving, but I told myself it was all part of the process.

"I think I'm making headway," I told Beckett. "He doesn't do that weird dance or anything."

Beckett smiled, taking a grape from the colander. "Remember when Carter made that snowman?"

I chuckled. "It wasn't Carter. I asked him at your parents' anniversary party," I teased. "He claimed innocence."

"You did not." He grinned.

"Are you sure you don't want me to take you to the airport?" I asked.

Beckett smiled. "Nah. I'm not great at goodbyes, and it's really a long haul back and forth."

The thought made my hopes sink. Hope of what? I wasn't sure.

He softly brushed his thumb against my cheek. "Cheer up. We'll see each other again."

I nodded, knowing that just because we'd see each other again, it didn't mean in the same capacity. He could find the love of his life wandering the Louvre, or who knows what could happen so many thousands of miles away?

"Can we have one more time?" I asked, smiling up at Beckett.

He instantly closed the gap between us and bundled me into his arms and picked me up.

Before I knew it, we were on his bed, kissing like we might never kiss again. His warm lips felt more urgent than last time. His hands skimmed me with determination, moving under my shirt and then pulling it off.

I nuzzled my head into the crook of his neck with an open-mouthed kiss. His body tensed as my tongue slid along his skin. He let out a deep, winded breath that turned me on like no other sound.

I wanted to memorize every single thing about him. The way he smelled of soap and the outdoors. The way his thumbs had little flat pads that he'd brush along my skin and make me tingle everywhere. The dimple in his cheek.

Kicking off my pants and underwear as he removed his own clothes created an unsaid frenzy between us. We both knew this would be it. This would be our last time together. I pushed down the uncertainty and focused on the man in front of me as he moved his hands down my naked body. The first time we'd been together, we were playful and exploring. Today felt different, charged with something I didn't realize was building.

Beckett brought his mouth back to mine as his hands swept along my breasts, teasing my nipples and stirring an aching desire deep in my belly.

"I will miss this," I said, careful to keep it about the act.

Beckett nosed me and shook his head. "I'll miss you."

The words shook me to my core as my hips wiggled toward him and he pushed inside me, making me so full. I curled my hands under the pillows and breathed a deep sigh of ecstasy as he charged into me again. His lips moved expertly along my breasts. His hands moved along my curves, tingling my entire spine with a current of need.

"Beckett," I whispered as he shoved deeper than before. My back arched in complete pleasure. "So good."

In an instant, we were trembling in bliss as our bodies joined together one last time. My hands hung lazily over his shoulders as I tried to catch my breath, my heart hammering in my chest.

Beckett opened his eyes, taking me in as we turned over and curled on our sides.

"I'm going to miss you too," I said softly, clutching his hands in front of me and closing my eyes. "Not just this."

As we spooned, I could still feel his length pressing

against my back. His warm breath feathered along my skin. Maybe, I'd be lucky enough to visit Paris. Maybe we could do this again one day.

I hugged Beckett's arm and let out a blissful sigh when I heard a funny noise at the foot of the bed. I looked down and didn't see anything other than Beckett's big feet. Tucking back into his arms, I heard it again.

But this time, the noise was in front of me from the side of the bed. The red comb of Blackheart slowly rose from the depths of jealousy, and we were eye to eye. The rooster wouldn't take his eyes off me.

"Beckett," I whispered. "We have a situation."

Beckett rose from behind me and started laughing as Blackheart changed his stance when he saw his hero.

"Scram," Beckett said, waving his hand at the rooster.

Blackheart tucked his head down and slowly padded toward the door. When he reached the doorway, he stopped and turned around to look at us both before going down the hall.

"Wow." I turned over to see Beckett scratching his head. "That was really dramatic."

"That was intense." He laughed, shaking his head.

My phone buzzed as we laid back down, and Beckett handed it to me from the nightstand.

"Looks like your sister Grace," he muttered, nestling back into me.

I slid up the screen on my phone to see a text message.

Grandma just called.

My heart froze. Was she okay?

Dad is at her house. We're headed there now.

Tears stung my eyes while my body stilled. Numbness coated every cell as I readied myself for what was in store.

"Nina, what's wrong?"

My body trembled with the news. I slid my phone to Beckett. He read it silently.

I turned over to face Beckett as I forced the lump in my throat down.

"Are you okay?" His tender voice pulled at my heart as I shook my head.

"No. I'm not, but I should go."

"I'm coming with you," he said, standing from the bed and reaching for his clothes.

I looked up at Beckett Knox and realized how much

I'd miss him once he was gone tomorrow.

"Are you sure?" I asked as he handed my clothes to me.

"I don't want you there alone."

"My sisters will be there," I offered.

"They have their partners." He smiled affectionately at me.

"I don't know what kind of shape he's in. He could be strung out or coming down or . . ." I didn't know what to say. Shame and sadness edged their way into my heart. "It's not something you need to see."

"And you do?" he asked, shaking his head. "But if you don't want me to come, I understand. I don't want to make you uncomfortable."

I'd pulled my clothes on and stood as Beckett walked over to me and hugged me.

"No, I think I'd like it if you're there." I nodded, hugging him back.

We led Blackheart into the garage where there was a pen set up for him. He stared at me as if this were my doing.

Oddly, the rooster became a bright spot in a completely unexpected turn of events. I clutched my phone as if it were my lifeline, but I was afraid to ask any more questions. I just needed to get to the house. I needed to see for myself.

Him.

The man who'd always chosen substances over his daughters.

As we pulled out of Beckett's garage, I drew a deep breath and rested my head on the seat as we drove toward my grandma's house.

There were so many questions spinning their messy webs in my mind.

Would he be high or coming down? Would Nate need to come handle things?

Beckett took my silence as the worry it truly was and squeezed my hand as we made our way to my grandma's house.

It had always felt like a protective force, the one place my parents' drama and poor choices couldn't touch us, but now he'd penetrated that force. My dad was no longer just a shadow of my memory. He'd made a choice to become front and center.

The worry started to etch its way into anger as I thought about my grandma, and everything she'd tried to make her son and his wife, my mother, better over the years. The worry and pain that drove her to pray until she had no more prayers.

271

Those tears . . .

I thought back to when my grandma cried after the book club session, and it suddenly made me wonder if she knew that my dad was coming to town.

Beckett pulled down the gravel drive nestled between snowbanks where Grandma Millie's home anchored the property and my heart. The bright green shutters and door on the old farmhouse brought a sense of calm as we drove toward it to see my grandma's car, along with Maya and Grace's.

I bet my father didn't even know Grace was pregnant with his grandchild.

Beckett pulled up next to his brother's Jeep and looked at me. "You ready for this?"

I nodded, feeling a catch in my throat. "As ready as I'll ever be."

We climbed out of Beckett's SUV, and he came over and met me. Holding hands, we made our way up the steps to the porch and opened the door to voices down the hall.

It sounded peaceful.

We made our way to the kitchen, and Grandma Millie appeared in the doorway with her Jackson behind her while Grace's Jackson stood next to her, rubbing his pregnant fiancée's shoulder.

"I'm so glad you got my message," my sister said

softly.

"Is everything okay?" I asked, reaching for the pot of coffee.

"I . . ." Grace shook her head.

How would we know?

Grandma Millie's red eyes were rimmed with tears, but she stayed anchored with her boyfriend, which was unusual for my grandmother. Usually, she flitted about all over the room, making sure she could make everyone comfortable.

Maya and Cash walked into the kitchen from the family room.

"Is he not here? Did he run away already?" I asked, feeling the odd mixture of betrayal, disappointment, and sorrow.

Maya shook her head. "He's taking a shower upstairs. He's had a long journey."

I looked between my sisters and shook my head. "What's that supposed to mean?"

My grandmother drew a long breath as the room fell silent. "My son is clean. He's completely sober."

The tears in grandma's eyes welled up again, and I knew she couldn't even comprehend what was coming out of her mouth. There had been so few times I'd even witnessed a sober Dad that I didn't even know what that meant. But my grandma, her son . . . she knew his life before the mess of drugs and alcohol. She knew the person she was missing and the person he could have become.

Without waiting another second, we dashed to Grandma Millie and hugged her as we all secretly prayed that this time was for real.

Someone cleared his throat, and I realized it was my father. We all stepped back from my grandma, and I turned around to see the man who'd been missing from most of my life.

Grace gasped and slowly brought her hands to her mouth. She was the only one of us who'd seen him recently. She'd tracked my parents down at a tent city back in Seattle, but they couldn't even get Grace's daughter's name right. They kept calling her Sammi instead of Izzy. Just one of the many things that pained Grace to no end, but she'd had closure with my mom. Her own form of closure. But obviously, she was seeing something different with this form of our father.

My dad stood in the hallway with his shoulders pushed back and more clarity in his eyes than I'd ever seen. He smiled, missing teeth and everything, but I saw a little spark, a little sparkle behind his eyes like my grandma's, and I realized for the first time that I was seeing who my father was meant to be.

Chapter Twenty-Four

Beckett

The moment I stepped into my apartment in Paris, I knew I needed to go back to Nina. I had no idea what mess I was leaving behind, but I didn't feel right staying here.

Nothing felt right without Nina.

I flipped on my light in the living area and sat on the couch. Everything here felt so cold when for years, it had been home. I stood and walked over to the window overlooking the exterior of the neighboring building. If I strained my neck, I could see the overcast sky looming overhead.

The world felt dreary being back.

I made my way to the bedroom and collapsed on my bed. The room was small and nothing like I had back in Wisconsin, but it had been enough.

Until Nina.

The truth was that I saw a future with her. The moment she came into the kitchen at her grandmother's house sold me on her. She was creative, funny, and a free spirit, all wrapped up in a cute grandma gown. The thought made me smile. Just thinking about her warmed me up.

She wasn't shallow. She understood how the world worked, injustices and all. Yet, she didn't let herself be strapped into one way of existing.

I pulled a pillow on top of my chest and just stared at the ceiling.

"Beckett, don't be an idiot." I groaned, rolling over. "She's got enough going on."

Before I left, I'd thought about leaving her with a plane ticket to Paris, but she'd said something one day about never wanting to be a charity case, and even though it would be a small gift on my part, it might not come across that way.

Nina had been screwed over enough between having parents who were never there for her and an ex who took everything from her. I didn't need to make Nina feel like I felt sorry for her.

I didn't. I admired her for pushing through and still being able to smile after everything.

And then to have her dad show up out of the blue?

I pulled my phone out of my pocket and dialed Nina's phone. It went to voicemail. I just left a quick message, letting her know that I'd made it back to my apartment, and then added that I missed her already and I hoped things were going okay.

It was late afternoon, and I probably had a good hour or two before it rained. I grabbed my coat and took off to wander the sidewalks of Paris. There was a little gallery I'd been meaning to stop into, and now was as good a time as any.

I walked along the street and admired the beautiful architecture that I'd passed by for years. It never got old seeing it, but I hoped I could share it with Nina.

I blew out a breath and a puff of cold air lingered. Still nothing like Wisconsin cold. The thought brought a smile to my lips.

My parents were probably in the family home, reading and planning the day, talking about dinner or some book that my mom just started for the Sunshine Breakfast Club.

Cash was probably crawling around some new fixer-upper he snagged to repair and rent out.

And Nina . . .

And her grandma.

Ah, the book club matchmaking that wasn't. The thought kind of rubbed me the wrong way when I thought about it. I couldn't quite figure out why they felt Hunter was a better candidate to focus on than me. Not that it mattered, but it got me wondering.

Did I have a stamp across my forehead that read

Forever a Bachelor?

I spotted the gallery and decided against going in. I would save it for when Nina came here. One way or another, I'd get her here.

My pace quickened when I thought about where I needed to walk. There was a beautiful cemetery a few blocks away. Maybe a few photographs of the gardens would pique her interest, distract her from everything that just landed on her grandma's doorstep. Maybe give her a chuckle.

Maybe that was a bad idea. She had a lot going on.

I couldn't even imagine my parents missing in action, let alone suffering from addiction, but it was a cruel roll of the dice. I shook my head in disbelief when I thought about Nina.

Nina as a whole person.

Not just the woman I was falling in love with.

She grew up with addict parents. She helped raise her sisters. She pushed herself to be successful and go to school in a field she loved. She traveled the country. She'd been to some wild festivals and managed to have a successful gallery for years. Until a criminal got the best of her heart.

I shook my head, thinking about the guy. Travis. I think it was? The thought of him sitting in jail unable to afford bail was the only bright spot in that story.

My phone buzzed, and I quickly answered, thinking

it was Nina.

But it wasn't. My brother's grumpy mug popped up on the screen.

"It's Cash," my brother said, clearing his throat.

"Yeah. I'm actually pretty good at guessing your voice after this many decades with you." I laughed. "Not to mention, there's this handy feature on phones nowadays that lets us see who's calling."

"Ah, a funny man once you're back in Europe again." Cash laughed and let out a sigh. "Did you just get in?"

"Yeah. Why?" Panic raced through me. "Is everything okay with Nina?"

"Nina? Oh, yeah. She's great. I just got done helping her move some of her things to your house. Her dad's staying in town for a little bit."

"I don't blame her for wanting a little bit of space."

"Totally," Cash agreed.

"I can't imagine you called just to check in on me, so what's the word?"

Cash sighed. "I think something is up with Hunter."

"Up as in he's not falling for the Sunshine Breakfast Club's obsession with hooking him up with Daisy?"

Cash chuckled. "Maybe that's part of it, but he hightailed it back to Madison after our parents' party. Said his staff needed him down at the bar."

"Maybe they did," I offered.

"I think it's that girl Brielle. You never met her, but she was a nasty one. Toyed with his heart really good."

"Oh, right. The one who ghosted him?"

"Yeah. Mom couldn't stand her."

"I heard."

"But she loves Nina, and she loves Daisy."

"I'll keep that in mind."

"Anyway, I was hoping you could call him when you get a chance. I tried, but he won't open up to me."

"I can do that. Anything for my younger brother." I nodded, walking into the cemetery. Being that it was the dead of winter, there wasn't anything in bloom, but the landscape was still striking.

"What are you up to?" Cash asked.

"Just got to a cemetery."

"Oh, no. I'm so sorry. I didn't know anyone passed away."

I laughed. "Many someones passed away. This cemetery is like three hundred years old or something crazy."

"Okay . . ." Cash wasn't following my lead.

"I just come here to clear my head sometimes."

"I—" Cash stopped himself. "You know what? Never

mind. Maya has taught me to be more thoughtful in my reactions."

I chuckled and shook my head. "I knew I liked her."

"I'll let you go be one with . . . whatever there is to be one with there, I suppose."

I snickered and said goodbye to my brother.

And for the first time in years, I let myself miss what I'd left behind in Wisconsin.

Chapter Twenty-Five

Nina

"I want to thank you for sending me that money, Nina." My dad's gaze landed on me before looking over at his mom. He had more clarity in his eyes than I'd ever seen before.

Beckett had left this morning, and I stayed at his house with Blackheart to sort out my thoughts before heading back over to my grandma's house. Last night, Beckett said I could stay at his place for as long as needed. He didn't have any vacationers coming for a month. The thought was appealing because I honestly didn't know my dad, and that was obviously where he would be staying for, I assumed, the foreseeable future.

Grandma Millie eyed me at the revelation. I'd never told her I'd sent money after my mom died. But there were a lot of things I'd failed to mention.

The guilt spinning through me only amplified as my dad studied me closely. I'd sent the funds to him to make him go away while I focused on my own problems. Usually, I wouldn't have sent a dime because it always went to things that made them, him, worse. But I just needed a few months of peace—no late calls, excuses, pleading. And then when it went silent, I assumed it was the money I sent that killed him. They just hadn't found him yet. Living with that kind of guilt does something to a person. It changed the way I viewed a lot of things in the world.

"It wasn't exactly sent with pure intentions," I confessed, toying with a napkin left over from a breakfast sandwich from the coffee shop.

Grandma Millie tilted her head and narrowed her eyes on me.

"I was going through some things personally and was caught off guard, Dad." I shook my head. "Normally, I wouldn't have bought into your I'm-going-to-rehab excuse."

My dad smiled and nodded. "I wouldn't have either with all the lame reasons and excuses over the years why I needed to borrow some coin."

Grandma Millie reached for my dad's hand, and I just prayed he would stay clean, that he wouldn't destroy her. "But you're here now, and you're clearheaded." She grinned. "That's all we can ask for."

My dad kept his gaze on me. "I mean it, Nina. Thank you. I was able to use the money for travel to the facility. I qualified for an in-house treatment program covered under a government program, but they didn't cover the cost of travel."

Fear pummeled through me. I didn't want to be the fool who believed this time would stick, even though I desperately wanted to believe in him.

"I'm glad I was in a place where I could help." Because I certainly wasn't in one now.

The sincerity in his gaze made me uncomfortable because I wasn't in control. I didn't know where to place him in my life anymore. What would make him be able to stay away from the drugs and alcohol this time?

Grace let out a sigh. "I'm so glad to see this side of you, Dad. With Mom gone and never being able to see her sober . . ." My sister cleared her throat. "It's just nice to see who you can be."

My dad nodded. "And I intend to stay this way."

Grace nodded and glanced at me with uncertainty. I knew what she was wondering. Would I feel comfortable staying here with him?

"You know my rule, Joe. As long as you stay clean and sober, you have a place to stay. You can take the primary bedroom." Grandma Millie squeezed his hand again.

I nodded. "Absolutely."

My stomach clenched at the thought. I'd definitely be

staying at Beckett's while I got to know my dad.

"Joe Bailey," Maya said softly. "It's hard to believe you're here. We've lived a lifetime without you."

My dad nodded and drew a slow breath. "And there's not a damn thing I can do about that but live with the regret of being a piss-poor parent and apologize. I was weak."

"Your weakness brought out the strength of my three girls." Grandma Millie sat up straighter.

Hearing her refer to us as *her girls* made life okay. I still had a place. We all had a place.

Grace dabbed some tears away and sniffled. "Sorry. Hormones from the pregnancy."

"I actually have more news," my dad began.

The acid in my stomach flew up my throat, but I pushed it down as I waited with the rest of my family for his next bombshell.

Because my parents always came loaded with ammo.

"I'm actually only here for a week until the sober-living facility is ready for me down in Madison."

Surprise flashed through all of us.

Maya let out a deep breath and shook her head. "Thank God for that."

My dad laughed and nodded. "Truer words."

Maya had a Ph.D. in Psychology and practiced for

well over a decade. She knew better than most of us about the underpinnings of addiction.

"For how long?" she asked.

"As long as I hold a job, stay clean, and follow the rules of the house . . ." My dad licked his lips. "Two years."

"Praise the Lord," Grandma Millie said, smiling. "I knew you had it in you."

She was surer than the rest of us, but she knew her son, and we never knew our dad, not our real dad. We only knew our dad in the throes of a tragic disease.

A thought occurred to me. Maybe my dad had been trying to work up the courage to talk to us on the phone. A bit of hope twined through my veins. "Dad, did you ever try calling here?"

My dad looked embarrassed, and relief flooded through me.

He shook his head. "I couldn't remember the number for the life of me."

"Oh." I couldn't hide the disappointment.

"Why?" Grace asked.

"Just some weird phone calls recently." I waved them off like it wasn't a big deal, and they probably weren't.

My dad clenched his fists uneasily as silence hung thick in the air. He let out a deep sigh and turned his attention to us. "And I was hoping that maybe I could have my wife's ashes. Unless you already did something with them. I understand if you did since you hadn't heard from me. There are a lot of beautiful places in Wisconsin to spread them."

Oh, no.

I sucked on my bottom lip and looked at my sisters before turning my attention to my father.

"Dad, I have some bad news about those." I cleared my throat, trying to buy some time. I hadn't even told my sisters.

He shook his head and put his hands up in the air. "Totally understand if you already laid her to rest."

I wiped my palms on my pants. "It's not that simple."

Grandma Millie cocked her head. "What do you mean, it's not that simple?"

I blew a big gust of breath to steady my nerves. "Mom's ashes were stolen."

My sisters gasped, and Grandma Millie's eyes widened.

My dad frowned and shook his head. "Stolen?"

"I had a bad man for an ex, and when he saw that I'd caught onto the fact that he was swindling money from me, he made a sweep through my house and stole what items he thought had value. Silly me, trying to be respectful to

Mom . . . I put her ashes in an expensive urn."

"Oh, my," Grace muttered, unable to look at me.

"I've tried to get the urn back, find out where Travis sold it, but he won't answer any questions about it since that would obviously incriminate him and he's already sitting in jail."

"Travis is the fellow who stole from you?" my dad asked.

"I'd say the man ruined her," Grandma Millie answered. "Financially, that is. You can't destroy a Bailey woman. We always come out on top."

I laughed, loving my grandma's confidence while praying it was true.

"Anyway, I didn't know how to tell you." I looked at my sisters. "I'm sorry for not coming clean sooner."

Maya chuckled and shook her head. "It's not like we asked."

Grace nodded. "And I'm not sure how you'd bring it up. You have enough going on."

I turned to my dad. "I'm really sorry. I hope I can figure out how to get Mom back somehow."

My dad smiled kindly with his missing teeth and nodded. "With everything we've been through, and everything we've put you girls through, that's the least of my worries. I only hope I can somehow prove to you how important you girls are to me."

Grace looked away, and I wondered if she was feeling the same level of desperation and confusion pummeling through me. It was a lot to take in, and I didn't want anything to complicate her pregnancy.

I looked over at Grandma Millie, who looked like the happiest version of herself, and I knew these two needed time more than we did. My sisters sensed the same, so we moved to the family room to give my grandma and her son time to talk.

"I hope he doesn't destroy her," Grace muttered under her breath, sitting next to me on the couch. "I will never forget what it felt like when I showed up to see them this summer. They didn't even remember Izzy's name and called Jackson by my late husband's name."

I nodded and drew a silent breath. "It's one step at a time. I just . . . I wasn't expecting it."

Maya nodded.

We all looked at one another, unsure of what to say or do next, but for the first time in a long time, we didn't have to worry whether our father was dead or alive. I just didn't know how long that would last. The house phone rang, and I quickly picked up.

"Hello?" I asked.

Silence.

A chill settled over me as I hung up the phone, realizing it wouldn't be a debt Collector. They'd want to track me down, talk to me, scare me.

"Who was that?" Grace asked. "Wrong number?"

I looked around the family room and closed my eyes for a few seconds. "Don't think I'm crazy, but I swear I'm getting prank called from my ex."

"Isn't he in jail?" Grace asked.

I nodded. "As far as I know. I checked last week with my attorney, and he confirmed he was, but I don't know who else it could be. It's getting creepy. I can hear breathing."

Maya nodded. "That's why you asked our dad if he ever called the house?"

I thought back to my rooster. "I'm just glad I have Blackheart."

Maya frowned. "The bird?"

I nodded, and Grace laughed. "You're just as goofy as always, Nina."

"You haven't faced those beady eyes in the dead of the night. He's a lurker. I swear to you, if anyone tries to cross Blackheart's turf, they'll die of a heart attack if not pecked to death."

"Well, good," Maya said sarcastically. "I feel so much better knowing my sister is protected by a guard bird."

Chapter Twenty-Six

Beckett

The deal had been finalized. I was a free man. I no longer owned my company, and it felt good. There was a small part of me that worried I might regret selling it, but the truth was that I'd built it up as far as I could go with it. Technology was changing at lightning speed, and the business needed new leadership that understood the future. Besides, I highly doubted I'd get an offer like that again as the competition ramps up.

Sitting at one of my favorite cafés with an empty plate where a savory crepe once sat made me oddly lonely. Once again, I finished a meal with me, myself, and I instead of talking the time away and learning new things, laughing about old things, and just enjoying life.

I shook myself out of it and looked across the street where the familiar line of Haussmann buildings towered over one of the city's squares. Their cream-colored Lutetian limestone exteriors provided a uniform appearance across the city with their four-sided Mansard rooflines and elaborate windows. These were the things I wanted to show Nina, the cobblestone streets leading to eccentric storefronts, cafés, and bakeries. I could just picture Nina having the time of her life. That was something I wanted to keep imagining, Nina having the freedom to enjoy life as it was instead of always looking backward. I glanced up at one of the long balconies and smiled. Maybe this spring would be a good time for a visit. Usually, that was when flowers exploded from the city gardens of Paris with red geraniums dripping from the verandas. It was no doubt a beautiful city.

But urban planning and pretty buildings couldn't keep a person warm at night. Someone a few tables down lit up a cigarette, and it was my time to leave and go back to my apartment down the road.

I'd done as Cash had asked and spoke with Hunter a week ago. He didn't seem to open up to me any more than he had with Cash. I did pick up on a female's voice in the background, which told me things weren't all doom and gloom in Hunter's life. I'd passed on the message, which was returned with a thumbs-up emoji.

As I made it to my building, I saw a message come over from Cash.

Got a minute?

I wrote back a quick, *sure*.

My phone rang as I stood outside the building and stared at the vivid blue skies. Such a stark change to the rainstorms pouring down a week ago. It was probably snowing back in Wisconsin.

"Hey, Beckett." Cash's voice sounded a little more solemn than I was used to from him. Granted, he was rarely a butterflies and rainbows kind of guy, but something was off.

"What's up?"

"Have you heard from Nina recently?" he asked.

My blood froze. What happened to her?

"Just last night. Why? What's wrong?" I barked at my brother.

"So, she's probably mentioned to you about the crank calls."

I shook my head, pushing my thumb into my temple. "No. She hasn't mentioned them. What's going on?"

Cash let out a deep breath. "I'm sure I'm going to get in trouble about this, but Maya mentioned that Nina's been getting crank calls with silence and some heavy breathing."

"For how long?" I asked as panic set deep within my abdomen. I was all the way in France.

"For a couple of months, maybe? Maybe a month? Not sure." He coughed into the phone, which nearly exploded my eardrum. "Anyway, she's working with Nate on the issue, but I don't have a good feeling about things."

I groaned and kicked a pebble on the sidewalk. "Not good at all."

A few seconds of silence rested between us as I thought about what to do. She hadn't told me anything about the calls. She was fiercely independent, but that didn't stop the need to help I felt stirring.

"Wouldn't her ex be making collect calls if it were him?" I asked, thinking back to the conman behind bars.

"Not that I know from personal experience, but that's the impression I've gotten from Nate. So, I'm guessing it has to be someone else. She even asked if it had been her dad, but he said no."

"Great."

"I know she wants to handle this on her own terms, and maybe it's nothing, but I just wanted you to know."

"No, man. I appreciate it. I'm just . . ." I let out a deep sigh. "I'm surprised she didn't tell me."

We hung up, and I went inside my apartment building, climbing the stairs two at a time. By the time I reached my unit, I'd made up my mind. I was headed back to

Wisconsin.

I hopped on my laptop and started looking at availability on the travel website. Was I overreacting? Yeah. No. Yeah, I was, but no.

I groaned and laughed, shaking my head.

The first thing I needed to do was call Nina and see if she wanted to tell me anything. Second thing was to call the jail her ex was in to make sure he was still there.

Nina picked up almost immediately.

"Hey, sexy stranger," her voice rang over the phone

I laughed, feeling the goodness of Nina spread over me. "I got a call from Cash."

"I just saw Maya and him this morning." She sounded happy. Not worried at all. "They're so cute together."

"They are," I agreed, thinking we were even cuter.

Her voice rumbled into laughter. "Let me guess. Cash called you about the weird calls I've been getting."

"Intuition strikes again." Just talking to her made me feel better.

"They're nothing. Nate is working to track down the number. I tried to Google it, but I came up empty-handed."

"That's good." It was right on the tip of my tongue. *Do you want me to come back?*

"I'm sure it will all be worked out in good time, and

meanwhile, Blackheart is ready and waiting. My dad left for the sober-living facility this morning. I'll be headed back to Grandma Millie's house this afternoon with my guard rooster. Of course, he asked about my mom's ashes, and I had to let everyone know they'd been stolen. I feel awful about it. But I just have to keep focused, and I'm so grateful for the rooster."

I couldn't help but picture Nina and Blackheart, and it brought a smile to my lips. "You can stay at my house a little longer if you'd like. You know, with the calls and all."

"Ah, you're worried."

"Of course, I'm worried. While I think the rooster is a mean son of a bitch, he's not—"

Nina chuckled, cutting me off. "It's fine. Probably some kids around here or something."

"Kids usually get bored after a little while. Cash mentioned it's been going on for some time."

"I suppose."

I let out a deep sigh. "Look, I know you've gone through a lot. I completely understand that you can handle life on your own terms."

"Okay."

"But I wish you had told me. Maybe I could have helped."

Maybe I needed to prove to her that I could help. I

thought about the missing urn, the random calls, and her ex in jail.

She was thoughtfully quiet for a few seconds.

"When I made up my mind to sleep with you, I also vowed that I wouldn't bring you into my mess." She sighed. "And this ick is just more of it, Beckett. You have a great life. Don't let me ruin that for you. We had fun, and maybe we'll have fun again sometime, but my problems don't have to become your problems. Be grateful you're across the globe."

Her reply stunned me. Stabbed me in the heart, if I were being honest with myself, which I didn't want to be.

"I didn't quite see it that way, Nina."

"You didn't? I have a great group of protectors here. My family and friends will keep a lookout. I've got everything I need here in Buttercup Lake, and it took this to remind me of that. I don't need to keep pining over my old life when I'm building a pretty incredible new one with an unexpected twist."

I shook my head without answering and walked over to the window.

She sighed. "I know it may sound like I'm choosing Blackheart over you, but I'm not."

I laughed, realizing I had no idea what was going to come out of Nina's mouth next, but I knew what I wanted to tell her.

"Nina, I miss you. I miss you a lot."

"Me too."

A sudden commotion happened in the background.

And I hoped it didn't have to do with the surprise I'd sent her today.

"Blackheart. No. Off. Bad rooster. Off."

Some sort of scuffle ensued, and Nina mumbled a quick goodbye while I stood in my lonely Paris apartment, contemplating why I thought I was better off living somewhere other than my home state.

And that was when I'd decided I'd come up with a brilliant idea.

Chapter Twenty-Seven

Nina

"So good to have you back," Abby said with a wink. She filled my coffee cup as I sat in the book club circle and stared blankly at the buffet table of food.

"Thanks. I've been spending too much time with Blackheart." I shook my head. "I genuinely feel like we communicate better than I have with any of my exes."

Grandma Millie grimaced. "Definitely time to get out of the house then, dear."

I laughed with a quick nod as I stretched my arms toward the ceiling. "I thought so. Any Hunter and Daisy news?"

"Not much," Abby answered. "They've both been spending most of their time in Madison, which makes sense since she's working down there."

"We have some eyes down there who tell us there's good chemistry. We just have to get Hunter out of his head," my grandma added.

I stared in shock at my grandma. "You have sources

all the way down in Madison? Three hours away from here?"

Grandma Millie laughed and winked. "I also have word that Beckett is absolutely miserable in Paris. He wanders around cemeteries and eats croissants in pouring down rain." She shook her head. "It's a shame, but he never should have left. You were perfect for him, and he can't be foolish enough to think you'll go traipsing across the globe for a man after what happened with your last one."

I threw my head back in a fit of laughter. "Thanks, Grandma."

"Oh, absolutely." She winked at me. "But not to worry. The right fellow will come waltzing into your life when the time's right."

Abby traded a funny look with my grandma as I scowled.

Who said Beckett wasn't right for me? He seemed pretty damn right to me up until the part of his leaving for Paris.

My scowl deepened, and I realized my grandma might have a point.

"The good news is that we're starting a great mystery series," Abby told me as more book club members filed in.

Beckett's mom waved at me from across the room. She had a pan of something in her left hand that she put down on the table. "Hi, Nancy."

"Hi, Nina." She walked over. "How are you doing? Are you holding up okay?"

I looked at my grandma, who shrugged.

"Uh, yeah. Doing pretty good."

"I'm just so sorry."

I shook my head. "For what?"

"My son. He never should have gotten on that plane. Cash told me all about how much Beckett adores you and can see a life with you and then-*bam*!" She punched her palm, and I jumped a foot in the air from my seat. "Men. But don't you worry. We'll keep our eyes peeled for someone good when they come into town."

I shook my head, horrified. "Oh, no. No need. I'm doing fantastic. Really. I'm just, you know, focusing on myself and trying to just take life one step at a time."

Beckett's mom patted my shoulder. "You do that, honey."

I looked around the eager group of ladies, and I hopped up from my chair. "On that note, I'm going to go feed my emotions. I'll be back."

As I wandered toward the table, I could hear Abby, Nancy, and my grandma all talking about how well I was taking everything.

But it wasn't like I'd gotten dumped, right?

I mean, we weren't really ever *together* together.

Reaching for a paper plate, I scanned the incredible spread. I'd brought a ham frittata, but I reached for a gooey cinnamon roll to put on my plate first, followed by apple strudel, a cornflake egg and cheese dish I couldn't completely identify but which looked tasty, and then some salmon and asparagus with hollandaise sauce. Who cared that it was eight o'clock in the morning? I saw a tray of crepes and my mind drifted to Beckett, living his best life in Paris.

Which was perfect. Because I had a lot of straightening out of my own to do. I was more determined than ever to find the urn with my mom's ashes. If I could get some sort of clue out of Travis, maybe I could track her down.

By the time I sat down and started munching on breakfast, I was all fired up and ready to get to work. The first thing I needed to do was contact my attorney handling everything back in New Mexico to see if there were any obvious options.

The women all balanced a plate of food on one knee and their book on the other, but I just stayed focused on the food. I knew they'd wrap up last week's book before they started talking about this new one. And that was when Beckett popped into my head.

His texts had slowed down some, and we'd only Facetimed a few times. And then it occurred to me.

He'd found someone else. That was why everyone was apologizing and talking about more fish in the sea. They were preparing me in only ways that women could. Focus on the next catch. I slid a look at my grandma, who looked completely happy in her element. She was one of the few who busily scribbled notes rather than eating everything there was to offer.

I wondered what the new woman might look like whom Beckett was dating. Maybe he'd finally found a Parisian who wasn't scared off. Or maybe he found another American transplant.

The thought suddenly made me want to lose my breakfast. I set the half-empty plate on the floor and dabbed my mouth.

Don't be ridiculous, I scolded myself.

No one said he was dating.

But it would be okay if he were.

"What do you think about that idea?" My grandma was staring right at me.

"Idea?" I asked.

My grandma nodded. "Yeah. Hosting the next book club at the house instead of here. It will be at night, and it might be fun to do a potluck dinner."

I nodded, realizing I needed to move out of Millie's house much quicker than I realized. It was her house, and I was the lucky one to be living there, but I was at her mercy. I would soon be hosting an entire house full of women with a one-track mind.

"Great. It's settled. Potluck dinner on Friday at six sharp. Let's make sure we get to the fifty percent mark on this story so we can really get into it," Abby suggested.

I nodded, not really listening as I thought about Blackheart. He wasn't exactly friendly to strangers.

Or non-strangers.

Just really, anybody he didn't trust.

My grandma leaned over. "Don't look so concerned. I'll help."

I chuckled and nodded. "I was just thinking about my guard rooster. It's all good."

"Oh, right." Grandma Millie chuckled, and I got an unsettled feeling that there was more to this dinner than discussing this next mystery.

When I got home, I set the book down and waddled from my full stomach over to the photograph I'd been working on. It was from the night Beckett and I spent watching the Northern Lights. The images that came over didn't even look like they came from this galaxy. I'd created a replica collage and they would be offered as a pair.

I sat down in front of the work and stared blankly at them while thinking about the whirlwind that had become my life.

The idea that I could find someone who made me feel so good for such a short time gave me hope, but it also gave me reservations. I'd spent a lifetime trying to find someone, and it hadn't worked out very well.

Until Beckett.

I thought back to the better-luck-next-time euphemisms this morning and realized something very definitely was going on that I didn't know about.

Beckett probably found someone. It had only been a few weeks, but love doesn't subscribe to a schedule.

I frowned.

Love.

Beckett better not have fallen in love.

I picked up my phone and dialed his number. He picked up, and I already felt the smile coming through the phone.

That wasn't a man who'd moved on.

Although, my picker was off a bit, judging by the man sitting in jail.

But not Beckett. He was one of the good ones.

"How's it going?" Beckett asked casually.

"Pretty good. Just looking at a piece from the night we saw the Northern Lights together."

"I bet it's beautiful."

"Thank you." I smiled. "I saw your mom this morning at book club."

"Yeah? I should probably call her back. She left a message last night."

I chuckled. "Probably a good idea."

"They're not very happy with you for flying off to France without me," I joked.

"Oh, yeah?"

"Yup."

"I'm not exactly keen on the idea either, but I do have some work to finish over here and then . . ." His voice trailed off.

"And then we'll see," I finished for him. "I'm trying to tidy up my life too. I realized I gave up a little too easily."

"Gave up on what?"

I stretched my legs in front of me. "I don't know . . . just paying off all the bills that kept coming and hoping that the restitution might help someday versus being the pit bull I normally am going after what's rightfully mine."

Beckett chuckled. "I think you and Blackheart have more in common than you think."

I laughed, realizing how good it felt to talk to Beckett. "I think you gave me a reminder of who I was."

"How so?"

"You didn't treat me with kid gloves or like I was pathetic or stupid for falling for the scam."

"Well, there's an easy reason for that," he said softly.

"What's that?"

"You're the smartest person I've ever met, with a drive like no one else."

My cheeks warmed even though he wasn't in the room with me. "Thank you, Beckett. I needed to hear that."

"But I do think it's okay to let people in a little bit. At least people like me."

I grinned. "I'll have to remember that."

We didn't say anything for a minute or so, but I didn't want to hang up.

"This is probably a crazy question."

He laughed. "The crazier, the better."

My hands got instantly clammy. "Are you seeing anyone over there?"

He choked on whatever he was drinking. "Here, as in Paris?"

"Yeah. I just thought maybe the ladies knew something I didn't."

"Nina, I obviously haven't done a good job of telling you this, but I can't stop thinking about you. I can't wait to see you again."

Relief spread through me, and I couldn't wipe the permanent smile off my face. "I feel the same way, but I want things to be different."

"What do you mean?" he asked softly. "They'll be how they'll be."

"No." I shook my head. "I want things to be cleaner, tidier. I don't want parents showing up out of the blue or criminals doing crank calls. I want everything tidied up."

Beckett let out a deep breath. "Nina, life isn't tidy. It's messy. What matters is finding the person you want to tidy it up with."

Chapter Twenty-Eight

Beckett

This girl was killing me.

No. She was ripping out my heart and tearing it into little pieces before handing it back to me to use.

The distance wasn't helping matters, either. I didn't know what the Sunshine Breakfast Club was busy telling her, my mom included, but it had to be something because she was doing pretty well until the latest book club meeting.

I was taken aback when she asked whether I'd started dating someone. Where'd she get that idea?

Shaking my head, I reached for a pastry and took a bite. I'd managed to speak to the detective who'd worked on Nina's case, and I discovered a lot of interesting things. My hope was that at least half of them were accurate. He did mention that I could visit Travis and maybe get some more answers.

After calling every pawn shop I could find in the directory to inquire about a vase or urn with something inside it, I came up empty-handed. But that was the point.

I didn't want to show up on Nina's doorstep empty-handed. I wanted to show her that everything didn't have to land on her shoulders to solve.

And judging by our call a couple of days ago, she was starting to think about another way. But if I weren't there to lend a hand, how would she ever know?

I shook my head, knowing I had to get back to the States.

I grabbed my wallet and left my apartment. There wasn't a lot I could do from Paris, but maybe if I could convince the book club to lend a hand, they could distract Nina long enough to get me over there and for me to find the items I needed to find. I knew the urn would be like finding a needle in a haystack, but if I could pull it off, I think it could really give Nina the hope she needed to believe in things turning around.

The chilly air reminded me that it was still winter in France, just a different winter from Wisconsin's. I smiled, thinking back to Nina's legs dangling out of a second-story window on the first night we met. She was a survivor, alright.

But that was the thing. It felt like she was always in fight or flight mode, kind of like the rooster.

I wanted to show Nina that things didn't always have to be that way. And I understood wanting to protect her heart.

She'd had a lot happen to her from a young age that most couldn't even fathom, but I saw the vulnerability in her, and I wanted to share in that.

As I wandered the streets, admiring the Paris that I'd fallen in love with, I realized that I'd fallen even more in love with Wisconsin.

In showing Nina all the fun things about Wisconsin, it reminded me how special of a place it was and could be. But what I realized most of all was that I didn't care if I was in Wisconsin or France or Portugal. I just wanted to be with Nina.

That was all that mattered, and if I could make her life a little better by possibly finding that needle in a haystack, then maybe she could see a future.

I pulled out my cell and dialed my mom's number. She picked up quickly with a motherly hello.

"Hey, Mom."

"Are you missing us already?" she teased.

"Actually, yeah."

"Really?"

"And I'm missing Wisconsin."

"Does this mean you haven't gone on any successful dates since you got back to Paris?"

I couldn't tell whether my mom was serious or not, so

I just laughed. "I actually need some help with a matter that seems perfect for your book club."

She chuckled and sighed. "I thought you'd never ask. She's The One, isn't she?"

"Mom, hold your horses." I laughed, shaking my head.

But for the first time while talking to my mom about my love life, I felt excited . . . not the dread that usually accompanied these conversations.

"I just think that she needs time to realize that maybe she misses me a little bit."

"Oh, you're playing hard to get. I like that angle." My mom laughed. "I had a feeling about that."

"What do you mean?"

"Well, I might have implied that it's better she move on from you."

"Is that so?"

"Yeah. I could see those wheels spinning."

"Nina is going to kill me."

My mom laughed. "The secret is safe with me. I promise. So, what would you like me to do? The book club is actually meeting at her house—well . . . I guess it's Millie's house, but Nina is hosting us tomorrow."

I laughed, glancing up at the sky. "That's perfect."

I proceeded to tell my mom the plan, and she wholeheartedly agreed with it. By the end of it, I wasn't even sure I was the one who'd come up with the plan. In fact, it almost felt like I'd just played into my mom's hands. I didn't even know anymore.

My mom hung up the phone, and I felt the urge to call Nina. It had been a few days, and the fact that I was closer than ever before to seeing her made me almost ache because I still didn't have her yet.

I wandered in the direction of the Louvre. It was many blocks away, but I often took this route to clear my head. As I made my way over, I saw several groups congregating along the open space in front of the glass pyramid. I wanted to be able to take Nina here sometime. I just hoped I could.

As I dialed her phone, I thought about her life in Wisconsin and how much I'd missed since I left.

"Hey, Beckett. Couldn't stay away?" she answered.

I laughed, loving her fire. "Not really. Guess where I'm standing?"

"Hmm. A cemetery?"

"Close. There are lots of old antiquities here and some fine art."

She let out a blissful sigh. "Ah, the Louvre. I can picture it now."

315

"I'm standing by the glass pyramid."

"Someday, I hope to see it."

"I hope that too."

My heart ached over the distance between us.

"Well, if my sales keep climbing like they have been, I just might get over there before I know it. Of course, I have to hope some Parisian woman in high heels and red lipstick doesn't swoop you off your feet."

I chuckled, shaking my head and wondering if she were just testing the waters. "Hasn't happened yet. I find myself attracted to the Bohemian type."

Nina gave a breathy laugh. "Is that how you see me, Beckett Knox?"

"I see you as many things, but today as I stand in front of one of the world's most magnificent museums, I see you as that."

"I'll take it."

I smiled, knowing I couldn't take being away from Nina much longer. "So, how's that tidying up going that you mentioned?"

"Not as fast as I'd like." She groaned. "I'm a little messier than even I knew."

"We all are, Nina."

"I guess."

"How's your grandma and sisters?" I asked.

"Awesome. Grace picked a wedding date, and so did Maya. Grandma loves the idea of it all."

"Yeah? When?"

"Well, Maya wants to elope in July, and Grace wants to have a small wedding out of the country."

"Like Paris, perhaps?" I joked.

"She hasn't gotten that far." Nina laughed. "The fact that she chose a date is a miracle, but I don't think she's given much thought to traveling with a newborn to some exotic wedding locale."

I snickered. "Sounds about right. What about you? When and where do you want to get married, Nina?"

Nina laughed. "Oh, first I have to find the perfect man. Maybe one who lives overseas most of the year."

I chuckled. "You know what they say. Distance makes the heart grow fonder."

A horrific squawk erupted on the other end of the line again.

Nina said a quick goodbye, and I had to hang up, wondering if that was just another coincidence or if she'd trained Blackheart to disrupt on demand.

Chapter Twenty-Nine

Nina

"You're a little lifesaver, you are. Yes, you are," I told Blackheart while dangling one of his favorite toys in front of him. "That could have gotten awkward really fast."

Blackheart pecked at the toy and eyed me before taking off toward the fireplace in my grandma's house. My heart ached from the words I told Beckett, but it was the truth. Ever since my dad showed up, I just felt like my world was becoming crazier and less stable with each passing second. The extra phone calls only added to the chaos.

I slid the phone onto the end table and leaned over with my head in my hands. What was I suddenly so afraid of with Beckett? Would I like him here while I figure out who's making the creepy calls? Totally. So, why wouldn't I just say it? Why wouldn't I tell him I want him home?

Nate had called a little bit ago to let me know that while the area code put the caller in Wisconsin, it was actually a VOIP number, a virtual phone number that makes it look like they're making the call from anywhere they choose. The truth was that Nate tracked down the origins of the accountholder, and the person was in New Mexico.

Nate also confirmed it was extremely unlikely to be Travis because his call would come with a warning that it's a jail call and ask whether or not I'd accept it.

I stretched, reaching for the ceiling as I wondered why I didn't tell Beckett any of this. A lot of what I told him was true. I didn't want to bring him down into my muck. But there was something more that I didn't understand, and it didn't really matter.

The facts were that Beckett lived in Paris, and I lived in Wisconsin.

End of story.

Besides, I had too many loose ends to tie up before I could think seriously about anyone. What was the old saying? We had to love ourselves before we could love someone else? And right now, I was pretty disappointed in myself. For starters, when did I become idiotic enough to fall for a conman?

I glanced at Blackheart and smiled. He'd gotten used to me the last couple of weeks. I think when he realized Beckett wasn't coming back, he threw up his wings in defeat and gave in.

"Nina, are you decent?" Grandma Millie called from

the entry.

I laughed. "As far as I know."

My grandma wandered into the family room with a book in her hands and stared at the rooster.

"Is that thing potty-trained?"

I chuckled and nodded. "Believe it or not, yes."

Sometimes.

"Well, I've heard what's been going on with some phone calls, and I don't like it one bit. I've been thinking about the situation, and I don't think you should stay here until we get it sorted out."

"Where do you think I should go?" I asked flatly. "Not many places take roosters."

Grandma Millie sat in her recliner. "Nate will take Blackheart until you return."

"Return from where?" I asked, shaking my head.

"France."

My brows shot up, and I looked over at Blackheart. He'd already had too much change in his life, and I had too many things to get straightened out before traveling.

Not to mention, I had no money.

I shook my head and smiled. "I love your suggestion, but I really can't fly anywhere right now. Not to mention, the book club is meeting here."

"Nonsense." Grandma Millie shook her head. "When I found out you sent money to your dad, I knew right then that I needed to do something about it. You needed to be reimbursed. And it's my house. I'll host the ladies."

I shook my head, not following.

"Your parents pulled you down long enough. He's my son. That expense is mine." She pulled out an envelope from the front pocket of her flannel jacket. "He told me how much you sent, and I have that amount in cash for you, along with your confirmation number for your flight to get to Paris."

Panic set in.

"I can't go to Paris." I shook my head. "Absolutely not."

"I thought you might say that, so I bought a non-refundable ticket. I know how cheap you are, and I know you won't waste it."

I groaned into my hands as Grandma Millie hopped up from her chair and made her way over with the envelope.

"Go on. Look inside. Your sisters chipped in some fun money for you too." She stared at me. "As did the Breakfast Club."

My eyes widened in horror. I didn't want people giving me money. I was the one who always did the giving.

I slid the plane ticket out of the envelope and frowned.

"It's only a one-way ticket."

Grandma Millie's gaze filled with mischief. "Who knows how long it will take to sort out the phone calls?"

I shook my head. "I seriously cannot accept this."

"This money belongs to you." She grinned. "If it makes you feel any better, the club actually purchased one of your pieces for the community center."

I narrowed my eyes at my sneaky grandmother. "Which one?"

"The one with the stack of books."

"I just hung up from Beckett, and he has no idea," I explained. "This could really backfire."

"Live a little, Nina. You've spent your years always driven by goals. Relax." She handed me a book. "And read this on the plane. That's my one stipulation since you skipped out on this week's book club selection."

I turned it over and laughed when I saw the cover with a cute couple on the front and an Eiffel tower behind them.

"Really great love story. I actually heard they're turning it into a movie."

I shook my head and smiled. "You are really something."

Without warning, a little bit of excitement erupted in my belly. Paris? I might be going to Paris?

"Who all knows?" I asked.

"Everyone." She shrugged. "Your sisters already packed your bags, and your passport is in your purse upstairs."

I shook my head and sat back on the couch. "Do you really think Nate will figure out who's making the calls?"

"If not him, someone will," she assured me.

"Because I can't stay away forever."

The doorbell rang, and a strange shot of electricity jolted through me, and that was when I realized just how scared I was about the unknown calls.

"Be right back," I told my grandma.

When I got to the door, I saw our local florist's delivery truck out front and a floral arrangement on the porch.

I waved to the driver and picked up the flowers. Red Gerbera daisies and white roses overflowed from the vase. I tugged on the card and opened it to see the sweetest thing ever.

Happy Groundhog Day!
With love,
Beckett

I held the card to my chest and sighed, suddenly not wanting to leave the arrangement. As I walked into the family room with my flowers, Grandma Millie's brow quirked.

"From Beckett," I explained. "To celebrate Groundhog Day."

She tilted her head slowly and studied me. "He knows that's your favorite holiday?"

I nodded, still holding onto the card.

"Does he know why?"

I shook my head.

"Well, maybe this trip is the perfect time to tell him."

"Will you take the flowers for me? I don't want them to go to waste."

She nodded "Absolutely. Well, I should get going. Nate will be by later to pick that bird up."

I gave my grandma a long hug before letting go. "Thank you, Grandma. I think you're right. The calls have been a little more unsettling than I wanted to admit to myself. I even freaked out inside when the doorbell rang."

"They'd scare the crap out of me," she said, pressing her lips into a thin line. "But this too shall pass, Nina. This is your home. We are your people. Things will get figured out, one way or another."

"Thank you." I nodded, feeling a weight slowly start to lift.

"But you really need to share more, Nina. Open yourself up a little. I had to find out about what all that man did to you by reading the local paper in your old town and calling around. Don't do the same thing to Beckett. He's not the bad guy."

I smiled, knowing she was right.

And a little part of me couldn't wait to see what book the Sunshine Breakfast Club cooked up for me to read.

By the time Nate picked up Blackheart, I'd sent messages to my attorney and stopped by the bank to deposit the money, and then the adrenaline started to kick in.

I was truly headed to Paris.

I was going to see Beckett again.

Sitting in the kitchen, drinking a cup of coffee before Jackson came over to take me to the airport, I thought about what I wanted out of this trip. Back at home, I hoped they'd figure out who was trying to scare me with the calls, but in Paris, what did I want?

Could I be brave enough to tell Beckett how I truly felt?

I swallowed down the sudden worry as thoughts shoved their way into my psyche. I took my last sip of coffee just as the house phone rang. I answered it to hear a man's voice.

"Have a good trip, Nina." The robotic cadence shocked me to my core.

And I heard the familiar click.

With my hand trembling, I called Nate.

And I couldn't wait to get to the airport.

Maybe these calls were a little more serious than I realized.

Jackson and Nate showed up at the same time. I explained to them both that this time, what sounded like a computerized man's voice told me to have a good trip. Nate wrote feverish notes and decided to look around the house with the promise that he'd lock up after.

By the time I got to the airport, I knew I had one text to send before takeoff.

So, I slid my phone out of my purse and sent a quick text to Beckett. And I got on a plane in the opposite direction.

Chapter Thirty

Beckett

Oh, no. I let out a heavy sigh as I scanned the Albuquerque Airport. I'd just turned on my phone and rolled my carry-on to the rental car counter when I saw Nina's text pop over. She was headed to Paris.

To see me.

And I was no longer there.

Something had to have gone wrong. This wasn't part of the plan at all.

I handed over my identification and credit card to the customer service agent and texted Nina back. It didn't show as delivered, so she must still be in the air.

It was about nine in the morning, and I'd planned on getting to the jail for visiting hours by ten.

But the thought of Nina stuck in France without me made my blood curdle. This Travis punk really screwed a lot up for Nina and me.

As I thanked the customer service rep for the

327

directions to my new car in the parking lot, I thought about what to do.

All I wanted was to talk to Travis to see where he took the items he stole from Nina's house. Seemed simple enough. But I knew it wouldn't be.

I plugged in the directions to the county jailhouse and turned onto the highway. The destination was about forty minutes away.

I called Cash and told him about the predicament, and all I got was a loud groan in the background.

"You've got to be kidding me," he finally said.

"Wish I were, but I wanted to talk some sense into this guy and at least get the urn back for Nina."

"She's gonna be touching down in about three hours."

"About the time I'll be talking to Travis."

"We'll get this figured out," Cash muttered to me before quickly explaining to Maya what just went catastrophically wrong.

"Have you heard anything more from Nate about the prank calls?"

Cash let out a deep breath. "Well, before she left, there was another one. And this time, they wished her a good trip to Paris."

My hands gripped the steering wheel. "How long had

the trip been planned?"

"That's the thing. Nina didn't know anything about it until her grandma came over to give her the ticket. It was a surprise from the book club."

I shook my head, trying to make sense of the mess. "That's impossible."

"But it happened. Nate found a bug, but he couldn't trace it." Cash sighed. "Anyway, Paris is probably the best place for her at this juncture."

"Not if they know she's going there, and I'm not with her."

Part of me wanted to turn the car right back around and try to get on the next flight to Paris, but the other part egged me on to meet Travis.

"I think the person I'm going to see holds the key."

"I hope so. Meanwhile, Maya and I will get ahold of Nina."

"There's a hotel across the street and down a little ways she can stay at until I get to town. I don't have any extra keys hidden or I'd let her stay there."

"Okay. Sounds good. Drive safe, and we'll be in touch."

The rest of the drive felt like time stood still with minutes stretching to hours and hours. By the time I got to the facility, I was more than ready to confront the man who'd made Nina's life so miserable. If he wasn't the one making the calls, I was willing to bet he knew who was dialing her number.

I found a visitor parking stall and turned off the car. A chill cascaded over me as I made my way to the entrance. I'd requested a visit with Travis before I left France, and he'd accepted. It wasn't in-person, but it would be via video conference.

As I checked in and handed over my cell phone and wallet, I hoped this would lead to something useful. They led me through the security doors, and my pulse quickened. It was definitely a place I didn't want to be. The guards put me in a small room with a monitor set up on a table. I took a seat as the guard gave me the instructions and turned on the screen. Within a few minutes, a man dressed in orange was led to the empty table I'd gotten accustomed to looking at via the video. He took a seat and stared at me.

Travis.

"Do I know you?" he asked.

I shook my head. "No."

The man had dirty-blond hair, a tan, and cold brown eyes that looked into the camera, waiting for me to say something.

"I'm here because of Nina."

He shook his head. "I have nothing to say."

"Are you aware that she's getting calls?"

Shock registered across his features. He didn't know.

"What's your name?" he asked.

"James," I replied, hoping I wouldn't be corrected by the guards, but they didn't appear to be listening. "She's been getting a lot of prank calls. They're coming from New Mexico."

"What does that have to do with me?"

"I was hoping you might know who they're from."

He let out a deep sigh and started blinking quite a bit.

"What about the urn you removed from her house?"

"That was mine fair and square." He stared at me.

"It had her mom's ashes inside."

Travis's eyes widened.

"Do you know where it is?" I cleared my throat and watched the man shift uncomfortably. "Like you said, it was yours fair and square. But do you know where it is?"

"Yeah. I know. It's with all my other stuff, over on San Mateo Boulevard."

"An apartment?" I asked.

"A storage unit." He watched me for a minute. "I didn't know there were ashes inside the vase."

I gave a curt nod.

"It's unit 271. If you could, replace the lock when you're done." He eyed me cautiously. "Who are you?"

"Just a friend of hers."

He nodded. "She's getting calls?"

"Yeah."

Travis let out a deep sigh. "There's a guy I owe money to. It might be him."

He gave me his information, which I committed to memory since I didn't have my phone to write it down on and stood up.

"Is she doing okay?" he asked.

And I realized how easy it was to get conned by this guy. He looked like he really did care. He managed the concern in his voice, the curiosity in his eyes.

"She's doing great, actually. Living her best life out of the States."

"Wow."

"Yeah. Wow." I turned and walked toward the door, which the guard on the other side quickly opened.

By the time I'd fetched all my items, I went to the car and typed down all the info Travis had given me. I sent off the info to Cash for him to hand over to Nate about the possible loan shark out here.

Poor Nina. She didn't deserve any of this.

I found a hardware store where I bought a bolt cutter and a new lock and followed the directions to the storage facility. I located his locker quickly and snapped the lock off, hoping no one would glance at the security footage, but there was at least a video of Travis telling me where to go. The rest was implied.

The small unit was packed, but toward the center, I spotted an urn with brilliant wildflowers painted around the porcelain. That had to be it. But I didn't want to do this twice. I took a photo and sent it to Nina's phone, hoping she'd already landed in Paris.

Within seconds, I received a text back.

Where are you?

I bit my lip and thought how best to explain things. Deciding against that idea, I just answered.

New Mexico

She wrote back.

That's the urn. Plus, I see a jewelry box of mine in the

background.

Bastard. He probably got arrested before he had time to pawn the stuff off.

I shook my head and smiled as I texted the next message.

Did Cash tell you which hotel to go to? There's one across the street from my apartment.

She texted.

I'm not in Paris. I needed to finish up some loose items in New Mexico. Didn't you see my second text?

I let out a laugh and shook my head.

You're in New Mexico now?

I could picture her smiling and texting me back.

And you are too?

I laughed and shook my head. I should have known

Nina would figure things out on her own. I wrote a text back.

Should we meet up or pretend this never happened?

Nina called me, and I picked up right away.

"Are you seriously here now?" she asked breathlessly.

"Yup. I went to visit Travis, and he seemed genuinely concerned about taking your mom's ashes."

Nina chuckled. "Oh, my gosh. I think I know what happened. My attorney was in contact with his defense attorney. He probably thought you were part of the plea deal."

"In exchange for some information, they offered to drop a few of the charges." She laughed harder. "But he gave you the information. Not anyone who counted. Oh, my word. I never delight in others' bad luck, but this one is good. You got the information, and there was no plea deal. He hadn't accepted it yet."

"That is bad luck." I nodded. "He also gave me a name. Someone Travis owes money to. He thought maybe he was the one making the calls." I scrolled through my notes and sent her the info.

"I don't recognize the guy."

"I forwarded the info to Nate."

"Thanks." She let out a deep breath. "Are you hungry?"

"Starving."

"Okay. Maybe I can swing by the storage unit and grab the items that I recognize, and we can grab something to eat?" She sighed. "And then somehow fly to Paris so no one knows that we're master sleuths?"

"I'd like that."

"Send me the address, and I'll be there soon." Nina's voice sounded lighter. "I've missed you, Beckett."

"Same," I said softly, hoping this might be the start of something new.

Chapter Thirty-One

Nina

I called my attorney, who got a good chuckle out of things, and I'd be lying if I didn't feel a little guilty about what just went down. Travis probably thought the deal had been accepted and that Beckett was the guy he needed to talk to. Or I could believe that it had nothing to do with what was on the table for him, and he'd just turned into a nice guy. But that was what always got me into trouble.

As I pulled into the parking lot, I drew a deep breath and followed the directions to the storage unit where Beckett was waiting.

A spark of something new and exciting zipped through me. Never in my wildest dreams did I think a man would go to this much trouble for me, for my family.

He opened his arms, and I immediately dashed to him, wrapping my arms around him as he spun me around.

"This is crazy," I said, muffled by his chest.

"I can't believe you're supposed to be in Paris," Beckett said, letting go and taking a step back. "Yet, here you are."

"And here you are," I said softly. "What made you do this?"

"You sounded so certain that you didn't need any help, and I just . . ." He stopped himself. "I just wanted to prove that sometimes, going at things alone isn't necessary."

His words touched me in a way that I didn't think possible. "Thank you."

Beckett smiled, and his dimple surfaced again. I brushed my fingers against his cheek, and he smiled.

"I know you've been taken advantage of a lot in your life in ways that you never really thought about, but I want to be the guy who shows you what it feels like to be taken care of, at least when you want to be." Beckett shook his head and looked over my shoulder in a distant gaze. "Blackheart isn't the man for you. I am."

I laughed and nodded. "I agree, and thank you for the flowers yesterday."

"Your favorite holiday." Beckett smiled, lifting the metal accordion door up to reveal what was inside. "But I'm dying to know why it's your favorite."

I drew a deep breath and thought back to when I was a kid. "It was a brief moment in time when both of my parents were sober. I was ten, and it was Groundhog Day. They wanted to make up for all the holidays that they screwed up for us, so we had a big feast, some presents, and just…family time." I shook my head. "To this day, that was the only holiday that was like that. By Valentine's Day, they were messed up again."

"Wow." Beckett squeezed my hand, but I loved that he didn't try to make excuses. He just listened.

I turned to see the urn that held my mother's ashes. I saw two jewelry chests and several autographed books of mine. A lot of stuff was Travis's in this unit, but the things that mattered to me and I'd had to leave without were stuffed inside with the rest of his crap like they didn't matter.

But it all mattered. And what mattered the most was the man standing next to me who found what I'd lost.

"If I were completely batshit crazy, I'd go find the man Travis told me about and shake him down," Beckett said, leaning against the storage unit. "But I'm not. I think we'll just let the authorities handle that?"

I laughed and nodded. "Good call. I appreciate a sensible man."

"I'm nothing if not sensible. Going into that jail was something I'd like to forget."

I chuckled, reaching for the urn. I could feel the heaviness from the bag of ashes still inside. "I can only imagine."

"You've never been in one, right?" he joked.

"Only to pick up my mom when I was twenty. It definitely left an impression." I chuckled, holding onto the urn. "This whole thing is nuts."

Without warning, tears pricked my eyes, and I tried to blink away the evidence of emotion. But Beckett saw, and he took the urn away, placing it gently on a table, and pulled me into him.

"You don't have to fight life alone, Nina," Beckett said softly. "I might have gotten on that plane a few weeks ago, but it wasn't because I didn't want us."

I nodded. "I know, and part of me wanted to fly after you, but the other more rational part knew I needed to take time to figure things out for my own." I looked around the storage facility. "But it looks like I needed a little help along the way."

Beckett brought in a deep breath and let it out slowly. "It doesn't have to be Nina against the world."

I took a step back and studied him. "Then what would it be?"

He smiled and nodded. "There's this little word called *we*. It's pretty cool when used appropriately."

I laughed and looked into the storage unit that Beckett

had somehow managed to find and nodded. "I think *we* works pretty well between you and me."

"I saw a cart back by the entrance," Beckett told me, pointing over his shoulder. "I'll go grab it."

"Sounds great. Thanks."

I watched Beckett walk down the narrow hall and return a minute or two later, pushing a cart toward me.

"*Voila.*"

"Oh, speak French to me," I teased.

Beckett grinned. "I just did."

I rolled my eyes and made my way into the storage unit, sliding boxes and looking for anything else that might be mine but mixed in with Travis's stuff.

"I'm still in shock that you flew out here all the way from France to help me." I glanced over my shoulder to see Beckett peeking into a cardboard box.

"It's been a week in the making," he joked and lifted his shoulders. "The more we spoke on the phone, the more I realized I needed to show you that we're in this together."

Beckett lifted up a pair of men's boxers and smiled. "I'm guessing these aren't yours?"

I chuckled, loving how he could always bring a smile to my face.

It didn't take long before my cart was piled with all

the items I thought were gone forever, and we pushed it out to my rental car to load up.

As he helped me with my mom's urn by placing some padding around it to secure it for the ride, his hand brushed mine, and I felt that crazy pull to him again.

"So, you're headed back to Paris tonight?" I asked, trying to think about the timeline he told me as we pushed the cart out of the storage facility to the parking lot.

"I can always change it," he offered.

"No." I shook my head. "I don't want you to have to do that. I've made the drive before. It's not so bad."

Beckett laughed and shook his head. "You're a really tough nut to crack."

I frowned. "How so?"

"I don't have any doubts about your capabilities to get yourself to Wisconsin. None at all. But maybe" —he held his hands up in the air— "just maybe, you might find it more enjoyable to have some company."

I snickered, shutting the door. "Well, when you put it that way. And it might be easier to explain why I'm not in Paris if you're standing next to me."

"Exactly." Beckett nodded, taking my hand in his. "And I'm not exactly thrilled about things until we know who's really making those menacing calls."

I smiled, letting out some of the tension I'd been holding inside. "I'd like that."

"I've wanted to do a road trip for a long time," Beckett said, smiling.

"And winter is always a fantastic time to travel across the plains and the Midwest." I laughed with a smirk.

"Makes it better to stop off at some cozy hotels every so often." Beckett said, hugging me.

"You've definitely not gone on many road trips," I teased, looping my arms around his neck.

"Why do you say that?" His eyes stayed on mine, and I was brought back to the very first time he'd kissed me.

"Because there's very seldom anything cozy about the roadside motels that dot the highways we're about to travel along. I'd say there more like the Bates Motel meets the Shining."

"Oh, wonderful." Beckett laughed, glancing at his watch. "Maybe I do have time to catch my flight to Paris."

I chuckled and nodded.

"I have a lot to learn about these kinds of road trips."

I grinned, tapping his nose. "And I'd love to teach you."

Beckett kissed me softly. "Do you think I'm too old to go to Burning Man?"

I chuckled and shook my head. "Age is only a number."

"And what do you think about traveling the country this summer?" he asked.

I nodded. "Sounds fun."

"But maybe in like a nice modern trailer rather than the Bates Motel?" he teased.

"One step at a time there, Beckett."

Beckett looked at me. "You're a magnet for serendipity."

"I was more thinking a magnet for chaos." I took a couple of steps back.

"Not on your worst day," Beckett said, shaking his head.

We found a place to eat a few blocks away where Nina could stare at her rental car with her most prized possessions inside. The thought of trying to find everything again wasn't appealing and would probably never happen.

She took a bite of her cheeseburger and looked content.

"I wasn't being completely honest with you at the Frank Lloyd Wright house," Beckett said.

I narrowed my eyes on him. "About what?"

"I left some pretty important things out."

"You're kind of freaking me out," Nina said softly. "Like my mind is at its breaking point."

"I understand, but this is important. Before we take off, you need to hear it from me."

She nodded, swallowing down her bite. "Okay. What about at the Frank Lloyd Wright house?"

"I don't think I can do a no-strings-attached *anything* with you. No, let me be frank." He eyed me. "No pun intended."

"Darn. That would have been a good one," I teased.

"I can't do anything with you that's casual. I am completely and one hundred percent into you, Nina Bailey. The entire time I was in France, I wanted to be in Wisconsin with you. I'm falling in love with you, Nina. I know you wanted a fling and just something casual." He shook his head. "But I don't want that."

His words settled deep into my heart, nudging away the fear and worry that had gotten so used to hiding there.

I drew a deep breath and then took a sip of soda. "I've never gone on a road trip with someone before."

Beckett looked at me like *give me something more.*

"I've always felt at peace finding the quiet treasures of this country. It was something I didn't have to share. Something that couldn't be taken away from me. That became even more important as I got older. There were so many things growing up that were taken from me."

Beckett nodded silently.

"I remember one time, I was so excited because I'd finally gotten something that all the other kids at school had. I'd wanted it so badly, and I couldn't believe that I'd actually opened a present that wasn't already played with to death by some other kid. It was a brand-new, in the box, Cabbage Patch Kid. Grandma Millie and Uncle Renny sent it for my eighth birthday." I glanced out the window, thinking back on it. "Well, times got tough about a month later. My parents needed what they needed, which wasn't heat, and they pawned my Cabbage Patch doll. Turned out, she was a special edition."

Horror filled Beckett's gaze.

"I think if they'd pawned it for the heat bill, I wouldn't have given it much thought, but I knew what the money went to."

"I'm so sorry, Nina. You and your sisters never should have experienced that."

I smiled and nodded. "But we survived, and because of it—not in spite of it, but because of it—I can treasure the things that aren't felt and touched far more than the things at my fingertips. So, when I look at the Grand Canyon, I know that vision will never leave my heart. When I look into your eyes, I know I'll never forget how special you make me feel." My chest tightened. "So taking you on this trip back home with me is a big deal. I can't do casual with you either, Beckett."

He still looked stunned about my Cabbage Patch revelation, and I held his hand. "I'm really okay about the doll."

Beckett laughed, shaking his head. "I'm not."

"I gathered that."

"We all have different experiences that shape who we become, but I want to start shaping mine with someone of my choosing, who'll make me a better person," I said softly. "The side of Wisconsin you showed me proved to me that you got me. You understood what was important to me. No one has ever done that for me before."

"You do that for me, Nina." He shook his head and cupped my hands in his across the table. "I took you to those places, but you opened my eyes, Nina. You make me see things in a new way, and I don't want to let you go."

Chapter Thirty-Two

Beckett

By the time we'd rolled up to Buttercup Lake, I was pretty certain we'd be purchasing a top-of-the-line trailer or RV to try a road trip in. Between the lumpy mattresses, funny smells, and things that went bump in the night, we both agreed we were too old for the shady motels tucked along the side of roads.

I pulled up to my house, where Nate was waiting for us with Blackheart tucked under his arm with what looked like a muzzle on its beak.

"What in the world did he do to my rooster?" Nina craned her neck to see through the window.

She barely waited until the rental SUV had stopped before jumping out to see Blackheart.

Nate shoved him into her arms before even saying hello.

"That rooster is possessed," Nate said, shaking his head as I climbed the steps to my front door and unlocked it.

Nina scowled at our town cop and pushed by him. "Maybe you're just not a very good people person."

"He's not a people," Nate called after her.

"She sleep on the wrong side of the bed last night?" He elbowed me and waggled his brows. "Do you know what I'm saying?"

"I haven't the foggiest."

Nate followed us inside and closed the doors. "It's nice to see you two back in town, but I have to say everyone is going to be a bit surprised that you're not still in Paris."

"I had something to take care of," Nina told Nate as she unstrapped the muzzle from Blackheart and put him by the fireplace.

"And you?" Nate asked me.

"I go with her."

Nate smiled and nodded. "Does that mean you're sticking around these parts, Beckett?"

"For a while." I smiled, glancing at Nina, who was soothing our psycho rooster who was preparing to do the infamous dance. Nate was on borrowed time.

"Well, I might as well let you know that the fellow pestering Nina was indeed the guy Travis fingered."

Nina's gaze flashed to mine, and I knew she was trying to keep in a laugh from Nate's poor word choice.

"Right. Wow. Good news."

"Unfortunately, we can't do much since it's more menacing than anything, but he's had the cops stop by and let him know the jig is up. He's on our radar, and his type doesn't want any more added trouble."

"Thanks, Nate." Nina smiled.

He nodded. "Thank Beckett. He was the one who went in and got the info out of the perp."

I laughed, realizing how much fun Nate seemed to be having with the cop jargon. Other than the occasional rowdy rooster, there weren't that many opportunities to use it.

Nina beamed and nodded as the bird started to lengthen its neck.

I patted Nate's back. "Well, we don't want to keep you, but we can't thank you enough. I need to go grab some groceries while Nina gets Blackheart settled."

"Absolutely." Nate nodded. "I have to get back at it, but I didn't want to keep that thing a moment longer than necessary."

I spun around to see Blackheart's plumes settle down as he noticed Nate heading toward the door.

"Want anything special from the store?" I asked Nina. "I'll bring everything in before I take off."

"I'm good. Anything you get will be great."

As I led Nate out the door, I felt the chilly air hit my skin, and I couldn't be happier. For the first time ever, I felt like I was home.

It took me this long to realize that it had nothing to do with where I was at and everything to do with who I was with. I needed someone who got me, not the person they wanted to see but the person I was.

Nate drove away in his patrol car, and I unloaded the rental with all of the recovered items from the storage unit so many states away. It felt like I'd seen Travis eons ago, and finding her mom's ashes even longer.

As I set the last of the items down in the entryway, I looked around the bend and saw Nina petting Blackheart. She was humming and so peaceful. I just didn't want to interrupt, but she smiled and waved.

"Actually, do you mind if I come and maybe you can drop me off at Grace's store?"

"Absolutely." Just the thought of getting to spend any time with Nina made me a happier man.

She slipped her coat on and wound her arm around mine as we left my house.

Brilliant blue skies contrasted the stark white of the snow, and I knew we had at least another month of this weather . . . maybe more. But I didn't mind one bit.

"Is it weird that I can't imagine you not by my side?" Nina asked as we drove into town.

"I like hearing it."

"My dad is doing well at the sober-living place," Nina told me. "I just got a text from Grandma Millie."

"That's incredible to hear."

"I know I might get hurt again, but I'm at the point in life where I can't bear the thought of not living on hope. You know?" She glanced my way, and I put my hand on hers as I pulled in front of Grace's antique store. "It's just time to embrace where I am in life."

"And where's that?" I teased.

"With an incredibly sexy man who knows a thing or two about wild roosters and even wilder women."

I laughed and shook my head. "Want me to just pick you up after the grocery store?"

"That would be great." Nina moved her hand to the door handle. "I'm kind of fond of this rental."

"I'll take it back tomorrow."

Nina nodded and slid out of the SUV. I waved as she walked inside and slowly pulled back onto the road. I decided to surprise my parents at their house.

I drove slowly, taking in Buttercup Lake and all the changes and promises it held, and I couldn't wait to share with the world that Nina Bailey was mine.

As I pulled into my parents' drive, I saw Hunter's car.

"Good," I muttered. "I can tell him too."

I parked in front of the garage and made my way to the door.

My mom opened it seconds after I knocked.

"Beckett, what are you doing here?" Her eyes twinkled in surprise as I walked inside.

My dad wandered into the hallway and gave me a huge smile.

"Well, I didn't expect this."

I gave my parents a hug and looked for Hunter.

"Where's my brother?"

My mom chuckled. "Hunter is completely schnookered."

"He's drunk?" I asked, surprised. That was really unlike Hunter.

My dad shrugged. "I think he fell for a girl who didn't fall back."

"That'll do it."

"So, how long are you in town for this time?" my dad asked.

I looked around my parents' home. The same place I grew up, and the same place I could now appreciate. I'd always taken for granted the stability my parents had provided through the years. I suppose that's what stability did. It made you forget things could be unstable. That dolls could be sold for drugs. That parents could put their own needs first. But mine didn't, and it was something I could truly appreciate now.

"Until Nina gets tired of it."

My mom clasped her hands and jumped on her toes. "Just wait until I tell the ladies."

I scowled. "Tell them what?"

"That our plan worked."

I leaned against the table in the entryway. "And what was the plan, Mom?"

"We knew you were both too headstrong for us to do anything other than introduce you to one another. We also knew that you needed time to sort out your differences."

I laughed and shook my head. "You're ruthless."

My mom smiled wider. "Just hopeful. Now, if I could only figure out your brother."

"All in good time. Tell my brother hi when he wakes up. I have to pick up some groceries at the store for the house."

My mom swiped a kiss on my cheek, and I took off to the store. But I couldn't help but wonder what was going on with Hunter. He had it all. But sometimes, those were the guys who secretly had nothing. I would know because that used to be me.

Chapter Thirty-Three

Nina

"I've always wanted to visit Washington," I told Grace and Amelia.

Amelia was an owner of an antique store out on some island off the coast of Washington. Anyway, she'd heard about Grace's concept for her store by adding booths for separate antique dealers and an art gallery by local artisans.

"I could really see this turning around our sales and helping with overhead. Maybe even add in a coffee shop." Amelia smiled, glancing at my sister. "It's hard doing the traditional store where we have to search for and buy all the merchandise for the store and just pray it sells." I recognized the tension behind her gaze.

"It's a lot riskier," Grace agreed. "And I wasn't sure how well this concept would do in the middle of Wisconsin way up north, but so far, we've been really lucky."

Amelia nodded in agreement. "You've been written up so many times in magazines, I just had to come see, and I'm so glad I did. Is it okay if I come back tomorrow to pick your brain some more? I've taken enough time up today."

Grace beamed and nodded. "Of course."

I gave a quick wave as Amelia made her way out of the store when Grace turned to stare at me.

"Tell me everything. Like why you aren't in Paris?"

"Beckett got Mom's ashes back."

"How in the world did he pull that off?" She shook her head in disbelief.

"He's even more stubborn and determined than I am."

"He'd have to be." She smiled. "That's just wonderful news."

"I think I'm falling in love, Grace. Like true love. The kind that lasts forever."

My sister smiled, nodding her head in agreement. "I could have told you that a month ago."

I let out a happy sigh. "He's just so amazing."

"Speaking of amazing, here he is."

I turned toward the front door to see Beckett walking into the store with a tray of drinks.

He set them on the counter and pecked a kiss on my lips.

"I'd love to feel my toes again."

"I think you have to wait for May to do that."

"Sounds about right." Beckett smiled. "I thought I

might be late. Since the mayor put all those stop 'n go lights in town, I can never predict time."

My hand flew up to my mouth as a chuckle escaped.

"What's so funny?"

"Stop 'n go lights?" I asked, bemused.

"You know, the stop 'n go lights."

"Whether you want to admit it or not, you're a full Wisconsinite."

He frowned with a smile tipping his lips. "What do you call them?"

"Uh, stoplights." I grinned. "Like most of the country."

Beckett chuckled.

"Well, not to worry. I found myself cursing in cheese lingo the other day, so it's all good." I shook my head. "I'm already turning into Grandma Millie."

Grace nodded. "It could be worse."

"How so?"

"You could be turning into Jackson's Uncle Carter. He's been making obscene snowmen all over town. I think I know why Daisy is staying in Madison for the winter. She knows there's no controlling him."

"Yeah. I know. I was hit by him too. I even handed him the two grapes and a carrot, innocently thinking I was handing him two eyes and a nose." Beckett rolled his eyes.

Grace laughed. "Boy, you've gotta love it here."

My eyes connected with Beckett's. "Yeah, you do."

"So, what are your plans?" Grace asked. "Are you going back to France or staying here?"

"Well, I was thrilled to find out that even though my ticket was non-refundable, I could still change the date." I glanced at Beckett. "So, we plan on going back this summer. I want to be here for all the good things coming up."

Grace rubbed her belly and smiled. "There's a lot happening."

"What about you, Beckett?"

"That's my plan too. It's about time I start enjoying what's been right under my nose all these years."

The front door swung open and in walked Grandma Millie.

"The rumors are true. You're back in town. Both of you." She held out her hands and grinned from ear to ear.

"News certainly travels fast. Is there like a Bat Signal or something?"

Grandma Millie gave me a hug and then gave one to Beckett.

"Welcome home, you two."

"I couldn't imagine being anywhere else."

Grandma Millie beamed. "You just made an old woman very happy."

"You're not old." I shook my head. "You've got more energy than most of us combined."

"That's because I never stop moving. I just can't sit still."

It was true.

She looked at Beckett. "I heard Hunter's in town too."

Beckett nodded. "I heard the same."

"Well, he's being a bit more stubborn than I expected."

"With what?" Beckett asked.

"Life." Grandma Millie smiled. "But I've got some great ideas on how to uncomplicate his life."

Grace chuckled. "I bet you do."

"I'm serious. I know Daisy is the perfect match for him."

"You do keep saying that."

Grandma Millie's brows lifted. "And has the Sunshine Breakfast Club been wrong yet? Is it every day you get to be snowed in with a potential mate? Heck no. That takes hard work, determination, and pure grit."

I laughed. "By whom?"

My grandma chuckled. "All I'm saying is I know a

good match when I see one."

None of us could really argue.

Grandma Millie patted Beckett's arm. "Glad to have you home."

"Good to be here."

"Off I go. Enjoy your afternoon, you three."

We watched my grandma trundle off as Grace drank the decaf tea Beckett brought her.

"You've sold two more pieces," Grace told me. "I hope you have more inventory."

I nodded, thinking back to the Northern Lights one I was working on.

"I do. I've got a really gorgeous duo I'm working on from our time together experiencing the Northern Lights."

Beckett shook his head. "We can't sell that."

I giggled. "Beckett, we can't keep all my art."

He grinned. "Wanna bet?"

I smiled, knowing he was only partly kidding.

Beckett took his drink and wandered around the store while Grace looked at me.

"He's in love with you."

I glanced in his direction and smiled. "I know."

"Are you ready for that type of all-encompassing love?"

I smiled with a nod. "I sometimes wonder if he's too good to be true. There's moments I look at him, and I just don't get why he's with me."

Grace looked horrified, but it was a thought that had occurred to me a time or two.

"He's the lucky one, Nina." She winked at me.

I leaned over the counter a little and lowered my voice.

"I'm serious. He's so sweet and sensitive. And sexy and amazing in bed."

Grace put her hands to her ears. "La-la-la."

I chuckled. "It's true. Anyway, I just feel like one day, I'll wake up and it will all have been a dream. Like he might just go *poof* one day."

"Nina, not all heroes have to be painfully flawed." She squeezed my hand. "He's one of the good ones, and so are you. Enjoy what life has to offer you for once. Maybe let someone take care of you for a change."

Chapter Thirty-Four

Nina

Three Months Later

Blackheart was nowhere to be found. I'd searched our bedrooms, the family room, the kitchen, and the garage.

He was gone.

Missing.

Beckett didn't know where Blackheart was either, and Beckett was busy admiring the piece I'd just gifted him that captured the day he encountered the white deer. The piece had turned out better than I expected, and it had taken me months to perfect. It was nice to see him appreciating it, but I had to find our rooster.

I grabbed a glass out of the cabinet and filled it with my grandma's famous lemonade before wandering outside to look harder for our pet rooster.

We'd just finished planting the tomatoes, corn, and peppers in our vegetable garden, and the flowers were overflowing the bins from the weekend before.

Now, we just had to pray that a freeze wouldn't wipe out all of our hard work. Grandma Millie said planting anything before May thirty-first was asking for trouble.

"Blackheart, where are you?" I called again, searching under the raised beds that Beckett had built me out of cedar planks. "Come on, you little turkey."

My rooster always hated when we called him our turkey. It brought out the crazy dance every time.

But this time, just silence.

I glanced toward Buttercup Lake and saw something on our little boat pier. I squinted my eyes to see better, but I couldn't make anything out.

"Beckett, I'm going to the lake. I see something near the boat launch."

He poked his head outside and nodded. "Sounds good. I'll be right there."

I nodded and stomped through the grass tightly holding onto my glass of lemonade, praying a fox or wolf hadn't gotten to Blackheart.

But as I approached the lake, I saw a basket with a loaf of bread sticking out next to a blanket. Relief spun through me, but it was quickly replaced by confusion.

I heard Beckett coming up behind me, and I spun to see him walking toward me with Blackheart right behind him.

"Where did you find that knucklehead?" I asked.

Beckett grinned as he took me in, and I suddenly felt like he saw every single thing about me. The good. The bad. The confused. The nervous. The scared.

Our rooster strode his way onto the wooden pier and stared at the loaf of bread sticking out of the basket.

"Don't you dare, Blackheart," Beckett said, laughing.

The rooster looked at us like we were only there to cause him problems, but I was sure that was his way of showing love.

"What's the occasion?" I asked, taking a seat on the blanket next to Blackheart.

Beckett smiled and looked across the lake.

"It's been wonderful being back in Wisconsin, being with you." He smiled, and my heart skipped a beat. Even spending every waking second with Beckett Knox these last few months didn't tarnish the feelings of seeing him in front of me and claiming him as my own. Anytime we touched, I felt that same spark. Whenever I caught him looking at me, butterflies erupted in my belly. I knew someday, it might subside, but right now, I was enjoying every single second of the chemistry running between us.

Beckett sat next to me as we shared the picnic he'd made for us, tossing a piece of bread to our rooster every so often.

"There's been something I've been meaning to talk to you about." Beckett took my hand before pouring us each a glass of wine.

"Yeah? What's on your mind?"

He smiled and took a deep breath. "I want to make us more official."

I tapped my pale peach fingernails along his knee and smiled.

"It seems pretty official to me," I said softly. "I know I'm not letting you out of my sight."

Beckett smiled. "Same."

I rubbed my hand on his knee and took a piece of bread to smear some brie on top.

"It's so gorgeous here," Beckett said. "It's hard to believe that I wanted to run away from here."

"We all have our own paths to follow." I shrugged. "Besides, if you'd stayed here the whole time, you might have fallen for someone else already."

He laughed. "Impossible. I don't think it matters what alternate reality we wind up in. We're meant to be with one another."

I liked hearing that.

"I love you very much, Nina Bailey."

"I love you even more, Beckett Knox."

Beckett snapped his fingers in the air, and Blackheart waddled over to him, and that was when I noticed he had a little box tied around his neck. Beckett quickly untied it and turned to face me while our rooster left to go peck in the bushes.

"Nina Bailey, I didn't realize how much of the world I'd been missing until you came into my life. I just went through the motions, wondering why the world stayed the same. I couldn't figure out why no matter my successes in life, I always felt flat. I thought it was Wisconsin. I thought it was my job. I thought it was me. But it was how I was looking at life. Nina, you reminded me to see things beyond the ordinary."

My hands trembled with excitement as his eyes locked on mine. Every emotion and more swirled through me as he held the tiny box in his hands.

"Nina, I don't want to go another day without making you mine. Will you marry me?"

I brought my hands to my mouth as tears lined my eyes. I tried batting them away with my eyelids as I nodded yes and sniffled, brushing away the happy tears.

"Yes, Beckett. Yes a million times over."

He opened the box to reveal a beautiful diamond

flanked by smaller diamonds on the sides. It was beautiful and unique and completely me.

Beckett slid the ring on my finger and brought his lips to mine. "You've just made me the happiest man in the world, Nina."

I kissed him back, blinking my eyes open to see him. Truly see him.

Beckett was my everything and more. He knew me better than anyone, and I couldn't imagine spending my life without him. Blackheart made his way back over, and I ruffled his feathers before kissing Beckett again.

As our kisses deepened, I heard a gathering crowd behind us and stopped to see our friends and family, including most of the Sunshine Breakfast Club.

"For cripe's sake." Grandma Millie shook her head while rolling her eyes. "Get a room, you two."

I chuckled and kissed Beckett again, realizing that my life wasn't meant to go any differently than it had, and I couldn't believe I'd finally found a man who truly got me— my messes and all.

Dear Readers,

You are the best! Thank you so much for reading Nina and Beckett's story. Ever since I started this series, I was itching to get to Nina, and I hope you loved reading it as much as I enjoyed writing it. The next book in the series is *Christmas of Love* and it is Hunter's story! It's available for preorder on Amazon now. I'm also starting a new series that involves Amelia, the visitor to Grace's Antique store, which is also available for preorder on Amazon. It's titled *Heart of Curiosities*!

Again, thank you for making my stories a part of your library! I'm so grateful for you, and I'd love if you stopped by my Facebook group at Karice Bolton Book Buzz or signed up for my newsletter on my website. As always, if you loved my story a rating on Amazon is always helpful for new readers.

Warmest wishes,

Karice

KARICE BOLTON BOOKS

CURIOSITY BAY SERIES
HEART OF CURIOSITIES

THE SUNSHINE BREAKFAST CLUB SERIES
DASH OF LOVE
PINCH OF LOVE
SPRINKLE OF LOVE
CHRISTMAS OF LOVE

CLOUDBERRY INN SERIES
IMAGINING YOU
REMEMBERING YOU
LEAVING YOU
LOVING YOU

ISLAND COUNTY SERIES
FINDING LOVE IN FORGOTTEN COVE
LOVE REDONE IN HIDDEN HARBOR
TANGLED LOVE ON PELICAN POINT
FOREVER LOVE ON FIREWEED ISLAND
TEMPTING LOVE ON HOLLY LANE
CHANCE AT LOVE ON MYSTIC BAY
IRRESISTIBLE LOVE AT SILVER FALLS
LUCKY IN LOVE ON HOUND ISLAND
MISTLETOE MISCHIEF
ACCIDENTAL LOVE ON MEADOW COVE LANE
DISCOVERING LOVE ON CRANBERRY LANE
CHRISTMAS ON FIREWEED
IMAGINING LOVE ON WILLOW ROAD
CHRISTMAS CRUSH ON FIREWEED ISLAND
WAITING LOVE AT HAWTHORNE AVENUE
FOREVER CHRISTMAS ON SUGARPLUM LANE

BEYOND LOVE SERIES
BEYOND CONTROL
BEYOND DOUBT
BEYOND REASON
BEYOND INTENT
BEYOND CHANCE
BEYOND PROMISE

Sprinkle of Love

BEYOND the MISTLETOE

SILVER RIDGE SERIES
A HAPPY TRUTH ABOUT LOVE
A LITTLE SECRET ABOUT LOVE
A FUNNY THING ABOUT LOVE
A SURPRISING FACT ABOUT LOVE
A SIMPLE WISH ABOUT LOVE
CHRISTMAS AT SILVER RIDGE

LUKE FLETCHER SERIES
HIDDEN SINS
BURIED SINS
REDEMPTION
MIA

V MAFIA SERIES
BLAKE
DEVIN
JAXSON

THE WITCH AVENUE SERIES
LONELY SOULS
ALTERED SOULS
RELEASED SOULS
SHATTERED SOULS

THE WATCHERS TRILOGY
AWAKENING
LEGIONS
CATACLYSM
TAKEN NOVELLA (A Watchers Prequel)

AFTERWORLD SERIES
RecruitZ
AlibiZ
UprisingZ
BLOOD TORN DUET
BLOOD TORN
BLOOD CURSED